Shattered Hope

SHATTERED

BOOK ONE

KARIN WINTER

Contact the author: https://linktr.ee/karinwinter

Editor: Killing It Write

Cover Design: Inbal Ohana - Une Studio

ISBN: 978-965-93045-0-9

Progress, Not Perfection

Foreword

The shattered duet is a steamy romance containing mature content. It touches on subjects that some readers may find triggering or hard. Those include kidnapping, hospital trauma, graphic violence, and non-consensual situations.

This story is about overcoming tragedy, violent relationships, and finding your true self.

CHAPTER 1
Ayala

Manhattan is a good place to disappear.

Or at least, so I hope when I get off the train at Grand Central Station. I had already run away once, but I didn't get far, and he brought me back easily. This time I improved my plan. Without a passport and with little money, I believe New York is my best option. Over eight million people live here. No one will notice me.

I step out into the busy street and tilt my head up. The tip of the famous Chrysler building is visible from where I stand, shimmering in the sun, grabbing my attention. I've never been to Manhattan before, but I already feel like I know the city from what I've seen on television.

"Ouch!" I blurt as someone in a hurry bumps into me, and a wave of pain strikes my body, causing me to fold in two. Gosh, he didn't even say sorry. I glare at him, overwhelmed, as he continues on his way.

It's too much. I don't think I can make it here by myself.

I shake my head. There's no point in self-pity. I need to keep my emotions in check, or I'll fall apart.

I accidentally glance at my reflection in a shop window as I pass, seeing myself for the first time in several days, and I'm shocked.

My heart aches. I've tried not to look in mirrors since my escape, knowing that the face I will see will be unrecognizable to me.

I don't know this freak looking back at me. My face is so swollen—one eye is purple and essentially closed. Blue-purplish marks and swelling cover most of my face. A red and painful cut crosses my lower lip, barely allowing me to speak. My ribs still ache when I move. I wonder if I will ever go back to feeling normal. It's a miracle I'm alive.

I lower the cap on my head even further.

Maybe it's for the better. My beauty has only brought me trouble.

I raise a hand to the long wild blonde hair that I've been using to cover my face. "It needs to go," I mumble. I must assimilate and disappear into the surroundings. That's my only chance.

I don't need to check my wallet to know I don't have much money left. The little money I had almost ran out after I used it to buy the bus and train tickets to get here from California. I should have saved more, but the plan I had in place crumbled when he beat me to near death. I had to expedite my escape to survive.

The first thing I need to do is find a job and make some money. Buy food, rebuild my life. I can start from scratch here. But who will hire me when I look like this? I have to wait for the marks and bruises to heal first.

I sit down on the bench, rub my neck, and open the map I took from the station, trying to find a place to go.

A shelter, perhaps? Surely there are places in New York that accept homeless people or distribute food. Gosh, I'm so hungry. And homeless.

I. Am. Homeless.

I can't even say it out loud. But this is better than going back to him. I would rather take my chances and live on the streets for the rest of my life than go back.

After studying the map, I realize homeless shelters are not marked. I don't know why I even bothered to check. But since I left my phone behind, I can't think of any other way. I guess I will have to walk around and search for myself.

My stomach rumbles louder, reminding me I must eat soon. I already feel pretty weak after a day without food.

"Do you need help?"

The low, smoky voice surprises me, and I jump in panic and peek over the map. I glance at the polished black shoes and the hem of expensive-looking pants. I dare not raise my head. He hasn't seen my face yet, and for my sake, he'd better not. Perhaps if I ignore him, he will go away. But he remains, waiting for my response.

"Everything okay, miss? Do you need help?" he asks again.

I brace myself and tilt my head up, showing him my grotesque face.

I hold my breath as I peek at this man. Even in my hunched state, it is impossible not to be impressed by him. He has this rough look, like a cowboy fresh out of a western, though he's wearing a very expensive suit. With a firm jaw covered with two-day stubble and dark brown hair arranged in a fashionable and relatively long haircut. His light brown eyes, almost golden, stare into mine. He looks as though he just stepped out of a commercial. It must be illegal to look that good.

I blink.

He inhales when he catches my face, and his expression changes at once. His eyes fill with pity. Emotions I'm not interested in. I wait for him to turn away in horror, but he just asks, this time using a softer voice, "What happened to you? Do you need to go to a hospital?" He reaches for me, but I flinch, stifling a startled sob, and he pulls his hand back.

He is too close. My heart beats so hard that I can hear blood gushing in my head. My whole being screams *run,* and that's what I do. Running at as fast as my sore body allows, hoping this man will not bother to come after me because if he does, I have no chance of escaping.

"Wait!" he shouts and, to my worst fears, starts running after me.

"Leave me alone! Help!" I shout, running as fast as I can. Dear God, I can't win this race. He's going to get me. I glance back and realize some passersby stopped him, thinking he was trying to hurt me.

I run across Park Avenue and keep running until I'm sure no one is after me. Holding my aching ribs, I stop to catch my breath. I'm alone. No one is chasing me. I'm saved.

I continue to wander the city, looking for a place to eat. My stomach rumbles again. I'm about to give up when I spot a sign at the corner of the street that reads, "Community For All." A little arrow points to the left. I follow it, still holding my sore ribs. I find a small storefront with the same orange sign and go in to find a line of people, some older, some younger, all waiting for food. I join the line and wait, lowering my head and trying to blend in.

I take the soup and bread they offer, but there are no open beds left, I'm told. I'm not sure where to go or what to do from here. I need to spend what's left of my money wisely.

After finishing my meal, I go outside and consider my possibilities, deciding to change my hair before everything else. To change my appearance and not be identified is my number one goal. Though I'm far away, I don't know if he placed a missing person's ad or sent PIs after me. I walk back to the Duane Reade store I saw on my way and buy a pair of scissors, some hair dye, a mirror, and a few more items I need. Everyone here seems to be indifferent, and they don't take a second glance at me. This is yet another reason I chose a big city like Manhattan. The cashier doesn't even lift her head from the register. She just chews her gum and moves my products down the belt without saying a word.

I pay and go to the nearest subway station, locking myself in a stall. My distorted face is again mocking me from the mirror. It tells me I have no chance of succeeding here alone, but I refuse to give up. I didn't come this far to simply surrender.

I lift the scissors, but my hand hesitates. My blonde hair has always been long, falling on my back in big, beautiful waves. But my hair was part of the reason he noticed me in the first place, I remind myself. It has to go.

I cut it, piece by piece, stopping at chin length. Shorter would doubtless be better, but I can't. Even as it is, it feels strange. And besides, I need this length to hide my face. Cutting the back side is challenging. I twist in front of the mirror. When I finish, I dye it a very neutral shade of brown.

After half an hour and a makeshift wash in the sink, I look in the mirror at the new me with satisfaction. I imagine the bruises healed and gone and decide the new hairdo will make me look so different, and that is exactly my purpose.

Now I have to find a place to spend the night. What options do I have? A hotel or an apartment is out of the question, as I don't have enough money left. I'll have to sleep on the street, I suppose. At least until I find a shelter with an open bed. The dice falls on the subway. How lucky I am I got here during summer, so I don't have to deal with the nasty cold of winter. I hope to have a decent place to sleep by then. Every year the news reports some poor homeless guy dying from the cold, and I don't want to find myself in a similar fate.

The station on Thirty-third Street is big and scary. I look for a quiet place, curl up into a ball on the bare floor, and rest my head on my backpack. My hand closes on the pocketknife I've secreted in my slacks, my only weapon.

"Get up. You need to get out," a loud voice startles me.

I look up at the policeman standing over me, and my eyes widen. Shit.

"Get up. You can't sleep in the station," he says again.

"Okay, okay," I mumble while collecting my things, keeping my head down so he won't see my face.

"If you come back here, I'll have you in handcuffs," he shouts after me as I rush for the exit, tears rising in my eyes. He was so rude. I did nothing wrong.

I walk to the nearest park and lie down on a corner bench, cover my face with what's left of my hair and try to disappear into the background. Fatigue overwhelms me, and I fall asleep fast, even in the scared state I'm in. But the nightmares keep coming.

The shaded figure hides in the darkness, lurking for me. I know he is there waiting for me in the shadows. He comes closer. His icy hand grabs my throat and squeezes. No sound comes out when I try to call for help. There is no one to save me. I'm alone. I lose my breath. My chest rises and falls heavily, trying to grasp for air, starving for oxygen. I know what he is going to do to me.

"No!" I wake up screaming, bathed in a cold sweat. My eyes flutter open, and I rub the little scar on my clavicle while I take stock. I'm on the bench at the park. Far from him.

"I'm okay," I mumble. "I will be okay."

The bartender greets me with a smile. "What can I make for you?"

It's been more than a week since anyone smiled at me. To most people, I'm the scary homeless woman you have to look away from when she approaches. Well, I guess the makeup I applied at the nearest drugstore has its advantages. It hides what's left of the bruises on my face. Thank you, lord of cosmetics, for the invention of free samples.

"I saw the 'help wanted' sign on the window," I say.

"Yes. The owner is in the back room." He points to the left. "You can go to her."

I find the owner sitting next to a table loaded with piles of pages in a small, crowded room. She looks to be in her fifties, with some gray hair and a small crease between her eyebrows.

I enter the room with small steps. "Hello. I'm here about the job."

She looks up and studies me. "Yes, I'm looking for someone to clean around here. Are you willing to do that? It's hard physical work." She tilts her head to the side, her expression saying she doesn't believe I will agree.

"I'm ready to work hard." I can't be picky when I have just thirteen dollars left. "If you can pay in cash."

Her eyes narrow. "You don't have papers? We don't employ illegals."

"No, it's not that," I reply. "I'm legal. I'm American. It's just... I don't have a bank account," I explain, pulling out an excuse from the top of my head. I've already tried at least five places this morning. No one agreed to hire me without completing the personal details form, address, bank account information, and social security number—things I can't provide.

She examines my face in silence. "Are the marks on your face related to your lacking of a bank account?"

I touch my face. Probably the makeup faded a bit. I should have stopped to renew it. Why didn't I think about that before I walked in here?

Defeated, I stand there and lower my head. Another futile attempt. Well, there's always another day. I turn and start for the door.

"Wait," she calls after me. "Okay, you can start tomorrow."

"Oh my God, real–really?" I stutter. Did I get the job? "You won't be sorry. I'm a hard worker," I blurt.

"I've had my share of trouble," she says with a sigh, "and I remember hoping someone would come to my aid. Don't make me regret it."

I nod. She won't.

"I'm Dana Margolis." She extends a hand to me.

I shake her hand and smile. "Hope." I give the first name that comes to mind. I have hope now.

"Where do you live, Hope?" she asks.

"Here and there," I answer.

"Here and there, huh?" She stares at me like she can see right through me, piercing into my heart. "I have a spare room above the bar. It's not much, but you might want it."

My eyes widen in astonishment. Is she offering me a room?

"Don't get your hopes up," she says, hurrying to lower my expectations. "It's more of a storage place than a room."

I know she's figured me out, seeing everything I wanted to hide, and still, she wants to help. I'm scared, but her smile is genuine, and that's all I have right now, so I take her offer.

She accompanies me upstairs. It's a simple, small room. It has a mattress lying in one corner, and restaurant equipment fills most of the space. A side door leads to a cramped toilet and shower.

"It's a little crowded." Dana steps in, trying to pile up the equipment lying on the floor.

"No, this is great," I say with a smile. After a week and a half on the streets, sleeping with a knife at hand, the room looks like a five-star hotel to me. And I'll be here alone. No unwanted guests.

She hands me a key. "Do you want to go get your belongings?"

I lower my eyes and glance at my backpack. "I have everything with me."

"Hmm... More trouble than I thought." She sighs, then leaves.

I can't believe my good fortune. On the same day, I get a job and a place to sleep. I will work as hard as possible to repay her for this. She won't be sorry.

I look around. I have a shower. A real shower with running water! After more than a week of nothing more than sponge baths in public restrooms, the first thing I do is lock the door and get into that shower. I stand under the running water, close my eyes and enjoy the feeling of wet skin and soap. The little things I never appreciated in everyday life.

Tomorrow I'll buy some laundry soap to clean the dirty clothes in my bag. But right now, I'd rather go to sleep on a real mattress.

I wake up in terror as the nightmares return, and my stomach clenches in a severe spasm. I run to the bathroom to throw up and sit down on the floor, trying to calm my hasty breathing.

He doesn't know where I am. He can't hurt me anymore.

I return to the bed shaking and cover myself with the blanket I found tucked beneath the mattress. "He can't hurt me anymore. He can't hurt me anymore," I mumble over and over until I fall back to sleep.

CHAPTER 2
Ethan

My thigh muscles burn as I push myself to run the last mile. The first rays of the sunlight are already shining between the buildings. Beads of sweat drip from my forehead and my black gym shirt is soaked. Gosh, I need a shower.

I slow down when I get closer to my street, preparing to lower my heart rate, but stop in my tracks. Where did all these press vehicles come from? I find a hiding place behind a tree and watch them lingering outside my building with their cameras.

Fucking hell. How did they find out already? I didn't make an official announcement yet. Who the hell leaked it? One of the employees? Who would disregard my warning? I was hoping to have a few more days before publishing. I need the money from this deal to support the growth of Savee for next year. I can't afford for it to collapse because of stupid rumors. Nothing is set in stone.

I glance down at myself. My sweaty clothing is not exactly how I want to present myself in front of journalists.

I turn back on my heels and head down the alley that leads to the maintenance door at the back of the building. Thank God I always take my master key with me. I knew it would be handy someday. I move with care, making sure no nosy reporter is waiting for me there. Fuck, if one of them surprises me inside...

I greet the lobby security guard on my way in and enter the elevator, using my key to go up to the penthouse. Perhaps I should hire a second guard until they lose interest, just to make sure no one slips in.

Madeleine opens the door for me, her pristine white apron tied around her waist and a troubled look on her face instead of her usual smile.

"*Kýrios*, sir. The phone hasn't stopped ringing since you left. They're asking for you, and I don't know what to say."

"How did they get the number?" I wonder out loud and take a quick look at my cell phone. It doesn't look like they breached my mobile number. I type a message to my assistant to arrange a change of my home number immediately.

Madeleine's eyes open wide. "I don't know. I didn't tell anyone," she hastens to say.

"How long have you worked for me, Madeleine?"

"*Fanta*. Five years, sir. Six, actually, if you count the year I cleaned the building before you hired me to manage your penthouse."

"Six years. And have I ever accused you of anything?"

"No, *Kýrios*, of course not." A blush rises on her cheeks. "Never."

"So why do you think I'm worried that you gave them the number?" I smile. "Don't worry, Madeleine. All is well. I'll disconnect the phone, so they won't bother you." It hadn't even occurred to me she was the one who told them.

"What happened? Is everything okay?"

"It's nothing. I closed a deal to sell one of my companies yesterday. The journalists must have found out about the sale a little sooner than expected." At least, I hope that's the reason they are here and not because of any of my other secrets. I need to check the news.

"And this is a good deal?"

"Yes."

"You know I know nothing about it, but if you're happy, I'm happy." She smiles and turns to the kitchen. "The usual breakfast?" she asks, already opening the fridge.

"Yes, thank you." I stride to my room and jump into the shower, glancing at myself in the mirror. The sun is barely up, and I already look like shit. I have this deal to close and a fundraiser to go to. I close my eyes and take a deep breath. *I'm doing this for you, Anna.* No, I'm deluding myself. Nothing's gonna make up for what I did.

I pull on my suit, then button up the specially made cufflinks with the letter W engraved on them, slip on my jacket and head for the kitchen.

My protein omelet and vegetable salad are right on time, as always. I look down through the large living room window. They're still there, waiting. I focus my gaze on the park and inhale. No point in stressing out about the journalists. I need to get the job done.

I lay my jacket on one of the kitchen chairs, sit and check the headlines. Damn it, they even found the selling price. It's bad. How come my PR manager is not all over this already? Maybe it's time to replace him. I write a message to Ryan to hurry with the drawing of the contract and then to my PR manager to put out the official press release as soon as possible. We need to control the narrative before they write whatever they want.

I call my driver to pick me up. I need to draft a few more emails and require a few extra minutes. I prefer to drive myself, but in this morning rush hour, it would be a colossal waste of time. There are a lot of details to complete before signing the deal, and now with the journalists, the pressure is higher. I need everything done before the fundraising event.

The limo will be there for you at 7 pm tomorrow.

Olive
thumbs-up emoji.

Good. I need Olive by my side to keep Mom off my back, and I'm guessing there will be some extra press coverage today, so I also need to keep the gossip in check. A stable relationship always looks good in the investors' eyes, not that I'm sure why, as it has nothing to do with the way I do business. They should keep their noses out of my bedroom. But after years in the headlines, most of which were unflattering, I'm comfortable being out of the line of fire.

Olive is beautiful, one of those women who turn heads. And she's of the right status, knows what to wear for every occasion, and how to behave. Perfect for my lifestyle. Hell, she's an arranged date by my mother, so she couldn't be more perfect.

I enjoy taking Olive to these events, making sure to spark the rumor mill about a coming engagement, exactly as planned.

I finish eating and ask Madeleine, "Can you make Olive the cookies she likes?"

"Sure thing. And how is Miss Danske?"

"Lovely as always."

"I know it's none of my business, but can I ask you something?"

I nod.

"The newspapers write all kinds of things about you, and I know they are full of bullshit, but they say that you two are engaged?" She raises an eyebrow.

"I'm not engaged. You would know if I was." I smile. I didn't think she was reading the gossip about me. I will never get married. I'm too fucked up for a relationship.

She nods. "I assumed so, as you and Miss Danske never seemed... You know. Why do you let them write such things about you?"

"I have my reasons." Although I trust Madeleine, I can't tell her about the agreement Olive and I have. It's not my secret to reveal. "How's your daughter?"

"She feels good. To look at her now, you'd never know she'd been sick." Madeleine beams with happiness.

"If she needs anything else, let me know."

She nods again. "You've done more for me than I can ever repay you."

"I don't expect anything in return. You're family."

"You have a big heart, *Kýrios* Wolf." She hugs me.

I force myself to smile. A big heart? My heart is black. Nothing I will do will ever redeem my guilt for killing Anna.

CHAPTER 3
Ayala

"Oh, shit!" A shout comes from one of the men sitting at the bar, and I glance in his direction. Once again, someone spilled beer. What is it about men that they can't drink without spilling once they get a little drunk? And it's not even happy hour.

I take my towel and spray and approach them.

"Johnny, look at those tits," the man mumbles. "I'd fuck her. What do you think? Isn't she hot? Maybe we'll take her home with us. I would bend her over..."

Bend over the table now, whore. I cringe and freeze in my tracks. What did he just say? I'm unable to move, and he takes it as consent. He grabs me, and I shiver as the unfamiliar hand crawls up my leg. My legs start shaking violently. His hand is getting higher and closer, and I stifle a whimper.

"Hey, let her go," a voice calls behind me, and the drunk removes his hand from me at once. I inhale, trying to get air into my constricted lungs. My breaths are short and ragged as I try to hold myself together. I can't afford to fall apart in front of everyone.

"I think it's time for you to leave," Dana advises, tilting her head toward the door.

"She wanted it," the man argues. "I didn't do anything she didn't want me to do."

"Are you going on your own, or do I have to take you out?"

He throws his hands in the air in surrender, then stands, swaying from his chair. "Okay, I'm leaving. Nothing happened. Come on, Johnny, let's go."

The man sitting next to him gets up, reluctance in his every move, and I follow them to the exit with my eyes.

"Are you okay?" Dana asks, studying me with her all-seeing eyes.

No, I'm not. "Yes." I nod.

"Call me if someone is bothering you." She turns and walks back in the direction she came from.

"What's the matter this time?" Robin, one of the waitresses, grumbles to Nicky, who's working behind the bar tonight, as Dana leaves. "Since Blue Eyes got here two weeks ago, Dana has been hovering over the woman like she's fragile. Dana's even given her double shifts every day of the week."

I lower my head, not sure what to do.

"Why do you care how many shifts she gets?" Nicky asks. "She works in cleaning, not as a waitress. Do you want to clean the toilets? Shall I go tell Dana that you're interested?"

Robin twists her mouth. "No, I don't want to clean toilets. Blue Eyes here should just do her job and stay away from me." She picks up the beer glasses from the bar and places them on her tray.

I turn around to the bar to thank Nicky, who intervened in my favor, and smile at her gratefully. Ever since I started working here, Robin has acted as though she's got something against me for no obvious reason. I liked Nicky before, but now even more so.

When the shift finally ends, I grab a mop and start pouring

water on the floor while Nicky closes the cash register and cleans the bar.

"I saw the new episode of Law and Order yesterday," she tells me, starting a conversation. "Did you see it? They say it's based on an actual case. When I become a lawyer, a case like this is my dream." Nicky continues to chatter while I clean the floor. "That is if I ever manage to earn enough to go to law school."

It hurts me that I can't tell her anything about myself. I'm a fake. All I am is just one big lie. But I can't take the risk of her finding out about me.

"Hope. Hope!"

It takes me a few seconds to shake off my thoughts and realize that she's calling my name. My new name.

I turn my head to her. She's standing behind the bar, holding her phone.

"What?" What is so important that she has to stop me in the middle of mopping the floor? Most of the time, she doesn't mind having a one-sided conversation.

"I just received a message from my second boss. There's an event coming up, and he's short of waitresses."

"Okay, and...?"

"So you're looking for more income, right? You told me you were saving for school," she reminds me.

"Oh, yes." I nod. I did tell her that, even though I won't be attending school any time soon. Just another one of the many lies I've told since I got here.

"He's missing waitresses for tomorrow night. You know how to serve, don't you? It's not that hard. Just hold a tray and walk." She grins. "And the events are always for the rich and famous, so they give good tips."

Going to an event like this, being exposed in front of a lot of strangers... I'm not sure I'm ready for that. Working here, behind the scenes, away from other people, feels safer. But Nicky doesn't take no for an answer.

"Come on, you should. Last time I made two hundred dollars just in tips, not including the salary. And it's an easier job than what you do here."

I have to admit, it tempts me. Two hundred dollars is a lot of money. I'll have to find myself an apartment soon enough, as I don't want to be a charity case forever. I do need the extra money.

What can happen? It's just one evening, isn't it?

I show up at the exact time and address Nicky gave me in Soho. The sign announces that it's a gallery currently showing an exhibition by an artist named Paulino. According to Nicky, Paulino is one of the most popular artists in Manhattan today.

I enter from the back entrance into the staff room. Nicky welcomes me with a hug and registers me for the shift. Her boss, Mr. Nielsen, does not introduce himself by name and is portrayed as a stern-looking person with a hostile expression. It's a dislike at first sight.

Nicky rushes in to get dressed and motions for me to follow. I look at the provided outfit, which doesn't look too comfortable. A tight pencil skirt and a white button-down shirt. The tailored shirt is tight on my not-so-small breasts, and the buttons threaten to burst.

"Maybe I should go a size bigger?" I say as I continue to button up.

Nicky grins. "You look hot. Do you want the tips or not?" She hands me black stilettos. "Size five, right?"

I nod. Am I supposed to serve in stiletto heels? Though I'm used to heels, serving in them is a whole different thing.

I put on the shoes while looking around. The waiters and

waitresses around me are making final preparations. Dressed in elegant black and white, they are all good-looking.

Nielsen makes us stand in a line and scans us with his sullen gaze.

"There is a stain on your shirt. Go change," he says to one waiter.

"Too wrinkled," he says to another. "Go change."

I shiver. Michael would look at me just like that every time we left the house. I needed to make sure I didn't embarrass him with my appearance. There were clear rules on what I was allowed to wear in public. I tug on my skirt and straighten it, passing the Nielsen quality check.

"Take it." A full tray is pushed into my hands, and I barely balance myself to prevent it from falling.

"Be careful!" another waiter shouts at me when I try to find my way. That's it. I'm ready to drop everything and run. I glance at Nicky, and she smiles at me and raises a thumb. I take a deep breath and carry the tray of champagne glasses outside for the reception to distribute to the guests.

A small whistle of admiration escapes me at the sight of the place. Vast paintings decorate the walls. Most of the art is of women in a variety of poses, all with their backs to the camera, lying against an industrial landscape. The hall itself looks industrial. Huge lamps hang from the ceiling, and lots of vegetation is scattered around. Lots. Huge flower pots in every corner. Green plants and even trees that I wasn't expecting to see here. It's unique and emphasizes the contrast between the industrial views in the paintings and nature.

Men in tuxedos and women in fancy dresses that cost more than my monthly income fill the place. And I would know, as I was one of them until recently. They walk around, examining the art, holding up fake smiles. How meaningless these parties are.

Everyone looks so perfect, so serene. Yet no one knows you once you get home. No one cares.

Even my parents didn't care.

I offer the champagne, completely transparent in their world. They don't give me another look. It's good. I don't need the attention. I don't want it.

Just walk with a tray.

Just walk with a tray.

I see him too late, the photographer. He's not trying to take a picture of me, of course. He aims the camera at a beautiful and probably famous couple in their evening clothes. But I'm right behind them. The camera is pointed directly where I'm standing, and he will capture my face in the picture as well. The shaky universe I've rebuilt over these last weeks here is about to shatter.

I twist my body, turning my back to him. The champagne tray in my hand crashes into someone walking right behind me.

Shit.

Like a comedy of errors, everything plays before my eyes in slow motion, the sound of the collision, the glasses smashing on the floor, and the champagne spilling right on this man's suit.

From the force of the collision and the high heels I'm wearing, I fall backward, straight on my butt, and I find myself on the floor, a little shocked.

Look at the damage you made. You destroy everything you touch.

I close my eyes and inhale, then I look around at the destruction I've created. Please don't ask me to pay for the damage I caused, I pray silently. All the money I saved at Dana's won't be enough to cover the expenses. I start shaking as reality hits me.

"Are you okay?" the man whose suit caught much of the champagne asks in a low voice.

I know that voice. Shit.

A face appears in the corner of my eye. I look up at the man in the suit bending over to me.

My gaze finds his face, and I exhale. This is the top model from the street, the one from my first day here.

A strand of hair falls on his forehead, and for some reason, I have an uncontrollable urge to move it away from his face.

"Are you okay?" he asks again in that deep voice that sounds like it's bubbling from within, from the boiling fire he holds inside.

He reaches out to help me, my eyes widen, and I recoil in a panic.

For a split second, my damaged mind thinks he's going to hit me. It's just for one brief moment, but he notices. His outstretched hand freezes in place. I come to my senses and take his hand. I have to play the game. I can't attract any more unnecessary attention now.

He pulls me to my feet and doesn't let go. My full attention focuses on this point of contact, on the heat it radiates, as if there is an electric current flowing between us.

I pull my hand away and straighten my skirt and shirt, trying to make myself presentable again.

"Are you okay?" he asks for the third time.

I look at him, trying to understand from his expression if he recognizes me. But there is no glimmer of recognition. He doesn't seem to remember our previous meeting. Good.

"Yes, I'm so sorry, sir. I turned around too fast," I mumble.

An intrigued crowd begins to gather around us, and I try to make myself smaller. I wish I could just vanish. My eye catches Mr. Nielsen walking toward us, his gait stiff and a look on his face of pure rage. He turns to the man in front of me.

"I'm so sorry, Mr. Wolf. She's new. I'll make sure she doesn't work here again. How can I make it up to you?"

I just stand there, my cheeks hot with shame, and I keep my head down.

The man glances at me, then back at Nielsen. "I bumped into her," he says, "I dropped her tray. It's my fault. I don't want you to fire her."

His golden eyes, which had a fire in them until a moment ago, turn to ice. His jaw hardens. This is clearly a man who's used to getting what he wants.

"Of course, sir." Nielsen gives me another angry look, trying to kill me with his eyes, I'm sure. How could he agree so easily to his demand?

"Do you need help with the clothes, sir?"

"No need," Mr. Wolf answers in his low voice, and a shiver goes through me. The manager shakes his head and walks away from us with quick steps.

The man's gaze returns to me. The gold flecks in his eyes now sparkle with anger, but the anger is not directed at me.

"Why did you do that?" I can't help myself, and the question shoots out of me like a bullet. "Why did you defend a waitress you don't know?"

"I don't like people who enjoy feeling strong in the expanse of someone weaker. A boss needs to protect his employees, not demean them. This man will not work for me anymore." His tone sounds menacing.

Won't work for him? What does he mean?

"Ethan Wolf," he introduces in a softer voice, his hand extended for a squeeze.

The name sounds familiar. I think I read about him in the newspaper a few days ago. My mind swells as I try to remember. Damn, I should have read it more carefully.

"Hope," I introduce myself, not giving any last name. The electricity between us reappears when I shake his hand.

"You—"

"Excuse me, Mr. Wolf, your clothes." A man arrives holding a new suit, wrapped and looking freshly pressed. Mr. Wolf apologizes and excuses himself, leaving me to guess what he meant to say.

I manage to get through the rest of the evening without any additional problems. When I hear the low, sexy voice again over the microphone, I turn and discover Ethan Wolf—as I know his name is now—on the stage. He speaks with enthusiasm. His posture is steady and relaxed. I can tell this is a person who's used to being on stage. The new dark blue suit he wears can't hide his solid physique. I glance around, surveying the audience in the hall. He has their full attention, his charisma present in every corner. It's impossible not to listen to this voice.

A slightly older, impressive woman in a floor-length white dress comes up on the stage. Her coloring looks similar to his, but her beauty is more classic. Refined.

"I'm pleased to introduce my mother, Laura Wolf, the executive director of the Wolf Nation Foundation," he says, just as I wonder about their connection. Applause fills the hall.

I ponder as she speaks just as passionately on stage. Both have an impressive presence and dizzying beauty, each in their own way.

As she takes the microphone, Ethan Wolf leaves her to give her speech and approaches a woman in a blue dress that wraps around a thin body and endlessly long legs. Her face is doll-like, and her long dark hair flows over her shoulders. He walks up and kisses her, and my stomach clenches with longing. I once wanted to be loved like this. It used to be my dream.

CHAPTER 4

Ethan

"Are you satisfied with the donations today?" Olive asks me in the limousine after the event.

"Mmm...yes," I mumble, deep in thought.

She gives up on conversation and dives into her phone. Our fake relationship is everything I've ever hoped for in a woman, but without the sex. She looks great, gives all the newspapers something to talk about, and gets the nosy parents off us. And best of all, she knows when I'm not interested in talking and doesn't mind being quiet. No expectations, no disappointments.

The image of the waitress doesn't leave my mind. I keep replaying the event over and over in my head. I've never seen a creature so scared as this little waitress.

Where the hell do I know her from? It's driving me crazy. It's like this light bulb flashing in the back of my head, telling me I've met her before.

It's weird because I have an excellent memory for faces, yet I can't figure out where I've seen her. And she doesn't have a face I would forget. A delicate face, full lips, and huge blue eyes, so big compared to the size of her face, with the bluest color I've ever seen, almost glowing. And when she stood in front of me, I couldn't help but notice her magnificent body—endless curves, heavy breasts, and a narrow waist. My taste exactly.

The thought of inviting her home with me was overwhelming. I even asked my assistant to check where she usually works. But then I told myself the woman is too nervous for my taste, a scared Bambi. I prefer strong women with lots of self-confidence, so I decided I should forget about her.

But no matter how hard I try, I can't stop visualizing her long bare legs spread out on the floor in front of me as her skirt lifted, her chest rising and falling as she gasped, and her huge eyes wide.

I wanted to spread her legs right there on the floor and taste her. God, she must taste amazing. But I'm not a sixteen-year-old boy anymore. I can control myself. Well, maybe not completely. I still have needs. I text Adele and let her know I'm on my way.

The only downside to my agreement with Olive is that now my sex life has to be hidden under the radar. I have to sneak into my mistresses' homes like some criminal.

I don't like it. I don't like it so much that I almost canceled the agreement shortly after it started. But Olive needs it, and surprisingly, my investors are also more generous now. I look more "settled" to them when I walk with the right partner on my arm. This was an unexpected and very welcome side effect of the agreement between us, and no, I'm not ready to give it up yet. I need the investments.

I drop Olive off at her house and, minutes later, sneak into Adele's apartment from the back entrance. I need to blow off some steam.

I'm just finishing dinner, alone, when my phone rings. A glance at the screen shows it's Ryan calling.

"What's up?" I answer.

"Ethan. I fought with Maya."

"Well, what's new? You're always fighting. That's the downside of both of you being crazy about each other. Wait for reconciliation sex. Sometimes it seems to me that you fight only so you can make up later." Their fights happen about twice a week and always end in steamy sex. At least according to Ryan's stories.

"It's serious this time, Ethan. She left for her mother's. She said she wasn't coming back. I don't know what to do."

I sigh. "I'm on my way."

The black Porsche wakes up with a growl when I press the gas pedal. It's fun to drive at night. The roads are relatively free, and it's just me and the car. The trip isn't long, so I take my time to enjoy it.

I take the elevator up to Ryan's apartment, only to find him sprawled on the couch, wallowing in self-pity. It's definitely one of the lowest situations I've seen him in, and I've seen quite a few. We've been friends since childhood.

"How much have you had to drink?"

"Just a little," he says.

I think it's more than a little, but I don't contradict him. I pour us both a shot of whiskey from his bar, hand him a glass and sit on the sofa.

"I messed up this time," he says. "I don't know what happened. We were eating dinner and Maya started talking about children. I answered, as always, that I'm not ready for children. We're young, I want to spend time alone with her, and kids are a mess. We've talked about it several times before, and she always said we had time. But today, she went wild."

He downs the whiskey in a gulp, and worried, I study him. "She just took her things, said she was going to her mother's to think, and left. I don't understand what happened. She's never left the house in the middle of an argument. We always make up.

Making up is the fun part." His mouth rises in a grin at the memories.

I have a hunch about where this story is leading, but If he doesn't see whats in front of him, only Maya can enlighten him.

"Come," I order, "you need to get out of this house and get some fresh air. Let's go get a drink somewhere."

Ryan gets up from the couch. "There's a friendly pub on the corner."

"Let's go to Lunis. It's also close," I say and regret it almost immediately. I said I wouldn't chase after her. What the hell am I doing?

Lunis is a small neighborhood pub with a dim and pleasant atmosphere. As we enter, I see the bar is quite full, but it doesn't feel too crowded. A Pearl Jam song is playing in the background.

We take a seat in the empty chairs at the end of the bar. I glance around, examining the waitresses, looking for those unforgettable blue eyes. Ugh. She's not here.

"In memory of our debauchery days?" Ryan says, lifting his glass in a toast. "Thank you for being here for me."

"Always. Do you remember when we started Savee?"

He nods. "How could I forget? We got so many nos, and each time we drank into oblivion. I think we were drunk more than sober back then." He snorts.

"I miss that a little." At the sight of his puzzled look, I add, "Not the nos. I'm glad that's behind me. But our time together before you became a super-successful lawyer."

He smiles back. "Before you became a busy CEO, you mean. You keep me busy around the clock with all your companies. But you're right, we need to do this more. I miss it too."

A woman comes behind me to clear the counter of empty glasses for us.

I glance at her briefly, and my breath stops for a moment. It's Hope.

The blue eyes look at me, and I can see the glimmer of recognition flickering in them as her pupils widen and her lips form a circle of astonishment. This is not an illusion. It's her. She's here.

She looks down for a moment, and her long eyelashes cover her amazing eyes. Her gaze wanders from me to Ryan and back, but she says nothing.

"Hey," I say, but my voice only seems to startle her, and she hurries away. She's just a scared Bambi. Not what I'm looking for. Not the kind of woman I enjoy fucking. So why is my heart rate up to the pace of a marathon run? Fuck. I'm too attracted to her.

I follow her with my gaze as she hurries away, dressed in simple jeans and a black Lunis t-shirt. The shirt is too big on her, obscuring the amazing figure I know is underneath. She's bewitched me. There's no doubt. This girl is a witch. I can't think of another reason for how I feel right now.

But where do I know her from? This feeling of familiarity is so strong that I can't be wrong. I look around again. I've never been to this bar before. It can't be from here. Maybe she worked at another bar? Maybe she works at one of my companies? Fuck, I hope she doesn't work at one of my companies. I look back at Ryan, finding him studying me with great interest.

"Are you enjoying the view?" he asks with a chuckle. "I don't think I've ever seen you stare at a woman like that. They're usually the ones chasing you, you filthy bastard."

"I don't stare," I deny. "I don't," I reiterate to his annoying grin.

"Ask her for her phone number," he says, insisting on continuing his tormenting. Ryan is the only one who knows about my agreement with Olive. The only one who knows that I'm actually single and completely free. He drafted the contract between us.

"She's not my type," I say, even though it's obvious Hope is very much my type at first glance. But I've already decided that getting involved with her would not be a good idea. If I wanted to fuck her, I would have asked her then. So why the hell did I choose to come here? To torture myself?

The universe has presented me with a test, and I have to face it.

For the rest of the evening, I focus all my attention on Ryan, encouraging him and trying as much as I can to ignore the beautiful woman who occasionally passes by.

After we enjoy half a bottle of whiskey and a few other drinks, most of which find their way into Ryan's stomach, I realize that if I don't drag him home now, I'm going to have to pick him up because he's already dangerously drunk. He's a big guy, and I don't want to push my luck. I pay the bill and get him on his feet. I hope he's still steady enough to make it home.

I hold back from stealing one last look at those gorgeous blue eyes but can't deny I'm almost tempted to turn my head to see her again.

I drag Ryan's swaying body all the way home and throw him on the bed. Thank God we chose a pub close by. He's fucking heavy.

I'm too drunk to drive home myself. I'll have to sleep on Ryan's couch tonight. I collapse on it, but my thoughts keep coming back to her. I turn from side to side as her big blue eyes haunt me.

I can see her face, hear her moaning and screaming my name in ecstasy. God, I want her under me. I want to taste her. I haven't been this horny in a long time, so horny that it's disturbing my sleep. I don't understand why I want her so much. This startled Bambi style was never my cup of tea, but I do. There is no doubt about it.

After an hour of twists and turns, sleep still escapes me. I make a hasty decision to go back to the pub and try to get her number. I'm guessing, based on her level of concern, it will take some convincing. She won't be jumping into my bed tonight like other women I'm used to. But that's okay. I'm ready for a challenge. Maybe it'll even add a bit of interest to my life. I admit I've been bored lately. Maybe that's the thing. Maybe what I need is the challenge. My pretty face and my money always do the trick.

I make sure Ryan is okay before I leave and find him snoring peacefully in his bed. I think he'll have a colossal headache tomorrow, but he's perfectly fine now.

I go outside, and the chilly night air helps to sober me up a bit. I feel more alert when I reach the pub after a brisk walk, only to discover that Lunis is already closed. Shit. I'm too late.

No, wait. There's still a light on inside.

I bring my head closer to the door, pin my nose to the glass and try to peek through the slits of the blinds to see what's going on inside.

I see her. She's got a mop in her hand, and she's dancing. I smile. Even in those horrific clothes, she looks amazing. She sticks her butt out and shakes. Fucking hell, my cock hardens immediately.

I knock on the door, then harder, and after a few knocks, the shutters move, and I see her face in the window. Her eyes widen. She signals to me with her hands that the place is closed and returns the blind to its place.

I knock again, asking her to open the door for me. I see the hesitation on her face. She doesn't trust me. But after another brief hesitation, she opens the door, just a crack. I can get in easily. Her featherweight is no match for mine. But I have no intention of scaring her. On the contrary, I need to earn her trust.

"I think I forgot my credit card here. Can you check, please?" I put on a big smile, but she doesn't seem impressed.

She's examining me, trying to figure out if I'm a threat. "Okay. Wait here a minute." She closes the door again, and I hear the lock click into place.

I wait for her to look for my credit card, which I know isn't there, while I try to think of what to say to her.

A few minutes later, she opens the door a crack again. "I can't find your card."

"Hope, right?" I ask as if I don't remember her name, as if I hadn't imagined her naked for hours.

She nods but continues to stand there, looking at the floor. She must be at least a little interested in me. I just need to find the right thing to say.

"Can I'll leave my number so you'll call when you find it?" I hope to hide the card here tomorrow and make her call me under false pretenses.

"Sure. You can write down the number, and I'll give it to the owner tomorrow," she says without looking at me, and now I'm getting annoyed. How am I supposed to impress her like that? I place a hand on the door, keeping it from closing.

Now I've got her attention. She's looking directly at me. Her hands clench on the mop stick.

"Can I walk you home?" I ask. "It's late."

She smirks. "No."

I raise an eyebrow. Her reaction surprises me. Nothing is going as I expected. I like that.

"Why not? I'm a public figure. I'm not dangerous." I try to convince her of my trustworthiness, though my intentions are not so innocent.

"Just no."

Okay, it's not going as well as I thought at all.

"Then I'd love to take you out for dinner or something else if you don't fancy dinners. What do you like to do?" Normally, I don't do dates. They're a waste of time. Why spend unnecessary hours on dates when you can go straight to bed? And since my agreement with Olive, I try not to appear in public with a woman other than her. But it's clear to me that I need to soften this one up first. It's okay. I'm game.

"No, thanks." Her answer is short and concise. She tries to close the door, and I put my leg in the gap.

"So something else, maybe? I want to get to know you."

"No. Thanks," she insists.

I'm starting to lose it. "Well, give me a chance. I don't bite." Unless you want me to bite... I imagine myself biting her nipples and exhale. Oh, this is going to be amazing.

"I'm not interested. Leave your number, and we'll let you know if someone finds your card. I have to finish cleaning and close the place."

Seeing I'm getting nowhere, I relent and let her close the door. I did say I didn't want to scare her.

I bite my bottom lip. I was selected as one of the top one hundred most wanted bachelors in NYC. I've got money, I know I'm good-looking, and damn it, I'm also very good in bed. I make them scream every time. I'm known for my reputation. Why would someone refuse to date me?

I don't know how to convince her. She's so stubborn. It's not something I'm used to. But I know where she works, and I can be stubborn too.

The buzz I had from the alcohol is gone, and now I'm just pissed off. I can wait for her, though. She'll finish soon and go home, and then I can accompany her, leaving her no choice.

I decide to wait, but half an hour goes by, and there's no sight of her.

I stick my nose against the glass again to peek inside. The place is dark, and she's nowhere to be seen.

How did I miss her? There must be a back entrance somewhere. She must have seen me waiting for her. I circle the building but can't see her or an exit to another street. Odd.

The phone is already in my hand, and regardless of the hour, I text Jess. He's my *getter*. He's discreet, expensive, and can get me anything I want without asking questions.

Jess, I need the plans for this building in Chelsea.

I write to him and attach a picture of the building, adding the address to the message.

Also, get me details about the building owner and the owner of the pub downstairs.

It's a bit extreme, but I'm willing to go all the way. Whatever it takes, I will get her.

I wake up late on Saturday in my apartment after the long night and text Ryan to make sure he's okay. He doesn't respond, and I assume he must still be sleeping. I didn't drink anywhere near as much as he did, and I can still feel the traces of whiskey in my veins.

Madeleine doesn't work on the weekends, so I make myself coffee and toast while I go through and answer my emails. After I'm done with the important ones, I notice an email from Jess. He's the man. I have to give him a big fat bonus. I add a task to my list and open the email with curiosity.

There is an attachment that I assume is the building plans I requested. I read the message first. The owner of the building is Jeffrey Johnson. I've worked with him before. He's tough but fair. The information's helpful if I decide to do something extreme and need him, but I hope not to get there. The pub is leased to Dana Margolis, whom I've never heard of.

I open the file, and indeed, Jess has provided the building plans. I enlarge the first floor and look for the exits.

Yes. I knew it. I pat myself on the back. There's a side exit to what looks like a path, probably leading to the garbage area. How did I miss this yesterday?

I look closer. Shit, it seems that the path also leads to the main street, the same place where I was standing. If she left the building from there, I would have seen her. Unless... The exit doesn't look exactly like in the plans. It won't be the first time I saw plans that didn't reflect the situation on the ground. I'll have to go there and check it out with my own eyes.

I retrieve the Porsche keys, then remember I left it at Ryan's, as I was too drunk to drive home. Fuck. I can take the Jeep and send someone to bring the Porsche back, but I don't like letting others drive my baby.

I can run there. Change my routine and catch two birds with one stone.

I arrive at the pub sweatier and more tired than usual. The fatigue from yesterday is affecting me more than I expected. I finish a run like this without a problem on regular days.

I enter the side path and find the door. It's locked as expected. The road leads straight to the main street, exactly like in the plans. If she left from here, she would have had to go through me. How did she sneak out without me seeing? I wasn't that drunk.

In an irrational and reckless decision, I decide to do something I haven't done since I was a teenager.

Break in.

I did a lot of illegal things back then, struggling with emotions I couldn't handle at the time. But doing it now, when I'm a grown man with successful businesses, isn't exactly smart. If I get caught, it could cost me everything. But for some reason, I can't help myself. I have to figure this out, find the woman who crawled under my skin and now occupies all my thoughts since I met her. This place is my only clue.

The skill is still there, just like riding a bike. Someone needs to tell the owner to improve the security at this place. I use the alarm code Jess sent me to disarm it without harm. Some day I have to ask him how he obtains all this information. Or maybe it's better not to.

It's still early in the day, the pub is dark, and there's no one here, thank God. But also nothing that screams, "I'm a hint!"

It's just a pub. What was I thinking when I broke in here? What did I expect to find in a pub? I walk back to the door, disappointed, when my eye catches a faint light coming from the left. It's a door, and the light is peeking out from beneath it. I open it carefully, not knowing what to expect.

Stairs.

I recall the plans showing a small room and bathroom located on the second floor. I hesitate for a moment. Who knows what's there? Am I willing to risk it all? But the urge to expose the truth pushes me forward, and I start up, taking each step on my tiptoes.

I stop at the open doorway of a small room loaded with restaurant items, chairs, and electrical appliances piled neatly on one side of the room. On the other side, there's a mattress arranged on the floor with a blanket and a pillow, and next to it is a small wardrobe with some neatly folded clothes. A bottle of water is placed on top of it.

It looks like someone lives here. The owner? Or the girl I'm looking for?

I go to the little closet to take a closer look at the clothes inside. There's not much here, some jeans and t-shirts. Nothing out of the ordinary. But these could be her clothes. Could she be living here? In the pub? I reach for the black t-shirt with the word Lunis on it...

CHAPTER 5
Ayala

I get out of the shower, wrap myself in a towel, and rub the small mirror with my palm, trying to keep the steam away so I can brush my short hair.

Noises.

Burglar.

My hands start to shake, and I drop the comb. It's not Dana, she never comes here in the mornings, and she always calls me from downstairs. She never invades my privacy. No one else knows I'm here.

Michael found me.

He came to finish what he started. What should I do?

I have to get out of here, run away. I can't let him get me. I can't go back to that life again. Anything is better than going back.

After a quick look around, I grab the only object that can help, The mop.

I turn off the lights and step outside, wrapped in a towel, holding the stick high with both hands. The room is dark, and he doesn't notice me.

A man is crouching next to my bed and rummaging through

my things. It's not Michael, I notice with a sigh of relief. Not the same body type. Michael is narrow and not wide in the shoulders like this man. But it could still be one of his messengers.

I sneak up behind him, and he doesn't notice me. What does he think he will find in my plain shirts? There is nothing to steal here.

I lift my hands and swing the mop over his head with all my strength. And I hit him. I hit him hard. I can't believe I did it. I did it! The man falls to the floor, holding his head. He tries to get up, and I hit him again.

"I won't let you take me back there!"

I stand panting, the stick still raised in the air, ready for a third strike, but he doesn't rise again. He just lies there on the floor. I dropped the towel on the floor, but I don't care. It's time to get out of here.

"Bambi, is that you?" he calls in a weak voice.

I recognize that voice. The low, unforgettable voice.

It's him. Ethan Wolf.

What is he doing here in my room, rummaging through my things?

He called me Bambi. He knows. Damn, he knows. He found out my real name.

No. That doesn't make any sense. Who would know that the name Ayala means Bambi? I didn't know it until my mom explained it to me. It's not even in English.

"Hope," he whispers, and I stop at the door, not knowing what to do. He's now using my false name. He didn't mention Michael either. What is he looking for here?

I'm not of his class or stature. Not anymore, anyway. I have nothing that could interest a man like him. I have nothing to give. Should I stay or run away? If he wanted to attack me, he would have done so already, wouldn't he? He's had no shortage of opportunities.

Gosh, I opened the door for him last night when the place was closed, and I was alone. I knew it was dangerous, yet I opened it for him. For some reason, he doesn't scare me, unlike the other men who try to hit on me. Maybe because he protected me in the champagne incident?

No, it's just my imagination running wild. I don't know him at all. He could be a dangerous criminal, for all I know.

I turn back and look at him. He's lying on his stomach, moaning in pain. Blood flows from the back of his head and forms a small puddle on the floor. I cover my mouth with my hand in horror. Damn, it's bad, and I did it. I get a little closer, trying to catch a glimpse of his face, confirming what I already know. His sharp features are only partially visible, but there is no doubt it's him. I nudge him with my foot, but he doesn't move. This doesn't look good.

"Ethan Wolf?" I call and get only a moan in response. His consciousness appears to be fuzzy.

Shit, how do I explain to Dana why there is an injured man in my room? I dare and bend down next to him, trying to understand how he's doing.

He's wearing a sweat-soaked sports shirt and sweatpants. Did he come here from the gym? I stare for a moment at his bare, shiny arm muscles.

"Ethan," I call again, louder this time. Maybe I should call him Mr. Wolf? We don't know each other. But then again, he is here in my room. It's not exactly an official meeting.

I'm in trouble. Big trouble.

He moans again and moves his head a little. His beautiful face contorts in pain. At least I didn't kill him. I grab a shirt from the wardrobe and quickly pull it over my head to hide my naked body.

I pick up my only towel and hold it to his head to stop the bleeding. Why is there so much blood? It doesn't stop. God, what should I do? He'll bleed to death on my floor. Images of blood dripping through the floor to the ceiling of the pub comes to mind.

I think he needs a doctor, but how do I get him to one? And with what money? I don't know anyone, and there's no way I could carry him down the stairs.

You're worthless.

I shake my head, trying to quiet the voices.

Damn Ayala. Think. But I can't think of any viable way. I pace the room back and forth, afraid of what's going to happen.

Maybe I should pack my things and just run away. Every option I play in my head ends up with me being in prison for murder or on the streets again, this time with fewer options than before. If I run away, at least I'll remove the jail option. But I know that if I leave him like this, he'll die. I can't leave him to—

A ringtone starts playing and startles me. The ringing is coming from his pocket. Someone is trying to reach him. Should I answer?

I bend down and take the phone out of his pants pocket.

The screen lights up the name of the caller next to his picture.

Ryan Blake.

I recognize the picture. Isn't that the same man he was here with yesterday? Yes, that's him. I'm pretty sure. In a hasty decision, I answer. They seemed close, and their relationship impressed me. Maybe he's my solution.

I slide on the green mark. "Hello?"

Silence reigns for a moment on the other side.

"Who is this?" a firm voice asks. "Where is Ethan?"

"He can't answer right now," I say with a shaky voice. The caller doesn't sound like the sensitive man from yesterday.

"Call him to the phone, now. I don't care if he's asleep or in the middle of fucking," Ryan continues, and I cringe. My finger hesitates over the disconnect button. He's stressing me out. This is not what I expected. But as I look down at Ethan motionless on the floor, I remind myself that this man on the phone is currently my only option. I'll tell him what happened and hope he gets me out of it. If he can't help, all I have left to do is run away again.

"I need help," I say. "This is the cleaning lady from the pub yesterday," I add, so Ryan understands who I am.

He's silent for a moment. "From the pub? Oh, so he took the number... I should have known. He's such a whore." Ryan's snorting now.

What is he talking about? Whore? I don't understand what he means. I don't have much time. I glance at Ethan on the floor. There's too much blood.

"Help me, please." My voice starts to crumble, and tears begin to flow against my will.

Ryan stops laughing. "What? What's happened?"

"I... He's here in my room, and I thought he was a burglar, so I hit him with the mop, and he's on the floor. There's blood. So much blood. I didn't mean to hit him. I don't know what to do," I sob.

"Burglar? Blood? On the floor? I don't understand a thing you're saying. What happened? Where is Ethan? Explain to me slowly."

"On the floor. Passed out. I think." I hope so. Because the other possibility is that he's dead.

"Where are you? I'm coming."

"Lunis. Come quickly, please.".

"Lunis? I thought you said in your room? Nevermind. I'm close. I'll be there in ten minutes."

A few minutes later, I hear vigorous knocking on the door of the pub. The knocks are so loud that I'm afraid the door is going to fall in. I should have run away before he arrived, left the door open for him, and disappeared. Why didn't I think of this before? Now it's too late.

I think I made a mistake involving this man, but I don't know. I don't know what he will do. He could call the police.

I stand up, wipe the trails of tears from my cheeks, and hurry downstairs to open the door for him.

Ryan bursts in and asks, "Where is he?" The soft look from yesterday is gone now. He looks different. Sober and powerful. His dark eyes are fierce, like someone you don't want to mess with. Like Ethan. I think I made a mistake in my assessment. He won't help me. I'm going to jail.

I point at the stairs. "Up."

He rushes past me taking two steps at a time, and I follow him. He kneels next to Ethan and tries to wake him like I did but gets no answer except moans. "Fuck," Ryan mumbles while checking the condition of the wound, and his lips tighten into a thin line. "It's not good. He needs a doctor."

I know that.

Ryan stands and paces the room. I retreat to a corner, hugging myself. Ethan's going to die, and I'm going to prison for manslaughter. Or murder.

"What happened here?" Ryan turns to me, his eyes narrowing in accusation. "I don't understand. What is he doing here? Why did you hit him?"

"I don't know what he's doing here." I shake my head.

Ryan approaches me, looking threatening. "Why didn't you call an ambulance?"

I rub my neck, trying to move away from him. "I don't know. He scared me. I was in the shower, and he just appeared here in the room. I don't know how he got in," I say, raising my voice. "I thought he was a burglar." I thought he was Micheal.

"He broke in?" Ryan wraps his fingers around his chin. "He

hasn't done anything like that since..." The rest of his words are muttered under his breath. Words I can't understand.

His eyes scan me from top to bottom, and I hasten to pull my t-shirt down over my legs. I took the time to pull on underwear, but I'm not wearing any pants and feel naked under his scrutinizing gaze.

He doesn't speak, and I feel the need to interrupt the silence. "I don't want to get in trouble."

"I guess if you live here, you've already gotten into some trouble." He waves his hand and gestures to my room. "Is that why you didn't call an ambulance? Did Ethan do anything besides enter your room?"

I shake my head. Why would he think so? Has this happened before? Is Ethan dangerous? I didn't get that impression. But I've fallen into this trap before. Why don't I learn? Once wasn't enough?

"Okay." Ryan's voice brings me back to reality. "I'll make a deal with you. I'll handle the incident without anyone knowing you're involved, and you won't tell anyone that he broke in here. Okay?" His head is tilted to the side, waiting for my answer.

I nod vigorously. "Yeah, okay." That's exactly what I want. Make everything disappear as if it never happened.

"Come help me get him out of here," he says. "I have to take him to a doctor ASAP."

"Isn't it dangerous?" I ask. "To move him, I mean?"

"Would you rather I call an ambulance?" He raises an eyebrow.

I shake my head. "No."

"He'll be fine. I'll take care of him." Ryan kneels and pulls his friend's sprawled body to a standing position. I don't move. I haven't touched a man other than Michael in years.

"Well?" Ryan rushes me.

I go under Ethan's other arm, grab his hips and help support him.

How can a sweaty man smell so good? The same citrus scent I smelled from him last time, this time mixed with his natural scent. And his body feels so solid next to me...

"Let's move," Ryan says, urging his friend to stand on his own.

I shouldn't think of Ethan like that. I need to focus.

We go down the stairs, almost falling every other step, but manage to reach the bottom.

I'm panting heavily. Ethan is bigger and heavier than me, and even with Ryan's help, my whole body hurts. I notice the black Mercedes parked at the curb in front of the pub. Ryan leans Ethan against the car and manages to squeeze him into the backseat. Ryan turns to me again, and I can see the beads of sweat on his forehead.

"Forget he was here."

I nod. This is exactly what I want, to forget it ever happened. I'd be happy if I never saw Ethan Wolf again. I watch as Ryan gets into the driver's seat and drives away, leaving me standing in the street in my t shirt and underwear.

CHAPTER 6

Ethan

I blink against the blinding light in the room, trying to understand where I am. My head is throbbing in pain. I reach out and feel the small bandage behind my head. What is this?

"Oh, I see you've decided to return to the world of the living," I hear a familiar voice say, and my vision finally focuses on Ryan's face.

"Ryan," I groan, "What's going on? Where am I? How long have I been here?"

"You're in a hospital. It's been three months," he tells me, and I jump out of bed in a panic. My heart beats hard, and a wave of pain washes over me.

"Fuck. Fuck!"

He smirks. "Calm down. You've been here for about two hours."

"I'd kill you if my head didn't feel like a bowling ball," I moan. "Son of a bitch." Suddenly a few hours sounds good. For a moment, I believed I'd lost a few months. "How did I get here?"

"Don't you remember?" he asks, tilting his head to the side as if he thinks I've completely lost it.

Am I supposed to remember? I try to pull the details out of my evasive memory. "I remember going into the pub. There was a storage room upstairs, with a mattress and clothes, as if someone were living there." That's where I got hit? Yes. I remember the crippling pain in the back of my head. "I think someone hit me," I say. Not telling him that I remember a naked woman with a divine body bending over me. Someone hit me hard if I remember correctly.

"The waitress or cleaning lady or whatever she is, the one we saw yesterday in the pub. She's the one who hit you. She thought you were a burglar. And she wasn't wrong, was she? Ethan Wolf, a respectable businessman, breaks into a pub," Ryan says, imitating a dramatic newscaster. "What the hell were you doing there?"

His lips curl into a wry smile, but he continues without waiting for an answer. "She answered your phone. She was very stressed. Thought you were going to die there on the floor. It turns out you don't die that easily. Just a few stitches. Luckily they're not on your ugly face. And you have a mild concussion. Nothing serious."

Hope was there. Maybe my imagination is not deceiving me as I thought. She was naked, and I missed it. Fuck, I'd be ready to get hit again to see her naked.

"Is she going to file a complaint?" I ask.

"No. It was pretty clear she didn't want to call the police, so I used that to your advantage. Obviously, someone who lives in a storage room above a bar is already in some kind of trouble. I told her we wouldn't involve her if she didn't file a complaint against you." Ryan smirks again. "Luckily for you, she didn't realize how much money she could get out of this situation."

Who cares about the money? "She lives there?" That's what I thought, but I didn't have time to make sure.

"Looks like that. But really, man, what's up with you? Breaking into a pub? I thought we were past that stage fifteen years ago. You know, the situation is different now. Though I'm an excellent lawyer, I'm not a magician. I won't be able to rescue you if you get caught. You could lose everything you have. Everything you've worked for. I don't understand why you would risk everything like that." He shakes his head.

"I know. It was a mistake. It won't happen again." What was I thinking? If the word gets out, I'm done. My parents covered up my bullshit when I was young, but I'm no longer a kid. And I got over the shit with Anna. I don't do things like that anymore.

"Did something happen?" he continues. "Do you want to talk about it? You know I'm here for you, both as a lawyer and as a friend. You can talk to me."

I appreciate the gesture. I know he's there for me. He's a loyal friend, and I would do anything for him, just as he would for me. But I don't know why I did what I did. Something about this woman drives me crazy. This has never happened to me before. I have to figure out where I recognize her from., I think that's the problem. Maybe if I remember where I saw her, this obsession will pass.

I hear Ryan talking, and I shake off the thoughts as I try to concentrate and listen to him.

"So you broke in there because of that waitress?" he asks, and I nod.

"I don't understand. Why didn't you just ask her for her number?"

"I did," I say.

"She turned you down? Someone turned down the amazing Ethan Wolf? Seriously? How can that be?" I hear the mockery in his voice, but I ignore it. "And you think being a stalker will make her want you? Somehow I don't think so."

He's right, of course, but it just annoys me even more.

"It's not like that. I never thought she would be there. I was just trying to figure out a few things for myself. Who the hell lives above a bar?" There's something strange there. I need to get far away from it. It will only bring me trouble. But for some reason, I'm drawn to it even more. I want to solve this mystery.

"Storage room or not, I promised that girl I wouldn't report her. When they come to ask you what happened, tell them you fell and got hit by a table. Okay?"

I nod. "Do my parents know what happened?" I ask with sudden concern.

He shakes his head. "I didn't tell anyone. Your decision."

Thank God. I don't need any more preaching from my mother, as if I don't get enough already.

"I'll go call a doctor to release you, and I'll take you home. You need to get some rest. You've been unconscious for a few hours, after all." I can hear the tone of concern in his voice, the one he tries to hide with jokes.

Yes, my head is pulsing with pain, and I need to rest. But I also lost half a day on this adventure, and I have work to do. And I need to stay away from this woman. I have to stay away from her.

So why can't I wait to see her again?

The doctor comes and asks me all kinds of questions. I stick to Ryan's version and answer laconically.

"I fell."

"No, I don't remember what happened."

"I was not involved in a fight."

"No, no one hit me."

I know he doesn't buy it, but I don't care. If there's no complaint, there's nothing to investigate. The story's over. I'm not a child they need to protect.

They try to convince me to stay for observation, but I insist on being released. I take the painkillers offered to me, and within an hour, I'm outside, waiting for Ryan to bring the car around.

I don't call my driver to pick me up, but I ask him to return my car home, as I have no other choice now. I also didn't tell anyone else that I was in the hospital. Ryan will keep it quiet. No one needs to know about my stupidity.

I know it was a mistake. And a serious one. But I text Jess anyway.

> I want to know everything about a woman named Hope who works at Lunis.

Ryan drops me off at my penthouse. It's early afternoon, and I have to complete some work. I sit down in front of the computer, read the same email over and over, and still can't remember what I read. Half an hour passes by, and I've made no progress. I slam the screen shut and stand up. It's a lost fight. I have to talk to her.

A few minutes later, I'm in the Jeep and on my way to Lunis.

Again.

CHAPTER 7

Ayala

My plans to go shopping for winter clothes fly out the window. Instead, I spend most of my morning fighting a panic attack, pacing the small room.

I use an entire bottle of bleach on the floor and scrub at the blood stain, but a faint trace is still visible. Dana mustn't find out what happened here.

I pack all my things in my bag and unpack them again. I don't know what to do. Should I run? Should I stay?

What if I killed him? What if he dies?

And what if he doesn't die, but he won't agree to what his friend suggested and says I attacked him?

Maybe I should get out of here right now. Save myself from getting arrested. But where will I go? I check the money I've managed to earn in the last two weeks. It's not much, but I can buy a bus ticket and move on.

I don't want to leave after Dana has been so good to me. I have a job and a place to sleep. I like it here. But I see no other choice. Staying here is a risk I can't take. At any moment now, the police could knock on my door.

I start packing all my things again. I haven't had time to buy much yet, and everything fits in my backpack easily.

I go downstairs and hurry down the aisle between the tables, running my hand over the slippery wooden counter, the one I clean every night. This place has been my home for the past weeks. I sit behind the counter for several minutes, trying to engrave every detail in my memory. I know it's ridiculous, but I'm going to miss this place. Here I felt free for the first time in a long time. I was myself and not some fake character Michael decided I had to be.

I pull out a sheet of paper and a pen from behind the cash register and start drafting a letter for Dana. I thank her for the help, for her warm heart, and I apologize for leaving like this. I try to explain that I had no choice.

I put the note in her office and walk out with a heavy heart, only to find a familiar figure standing on the sidewalk.

Ethan Wolf.

I freeze as if I see a ghost. It's just a mirage. He's in the hospital. It can't be him. But it is him. Alive and breathing.

He's standing here as if nothing unusual happened this morning. Like I didn't hit him. Maybe he has a twin brother? But as he approaches, I see the bandage behind his head from the injury I caused. His face shows no expression.

He came to collect.

I should run away. But if he chases me, I have no chance against him. I'm not a runner. I go through all the options in my head quickly.

I can escape.

Return to Lunis and lock the door.

Let him catch me.

Scream.

Talk to him.

I decide to go back inside, but my legs are as heavy as stones, and I'm too slow. He catches up with me and stands in front of me, blocking my way.

His eyes glow in shimmering gold in the midday sunlight. He swallows, and it draws my gaze to his sharp jawline. He is so damn beautiful.

"Are you going somewhere?" He peeks behind my shoulder at the bag. The bag that contains my whole life.

I don't respond, and he continues. "I just want to talk to you."

I want to run away before you decide to call the police. That's what I want to say to him, while he just stands and stares at me in silence, waiting for my answer. *Before Michael comes to take me back.*

"Aren't you in the hospital?" I ask after my voice comes back to me. What a stupid question. Obviously, he's not in a hospital. He's right here in front of me.

"They released me. Mild concussion." He waves his hand as if something like this happens to him every day. "So, can we talk?"

"I–I'm...sorry," I stutter, assuming he wants to talk about what happened this morning. "I'm sorry I hit you. You scared me. I thought you were breaking in."

He looks at me, his pupils dilating, and his lips curve into a smile.

"Oh, don't worry. I kept the deal you made with Ryan. I didn't mention you. You're not in trouble or anything."

I release the air I was holding in my lungs. He didn't say it was me. No one is chasing me. I don't need to run away. Relief washes over me, and my muscles relax.

"I just want to talk. I'll accompany you wherever you need to go."

"I..." Now that I don't have to run, I have nowhere to go. I feel like a heavy weight has been lifted off my shoulders.

He continues to stand there, his gaze moving between me and

the bag. But it doesn't look like he's going to leave until he says what he has to say.

"Okay," I say with a shrug, "talk." I start walking without a definite destination, preferring not to enter Lunis again.

We start walking down the street, and silence prevails. He wanted to talk, but he remains silent, and I'm not going to be the one who starts this conversation. After a long minute of silence, he turns to me and asks, "Are you hungry? Because I'm starving. Let's buy something to eat and sit down?"

I nod. I'm hungry, but I agree only to break the awkwardness more than anything else.

He takes my hand and pulls me with him. I look down at his big palm holding mine in shock. I want to pull my hand back, but I don't want to at the same time. Is this even possible? A cold spot forms on my lower back and starts to climb up. In a few moments, I won't be able to breathe.

"I know an excellent deli here. We'll be there soon."

His hold on me stresses me to the core. A man is holding onto me and taking me to an unknown place.

I feel the panic attack coming and try to control it.

Inhale... Exhale... I look up at him and tug on my hand, trying to make him stop, but he doesn't notice my fear and continues to move forward, dragging me after him. I try to remember to breathe, but I feel like I have no air. The freezing cold grips my lungs.

We are on a public street. There are people here. Nothing will happen to me.

We speed through two blocks, and finally, he stops outside a small store packed with shoppers and drops my hand.

I hurry to put my hands in my pockets to prevent him from taking my hand again and try to ignore my heart that threatens to jump out of my chest. *He's not Michael. He's not trying to hurt me.*

I say it over and over in my head like a mantra while trying to keep a calm face.

"What do you like to eat? Do you have any allergies?" he asks, completely unaware of the storm raging inside of me.

You can't order for yourself. You're worthless.

What do I like? I haven't ordered for myself in years. I can't even answer a simple question. "I... I don't know."

"I'll order for both of us." He goes inside and leaves me to wait outside.

Should I go in with him? I decide to stay on the sidewalk and catch my breath.

Despite the long queue, I see he gets served right away, and after a brief wait, he receives a bag full of boxes from one of the employees and steps outside.

"I didn't know what you would like, so I bought a selection." He smiles and lifts the bag toward me. The smile lights up his face. He seems so young. More accessible. I wonder how old he is.

We keep walking, but this time he's holding the bag and lets me walk beside him without trying to grab me. I keep a safe distance until we reach a small park, and he hurries to place the heavy bag in the center of the bench. He sits on one side, leaving me to sit on the other.

I thank him in my heart for the space the bag created between us and pull my oversized shirt over my hips. Not what I expected when he asked if I was hungry, but the food smells good, and my stomach is rumbling.

He takes napkins out of the bag, hands me one, and spreads the other on his lap. Then he pulls out the boxes one by one and presents me with a large selection of salads and sandwiches that all look great.

I take the plate and fork he hands me and watch as he fills his plate with food and lifts the full fork to his mouth. He doesn't seem to care what he looks like.

He looks so relaxed, almost carefree. Just a few hours ago, I thought he was dying on the floor of my room. I don't understand it. How is he not angry?

He notices me staring at him and stops with the fork midway to his mouth. An embarrassed smile appears on his face.

"I eat like a pig. Sorry. I'm so hungry. I usually eat right after I run," he says, and I find myself smiling back.

He thinks I'm staring at him because of the food. I can't remember the last time I smiled at a man. I also don't remember when a man bought me food and sat down to eat with me on a bench. Actually, I do remember—it was never. I try to imagine Michael in this situation, and I just can't. A meal on a bench would shock Michael. Meals should always be served on a carefully prepared table.

I dare and eat some of the food. It's delicious. Salads and delicacies that I have never tasted before. I don't know what he wants from me, but at least the food is good. I eat but stay alert. Ready to run away if I have to.

"Do you live in that storage room?" he asks, and I look up to find him examining me. His eyes scan my face and then lock onto mine. There is nothing but curiosity in them.

I nod.

"Why?"

"It's a long story."

"I have time." He picks up more food from the plate and puts it in his mouth. I follow how his full lips wrap around the fork, and an unfamiliar heat rises in my stomach.

"I'd rather not talk about it."

"Okay." He bites his lower lip. "I know I've seen you before. I'm sure of it. I have an excellent memory for faces. But I can't figure out where. Maybe tell me where we know each other so I can put it behind me? It's driving me crazy."

Wait, does he remember our first meeting outside the station?

It was just an insignificant moment. He can't recognize me. My hair was long then and in a different color. My face was swollen from beatings beyond distinction. How could he remember that? It doesn't make sense.

"We don't know each other," I answer. That's true. A random meeting on the street does not count as an acquaintance. "I probably just have a familiar face."

He seems even more frustrated now that I haven't provided the answers he's looking for.

"You're too beautiful for me to mistake you for someone else. I'm sure I've seen you before." He runs his hand through his hair, pulling it back. "I don't know why but it's making me crazy that I can't remember."

Does he really think I'm beautiful? I feel my cheeks getting warmer.

He takes another bite and continues, still chewing, in a not-very polite manner, "I'm sorry for what happened this morning."

I don't understand. He should be angry. I'm the one who should be sorry.

"I thought it was an empty room," he adds. "I didn't know there was anyone there. Sorry for scaring you." He continues to apologize, and I just sit frozen and look at him in astonishment. This is not what I expected. At all.

"I'm sorry I hit you," I mumble again. "How come you're not mad at me?"

He smiles again. God, why does he look so good? It's distracting.

"It wouldn't be the first time I've gotten into trouble. You've got nothing to worry about. A few stitches and a headache. I've had worse."

I wonder why a rich man like him would get into fights, but I keep my mouth shut. I don't think he cares, and I managed to get out of it somehow.

I peek at his bare arm. He has a tattoo on the inside. In the daylight, I can see it well. The hummingbird looks like it's literally coming to life, and the curled letters below it spell out the name Anna.

I wonder who she is, but I don't dare to ask. Maybe the woman in the blue dress?

"Why did you buy me this meal?"

"Because I wanted to talk to you, and I'm hungry," he says. "I already told you that I'm interested in you. You didn't agree to go out with me, but it looks like I succeeded in making it happen." His mouth curves in an amused smile.

Indeed, he succeeded.

"So, tell me something about yourself other than the fact that you work as a waitress."

What can I tell him? I left everything I had behind. I have nothing. The new me has no history.

"You managed to drag me here under false pretenses, but you won't get anything out of me." I smile.

He tilts his head, and a small wrinkle appears between his eyes as he narrows them. "Under false pretenses, huh? Well, I still want your number."

I shake my head. "No."

"Why? You won't even give me a chance? Most women would kill to give me their number."

"I'm not most women."

His eyes are fixed on me again. "I see that. And yet..."

"I don't have a number to give you because I don't have a phone," I admit. I couldn't take the phone I had because Michael would have used it to track me. And I have more urgent expenses than a new phone. For example, a coat and shoes so that I won't freeze when winter comes.

"I don't think I've ever met anyone who doesn't have a phone. I also never met someone who lives in a storage room." He mumbles that part quietly, but I still hear him. "Why don't you have a phone?"

I shrug. I have no intention of explaining myself to him.

"So...can I buy you a phone?"

I arch an eyebrow. "What? Why would you buy me a phone? We don't even know each other."

"Oh, for purely selfish reasons. I want to be able to talk to you without breaking in anywhere." He smirks. "It's just a phone, not a marriage commitment."

I cringe. I will never marry. "I don't want to talk to you." I pause and then ponder the ridiculous idea for a moment. It is ridiculous. Why would I let a complete stranger buy me a phone? But on the other hand, beyond the cost, there is one distinct advantage. This device will have nothing to do with me because I won't be the one purchasing it. I won't have to give fake details and they won't be able to track me down through it. It would be safe. And I do need access to the internet. I need to connect to the world.

Suddenly the idea doesn't seem so bad. But this is not a casual meal on a bench. Letting him purchase a phone for me would create a commitment on my part. Not something I'm ready for. Michael also seemed kind at first, and look where that got me.

"There's no obligation on your part," he hastens to add as if reading my mind.

I bite my cheek. It's tempting. Too tempting. Disconnecting from the world is dangerous too. I don't even know if Michael is looking for me.

"Okay, but I'm not going to answer your calls if I don't want to," I say, and he nods.

"No problem. I already know how to break into your room if I need to," he says with a stern expression.

In any other situation, it would sound like a threat, but I smile in response.

CHAPTER 8

Ayala

I stare at my new iPhone, and self-loathing overwhelms me. I've been blinded by money again, letting my desire to be connected to the world take over my common sense. These things never come for free. I learned that the hard way.

How the hell did I fall for this again?

After all, that's how it all started.

I was in the second year of studying business administration, completely immersed in studies and work. Even with a scholarship, I still had to finance my living accommodations, so I spent all my evenings working in a call center.

The college experience went over my head. Parties and hanging out? Not for me. I knew I had to excel to keep the scholarship.

But when Katya, my roommate, celebrated her birthday, I had no way of avoiding it.

That party changed my life.

I met Michael Summers at that party. A third-year law student. Rich, handsome, charismatic. The king of the campus who had all the girls falling at his feet.

And as someone easily overlooked, I was a little too flattered that he chose to spend time with me.

We started dating, and he made me dizzy. We went to expensive restaurants, he drove me everywhere and bought me everything I wanted. I was the envy of the campus. I liked it.

Everyone convinced me I'd won the big prize. The most wanted man on campus loves me. I was blind.

Blind to the early warning signs. Blind to the fact that he didn't allow me to meet with anyone but him. Blind to the fact that he forced me to stop working so I could have more time for him.

I thought he loved me. What a fool I was.

I confused obsession with love. Only a few months later, I discovered the genuine face of the monster. And now I'm falling again. One meeting on a bench, and I've already agreed to this commitment.

You're worth nothing without me.

I bite my bottom lip hard until I taste blood. I have to stop this immediately and return the device to him. I need to keep my distance from men in general and from him in particular.

I wake up the next morning after a long shift to an annoying beep, and I remember that I now have a phone. A message from Ethan lights up my screen, and I defiantly ignore it. Despite the crappy way I got it, I now have access to the world. I need to see if Michael posted anything about me. But instead, I open a search and type quickly before I regret it. Ethan Wolf. I watch as the results unveil.

"He has a Wikipedia page, for God's sake," I mutter as the results appear before my eyes, and I click on the link.

Ethan Wolf, twenty-eight years old, single.

At the age of nineteen, he founded the high-tech company Savee, which is known for the phone application with the same name, intended to help victims of rape, violence, and mental support.

At the age of twenty-two, he founded Wolf Fortress, which deals with data security in the cloud. [Update] The company was sold in a successful exit that is valued at over a billion dollars.

Wolf also owns a venture capital fund known for its investments in new startups. He is the main investor in the well-known company Landen Gaming and...

I'm skipping some paragraphs that are less interesting to me, supplying additional details about companies owned by him. How many businesses does he have?

Where am I, and where is he? At the age of twenty-eight, he has a billion-dollar empire, and I live in a warehouse without a dollar on my ass and clean tables for a living. I don't understand what he wants from me.

I stare for a moment at the Savee company logo. I know this app. It's supposed to help women and men in need. I never installed it on my old phone, but I definitely considered it. I knew Michael had my phone under surveillance, just as he had every aspect of my life under surveillance. I couldn't risk it. I could only trust myself.

I look at the company logo again. Is this what I think it is? I enlarge the picture. It's a hummingbird. The logo is just an outline of the bird, but it's almost identical to the tattoo Ethan has on his arm. I look for data on the meaning of the symbol of the logo, but I don't find anything. Whatever the story behind it is, it's not public.

I continue reading and click on some of the links, reaching an article announcing he was chosen as one of the sexiest men in NYC. I enlarge his picture, a publicist photo of Ethan in a suit. He looks amazing, of course, but I remember how he looked sitting next to me on the bench in a t-shirt and a smile. Simplicity suits him better.

I open more pictures of him photographed with different women. One of the articles claims he has a girlfriend. I recognize in the photo the beautiful woman I saw with him at the event, Olivia Danske.

The slight tingling of irritation I feel annoys me, and I decide to push it aside. This is not why I ran away from everything. I need to start over and build a new life for myself.

Alone.

CHAPTER 9

Ethan

I wake up in the morning with a headache and realize the painkillers they gave me in the hospital yesterday have worn off. I hasten to swallow two more pills with a glass of water.

Ryan informed me that he's going to Maya's parents' place to sort out the issues between them and won't be available today. I tell him not to rush.

I kept him here until noon with the whole hospital drama, and I know that without it, he would have gone to Maya yesterday morning. I hope the delay didn't hurt their relationship.

I have the urge to run. My muscles tingle with need as I'm used to the daily exercise, but the throbbing pain in my head reminds me that I shouldn't. I was able to ignore the slight concussion yesterday, but it's still there.

I sit down and start going through emails. I sink into work for a good few hours. When I look up from the computer again, it's almost noon.

My fingers hesitate on the keys before I send the message.

Hi

I stare at the screen, trying to make it wake up with a determined look. Is she not going to answer me? I was sure I softened her up after the meal at the park.

I go to the kitchen and open the fridge with a little more force than necessary, and the beer bottles on the door rattle loudly. I take out the meal Madeleine left for me, heat it, and sit down to eat.

The phone beeps, and I rush to pick it up from the counter and pause for a second before opening the message.

What the hell is happening to me, jumping like a teenage boy at a message from a woman I barely know? I need to control myself. I put the phone back on the table. Pick up the fork and take a bite. Then another, all the while sending glances at my device. Ugh.

I lift the phone again, and my chest expands when I see that she answered me.

Hope
Hi

How can I be so excited by one simple word?

I want to know what her story is. Why does she live in a bar, and why doesn't she have a phone? Surely there is a story there, something she got involved in.

Hope
I'm sorry about yesterday. How's your head?

I've already forgotten about it.

I answer her with feigned nonchalance. I'm still in pain, but there's no need for her to know that right now. I want to convince her to spend time with me. I want to get to know her, remember where I know her from, and understand why I can't get her out of my head. But I have to be calculated. Inviting her to a restaurant earlier without thinking of the consequences was not very smart. The paparazzi will be happy to ride on it, and Olive will get hurt.

I run through the options in my head until an idea comes up. Mohonk Lake. I've stayed dozens of times in the house by the lake, and I know the surroundings well. The location is close enough that we can do a day trip. Hiking in the forest is one of my favorite things. It's a popular place and usually very crowded, but I know my way around. I know all the secret hiding spots. The nature, the silence, the noise your shoes make on the ground, the ultimate head clearing. There are also some simple routes there that we can take. A picnic by the water sounds good for a first date.

I've never taken anyone there. I always travel by myself, lost in thoughts. Am I willing to share the experience with someone else? And what's more, will she even agree to come with me?

I can convince her. There hasn't been a woman yet that I haven't convinced.

When do you have a free day, Bambi?

Hope
Bambi?

Hope doesn't suit you. So I decided on Bambi.

There is a slight pause while I watch the flashing dots that indicate she's typing.

Hope
I don't have a day off.

How is this possible? Come on. A minor obstacle will not stop me.

Find me a day.

Maybe that sounds a little arrogant?

Please.

Hope
I'm not interested in sleeping with you, so you can stop trying.

Oh, how did we get to sex? Well, then, I'm interested, but I have patience. When I fuck her, which will happen soon, she will beg for it. She interests me enough to want to invest the time.

There are other things I like to do.

She doesn't answer, so I keep writing,

I want to show you an amazing place. Come for a hike with me. Just walking. I promise not to try anything.

Hope
Nothing?

I promise. Friends only.

I see her typing, and I wait until she responds.

Hope
You have a girlfriend.

I don't have a girlfriend. Totally single.

Hope
Okay then. Saturday.

There it is. I knew she could be persuaded. Too bad it's almost a week away, but I have to work anyway. There are still a lot of details in the sale I need to close before I can go on Saturday with a clear head.

Hope
Where are we going? And what should I bring?

Nature. Bring comfortable clothes and sports shoes. Saturday, 7 am.

I hope she doesn't hate walking. Maybe I should offer the restaurant?

Hope
Okay. Smiling emoji.

I got a smile. I smile to myself and toss the phone on the sofa. The chase has begun.

I call Jess to catch up on all the tasks I gave him this week, but I'm especially interested to hear what he found out about Hope. I leave it for the end.

"Wolf, what's up?" he answers.

"What do you have for me?"

We spend the next ten minutes on updates regarding several companies that I was interested in purchasing and requested Jess do an in-depth investigation on them. I'm sorry to find out that one of the insurance companies has problems with the financial statements.

"Something isn't quite right there," he reports. "There are

expenses that couldn't be accounted for. Do you want me to keep digging?"

"No." I delete it from my list. No point in taking the risk. I have other options. "Who's next?"

The next company passed the investigation successfully, and I'm moving the report to the next stage with one of my managers for further review.

After we finish going through the list, I ask, "What about the personal assignment I gave you about Hope?"

"Mmm..." he says. "I'll have to get back to you about her. It's a complicated case. I couldn't find much. I'm trying to dig deeper."

Not good. Jess is the best in the field. "What did you find?"

"She's not listed anywhere. Not even a last name. She works at Lunis and lives there, as you already know, but she doesn't have an employment contract. Seems like something's fishy."

"Fishy, how?"

"She started working there about a month ago, and before that, she didn't exist. It's like she was born a month ago. No paperwork, no acquaintances, no friends, nothing."

"She also worked as a waitress at that event at the gallery," I say. "Did you check there?"

"Yes. A bartender at Lunis got her this job, but she registered there as Hope King."

"Oh, okay, so you do have a last name."

"Hope King is not her real name. And that was the only time she worked there."

That son of a bitch manager probably fired her after all. I'll no longer be working with him on my events.

"What is her connection to Lunis? How did she turn up there?" If she works there without documents, maybe she's related to the owner.

"I was unable to find any connection. I found no evidence

that she knew the owner or anyone else from there. The situation becomes a bit complicated when there's no last name. I looked in the police database for missing person reports, things like that, but there's nothing. I'm sure you'll agree with me that Hope is probably not her real name, either. I also searched her belongings, but found no documents of any kind there. I'm running her picture trough the wanted databases, so we'll see if we get any results. I also contacted friends at Interpol, thinking maybe she's not American. But that will take time. I'll owe them."

"No matter the cost," I add, understanding the hint in his words. This is weirder than I thought. "Maybe she's in the witness protection program or something?"

"It's unlikely. That program is very organized. If she was part of it, she should have had an organized identity with documents and everything. They would make sure she wouldn't arouse suspicion. But this woman has no identity at all."

"Okay, keep checking for me," I say with a sigh. Maybe on our trip, I can get some hints.

This week will pass so slowly.

CHAPTER 10

Ayala

This week went by quickly.

Ethan wrote to me that he would pick me up at seven. He didn't tell me where we were going, but I know it involves some walking.

He said to come in comfortable clothes, so I'm wearing my new black tights, a cotton shirt, and a long, wide hoodie over it, as I know it's usually a little cool in the morning. My backpack only has a bottle of water, and I'm debating whether I should have packed food as well. But it's too late now to go pick something up. I have nothing here. Damn, how did I not think of this before? Now I might stay hungry until tonight.

I head outside to wait at about five minutes to seven, shifting my weight from leg to leg and blowing into my palms to warm up.

At five past seven, I don't think he's going to come. Shit, he must be just playing with me, making me think the rich and handsome man is interested in someone like me. And I bought new clothes, especially for this trip. Fool. He'll leave me here on the sidewalk and then probably laugh about me with his friends. Or maybe this is his revenge for the blow I gave him.

Maybe I should go back inside.

A black Jeep comes barreling up the street and goes up onto the sidewalk next to me. I jump back, startled.

The dark window rolls down, and I see Ethan smiling at me through it. A feeling of warmth washes over me, and I swallow heavily.

"Good Morning."

I open the door and jump in. He's wearing dark pants with big pockets and a black t-shirt with The New York Knicks logo. Okay, at least my sporty clothes will fit. He runs a hand through his hair and smiles at me again. He seems about as excited as I am. This is surprising.

He leans toward me. For a hug? A kiss? But stops himself and leans back in his seat. I'm surprised by the small pinch of disappointment that runs through me. This is exactly what I wanted. He promised not to try anything, and so he doesn't.

"Do you like the Knicks?" I point to his shirt.

His gaze is clouded. "Someone I once knew loved them. We went to games together."

"And not anymore?"

He ignores the question. I look at him with interest, but I don't want to probe.

"I hope you don't mind a bit of a hike?" he asks, looking at me and testing my response. "Nothing hard, just a nice and easy route."

"No, no problem. I'd love to walk for a bit." That's the truth.

He reaches into the backseat and brings a cup of coffee and a hot croissant out of nowhere.

"Breakfast? I bought it on the way. That's why I was delayed a bit."

He seems so approachable compared to my expectations of someone who has unknown sums of money. I imagine any member of Michael's family in a t-shirt, and I shiver. They are the furthest away from approachable and lovable as possible. They are more like vampires.

He puts the Jeep in gear, and we are on our way. I bite into the pastry and peek at him out of the corner of my eye, taking advantage of the fact that he's driving and can't see I'm doing it.

"What kind of music do you like?" He turns his head to me. "No, actually, you know what? Take my phone and put on something nice." He clicks on the music app on his phone and hands it to me.

Oh, What should I play? I like old rock, but it's not for everyone. I'm not used to being asked my opinion. I haven't been given a choice for so long that the situation has me flustered.

I open a playlist of old rock hits and choose a song. The car fills with the rich sounds of bass and guitars, it's a song by the Rolling Stones, and for a moment, I can believe I'm in a club and not in a car.

"An interesting choice," he states, and his long fingers are drumming on the steering wheel along with the rhythm in a way that it's clear he knows and loves the song.

"You don't have a New York accent," he says, more stating than asking.

I'm debating what to answer him. I can't tell him anything about where I came from. "That's right, I'm not originally from New York."

"Will you tell me where you're from?" he asks, noticing my evasion.

I remain silent, and he continues. "Okay, so if you won't tell me where you're from, maybe tell me something else about yourself. I don't even know your last name. What do you like to do? How old are you? You know, the basics."

You can never find out.

"Mmm... I'm Hope B..." I hesitate for a moment, immediately realizing my mistake. I almost blurted out my real name. I should have thought of an appropriate answer beforehand. I can only hope he didn't notice.

"Hope Brown," I say. "I'm twenty-two years old. I work at Lunis." I try to think of something good to say about myself. But what can one say after being locked up at home for more than two years?

"I like reading and old rock music." I sound like the most boring person in the universe.

"Come on," he teases me. "There must be something interesting you can tell me. Is there something you want to do when you grow up?"

I know he's laughing and expects me to say that I'm studying a profession or that I'm an amateur artist, but he's hitting on my sensitive spot. I dropped out of college when Michael convinced me to. And now that I can't use my real name, I won't be able to finish or study ever again. It looks like I'm stuck with jobs like Lunis. Not that it's bad, but cleaning tables was never my dream.

Shit. I feel the tears welling up, and I turn my head to the window so he won't notice. The scenery outside is no longer urban, and we're speeding down the highway. The awkward silence stands between us for a moment, but then he starts to speak.

"Well, I'm twenty-nine. I have several high-tech companies that require too much of my time which is why I sold one of them recently. I love cars. I love running, and I run every morning. I like whiskey and beer, good movies, especially horror movies, and good food. And I love hiking in nature, climbing, things like that. But don't worry. I chose a simple and easy route for us today."

The words come out of him so easily. Well, it's easy when you're a famous and successful man and have everything to be proud of.

"Google said you're twenty-eight," I say.

"Google, huh?" He raises one eyebrow. "So you looked me up?"

He looks far too pleased with himself. "Don't flatter yourself too much. I wanted to make sure you weren't planning to take me into the woods to murder me."

"Do you think Google will tell you if I'm a serial killer?" He's laughing now.

God, he's so beautiful when he laughs. My stomach clenches, and I turn my head in embarrassment.

"Well, technically, I won't be twenty-nine for another week."

"Saturday is your birthday? What are you planning to do?"

"I didn't make any plans," he says. "I don't celebrate birthdays."

He's not celebrating? But birthdays are fun. I look at him. "Nobody's planning a party for you? Not even your girlfriend?"

"No parties." His voice is cold and stiff. So different from the light tone he used till now. "I don't like birthday parties. And I already told you I don't have a girlfriend."

I cringe a little and rub my neck. What did I say wrong? I wait to see what he'll say next, but he's silent. I decide to change the subject. "Do you really run every morning?"

"Yes." He states without taking his eyes off the road, still in the cool tone from before.

"Every morning?" I ask, trying hard to lighten up the conversation again.

"Yes. I mean, there are some exceptions, but I definitely try. I get up at five and go for a run. It clears my head. It helps me start the workday with high energy."

"Five?" I'm still fast asleep at that hour, but then, I typically only finish the night shift at two in the morning.

"I run for an hour, go back home, shower, eat, go to the office, sleep and work some more. That's my life. Busy." He smiles, but the smile doesn't reach his eyes.

It doesn't sound like he's enjoying his life that much. I thought a man in his position could do anything he wanted. "So, when do you manage to get into trouble?" I'm trying to be funny.

"Trouble?" He tilts his head, trying to understand what I mean.

"When we talked in the park, you said it wasn't the first time you got into trouble."

"And that's what you remember?" He's silent for a moment. It seems that he's not going to answer, but then he speaks.

"When I was a teenager, there was a time when I tried all kinds of things that I'm not so proud of today. I got into a lot of trouble, including fights. That time is behind me," he says and doesn't elaborate further. I can tell it's difficult for him to share it with me.

Every breath you take by The Police starts playing, and I hum along, unable to stop myself from moving to the sound.

I must be a poor dancer because Ethan turns his head to me in amazement and laughs. I don't know why I'm so open in his company. He just makes me feel so comfortable, like being with a good friend I've known for years. And I don't know why but I take it with both hands.

I have never had a male friend. In fact, for a long time, I had no friends at all. Not since high school.

To my surprise, he starts singing along. He knows all the words, and his voice is amazing. Low and hoarse, like a rock star. I look at him in amazement. "You can sing too?"

He stops, and I regret my comment. "I don't. I just sing in the shower sometimes."

That's not true. He can sing. "With a little training and voice development, you could replace the lead singer."

"Thanks, I guess." He doesn't look at me, and I think he even blushes a little. It's funny that little me manages to embarrass this strong man. But he doesn't sing again, and I'm sorry I ever said anything.

We approach a populated area, and Ethan slows down until he stops at an observation point by the side of the road.

We get out, and he's holding his coffee cup, stretching after the long drive. I can't help but stare. He's a prime example of a male figure. His shirt rises a little, revealing some tanned skin, and I feel the need to press my legs together.

"Come see." He offers me a hand, but I don't take it, remembering the near panic attack I had last time. He pulls his hand back, and the smile is erased from his face. He doesn't say anything but waits for me to follow him.

We move toward the rocks on the side of the road, and he points to a wooden path that leads down through the trees. We walk on the path, and after a few steps, the trees no longer hide the view, and my mouth opens.

In front of me is a pastoral lake surrounded by rocky cliffs. You can even see several boats in the water, although at the height we're at, they look more like small dots. What immediately catches my attention is a large building on the opposite bank, similar to a castle, with small red roofs, an eclectic fortress that consists of many buildings in different styles. It's strange and beautiful at the same time, and I feel like I've stepped into a fairy tale.

"Wow," I say.

Ethan signals me to keep walking until we reach a wooden bench and sit down facing the view. I keep staring at the castle and the lake. He sips his coffee, and I'm sorry I've already finished mine.

"I like to come here from time to time to clear my head and relax," he says with sudden honesty. I can understand why. This place is an escape from reality.

We sit in silence for a few minutes until he's ready to continue.

"I could sit here for hours, but I have other plans for today." He gets up and starts walking back, this time not bothering to try to give me a hand.

We get back in the Jeep and continue driving until the strange castle is right in front of us. Ethan parks, asks me to stay by the car, and enters a building that looks like a transparent restaurant. I watch him as he speaks to one of the workers, then returns holding a large basket.

"Food," he says briefly in response to my questioning look. It appears he brought food for me too. *Phew.*

"Ready?"

I nod, and we start walking.

The route is simple, just like he said. We hike between the trees and by the lake, most of the time in silence. He looks thoughtful, and I don't disturb him, enjoying the peace and quiet myself. After an hour of hiking through the forest, I'm starting to sweat. It's hot. I pull the hoodie over my head and fold it into my bag. I look up to find Ethan studying me. I can't decipher what he's thinking from the look on his face, but our gazes lock on each other for long seconds.

"I'm hot," I say.

"Me too. There's a lake here. What do you think?" A glimmer of mischief lights up in his eyes.

"What do I think about the lake?" I don't understand. But he's already hurrying down through the trees to the edge of the lake, so I hurry after him.

We get close to the water, and he stops. I wonder what he intends to do, and I get my answer. He bends down, kicks off the heavy shoes and the socks, and before I realize what's happening, he's already standing with his back to me, completely naked, with his clothes thrown on the rock. I notice another tattoo on his back and try to focus my gaze there and not on that firm and round butt. The tattoo looks like a wolf disappearing into the smoke, but I can't concentrate at all. My eyes keep going down, studying every muscle. It should be illegal to look like that. I don't know what I'm supposed to do.

I'm standing there, so mesmerized by the sight of his broad back, the way his muscles move when he walks, and before I can decide what to do, he jumps into the water. I release a breath and lick my lower lip.

He disappears under the water, then his head comes up again, and he pulls back his long wet hair.

"Come on," he calls for me. "The water is amazing."

He swims a little and moves away from the shore. I approach the water and touch it with my fingertips. It's cool, and he seems to be enjoying himself so much that I feel like joining.

"I didn't bring a bathing suit," I mumble in a weak voice. How could I be considering this? Go into the water with a naked man I barely know?

"Me neither," he says with a laugh. "But you don't need a bathing suit. Come on, there's no one here."

It looks so nice and cool in the water...

"I won't peek. Come on in."

I've never done anything like this. Swimming in the lake? And with a man? But he makes me feel adventurous in his company, like I want to try new things.

Alive.

Yes, that's the word. I feel alive.

Over the last two and a half years, I wasn't living. I was a shadow of a woman. I want to live again. I want new experiences. Isn't that why I agreed to this trip in the first place?

"Turn around!" I call and wait for him to turn his back to me.

I take off my clothes, with the exception of my underwear, and place them in a neat pile. All the while, I take quick glances at the water to see that he's not peeking as he promised. He stays with his back to me the whole time. I cover myself as much as possible with my hands and hurry to dive in before I regret it.

The splash I make in the water prompts him to turn to me, and he swims in my direction.

"Everything is okay?" he asks, observing me.

I nod. I feel great. The water is pleasant against my skin, and everything is perfect. How come I don't feel embarrassed to be in the water with him?

He swims up to me, a little too close, and I know that he can see me, my body, and the bra I'm wearing. The magical moment is broken, and I swim back, creating a distance between us.

He stops. His eyes are fixed on me, and I recognize the sparks of desire in his gaze. My heart rate goes up a few beats, and I'm afraid he can see it. That he can see his effect on me. He certainly has a lot of experience with women. A lot of experience with sex, unlike me.

"You're beautiful," he says, and I feel my cheeks getting warm. No. Take it back, I try to whisper to him telepathically. I just want us to be friends. I want to feel relaxed and calm around you. I don't want to fear the moment he tries to touch me.

And as if he can read my thoughts, he looks away and calls me to swim after him.

CHAPTER 11
Ethan

What the hell did I do? Now all I can think about is her almost naked body swimming next to me. I slow down, letting her swim in front of me, so she doesn't notice the looks I'm giving her.

You promised not to try anything.

You promised not to try anything.

I catch a glimpse of her butt as she swims by. Fucking hell, it's perfect. She's perfect.

Enough of this.

You promised not to try anything.

I keep repeating my promise, but I can't help but imagine how good it would be, how my cock is inside her as that perfect ass wiggles in front of me. God. She'll be the death of me.

She turns to me, laughing, and I can see the outline of her breasts. They're big and heavy, and I'm starting to get aroused more than I should. Maybe I should get out before I have to hide my erection. Lucky for me, the water is cold.

She surprised me with her music choice, the dancing in the car, and now the swimming. I didn't think she would have the courage, but here she is, by my side.

She seemed so closed off and shy, and she still does, but it turns out that it doesn't take too much for her to open up a little and try new things. She still recoils if I get too close, but I can tell I'm headed in the right direction.

"Do you know that the name Mohonk means 'place in the sky?'" I try to distract myself from her body with facts.

"It fits this place. It's magical." She smiles at me, and my cock hardens. I turn my face away from her and exhale. By the time we're done here, I'll have blue balls.

I feel a splash of water hit my back and turn just in time to catch another one straight to my face.

"So you want to play, huh?" I find her in front of me with a wide and playful grin on her face. I splash back at her. Her rolling laugh echoes through the surrounding trees. I swallow. All I want is to hear her laugh again.

"I'm getting out," I call as we both stop panting from the game and start swimming toward the bank.

She swims after me. I get out and go to the pile of clothes I left on the rocks. It would have been better if I could wait for a little and dry in the open air, but I get the impression she would be embarrassed if I remained naked. So I grab my shorts and start getting dressed.

"Don't turn around," she says in her gentle voice, and I stay with my back to the water to allow her to get out in private, although it takes all my will power not to peek.

"Are you dressed?" I ask after I finish dressing.

"Yes," she says in a shy voice. Where did the daring Bambi who swam with me go? I liked her.

The t-shirt she's wearing now is tight on her. She's wet, and it clings to her body like a second skin. Her heavy chest stretches the fabric, and the nipples are hard and noticeable. I turn around to adjust my pants to a more comfortable position.

She wants us to be friends, but I already know I can't be her friend. She has to be mine.

"Are you hungry yet?" I ask after glancing at the clock. I didn't notice the time, and after the drive, the hiking and the swim, it's quite late.

She nods, and I take the large blanket out of the basket and spread it on the ground. She takes the food out of the bags and places everything neatly in the middle. Too neatly. I have the urge to take the boxes and mess them up. Show her that there's fun in clutter as well.

I sit down on one side of the blanket, and she examines what's in each box, then takes a plate for herself. I wait for her to finish, but then she hands the loaded plate to me.

"Thanks." I'm not used to such gestures and reach out to take the plate from her. My fingers touch hers by accident, but the electricity passing between us sends shivers down my spine. She's electrifying and not only in my thoughts. The sex with her is going to be out of this world. I know it. She looks down, so I can't read her expression, but I have a feeling she's not indifferent to me, either.

We eat quickly. I put the plate on the blanket and stretch out on my back, tucking my hands behind my head. The treetops above me move in the wind and sweep away my thoughts. I still haven't been able to get any details out of her about her identity or where she came from. She gave me a name, but I don't believe it's a real one, even though it's a different name than the one she gave for the waitress job. She may have given me another fake name, but maybe it will help Jess. I have to know everything about her.

I close my eyes and surrender to the moment. To the rustling of the leaves and to the silence. I can feel her eyes on me.

When I'm not looking, she's braver. I keep my eyes closed to give her time to look at me as much as she wants. I like that she's checking me out. I think she likes what she sees. It's only a matter of time.

A rustling sound has me opening my eyes to thin slits. She moves the bags that stand between us aside and lies down next to me, so close that I can smell her hair, like tropical fruits.

I hold back from pressing my nose to her and inhaling deeply. This trip is proving to be more and more difficult by the minute. Why the hell did I promise not to touch her? That's the only thing I want to do.

I turn my face in her direction. She's lying, on her back, her short hair scattered around her face. This close, I can tell she has no makeup on, and still, she's so beautiful. I'm not used to seeing women without makeup around me. They're all fake in this town, but not her. She's real.

Wait a moment. Real? I don't even know her first name. She's not real. She's fake. Just like everyone else.

It's all an act.

But I can't believe it. An innocence like hers can't be an act. It just can't be. There's something else here. I just need to figure out what.

She turns her head to me, and our eyes meet. She doesn't look away this time, which is more proof that our relationship is progressing in the right direction. Her eyes are huge and so blue that I want to drown in them. Warmth spreads through my body. I'm sure she feels it too. Her pink lips twitch a little, and my eyes are drawn there like a butterfly to a fire. If it weren't for that annoying promise, my lips would be on hers right now.

"Bambi," I whisper, but it breaks the spell, and she sits up.

"Let's keep walking?" she says and stands.

Fuck. I scared her. Baby steps. I have to remember that. Baby steps.

I sit up and collect all the garbage and bags and put everything back into the basket, making sure not to leave anything behind, and we continue our hike in silence.

We reach a steeper part of the route and climb up on the rocks to the observation point on the lake.

"Holding up?" I ask as I see her panting. She just nods and continues to climb. I extend my hand toward her, offering my help, but she ignores the gesture and goes up herself.

We reach the lookout, and I'm panting a little too. The view from the top is spectacular and totally worth the climb, but the view that interests me right now is not that of nature.

Bambi is standing on the edge of the cliff, facing the landscape, and she's smiling. I managed to impress her. Well, the view did. But I brought her here.

I look down. The lake sparkles in the sunlight and looks golden. The boats are tiny from this distance, leaving a trail of white foam in the water behind them.

She turns her face to me, the smile still on her face, and she looks happy. Fuck. I would give a lot to fuck her right here, right now, on the ground.

I watch as she takes out the phone I bought her and takes pictures of the view from all angles.

I take mine out and pretend I'm taking pictures of the view too, but I'm taking pictures of her. She's more beautiful than the landscape.

"Thank you for bringing me here." She looks at me with sparkling eyes.

I smile in response. I'm the one who should say thank you. This place will never look the same.

We start our way back down. I go first, skipping through the rocks easily. We're about halfway down when I hear a startled cry behind me. I turn to find that she has lost her grip and is sliding down the path without being able to stop. She's dangerously close to the edge of the cliff. Fuck!

My heart pounds as I leap and try to catch her, but she's still too far away. I reach out, trying to reduce the distance between us. I manage to grab her arm and pull her to me. Her body collides with mine. From the weight of both of us, we continue to go down, stopping dangerously close to the edge. I plant my feet as hard as I can and lean my body weight forward, managing to stabilize both of us at the last second.

I breathe heavily, holding her in my arms. I damn near lost her. Her face is hidden in the hollow of my shoulder, and she's trembling. She's soft and tiny in my embrace, and I never want to let her go.

CHAPTER 12

Ayala

My heart is beating so hard, I can hear the blood rushing in my ears. I have no air. I can't breathe. He's here. Michael.

I shiver, waiting for the blows that are about to come, but nothing happens. I slowly open my eyes, realizing I'm in Ethan's embrace. It feels good. Pleasant. I stay close to him, in his arms, my emotions changing with dizzying speed between fear and confidence, and the change completely unsettles me. His body is warm and firm, and his pulse is strong and steady against me. Against all logic, a warmth starts spreading from my lower abdomen to the rest of my body, setting me on fire and making me boil from the inside. What's happening to me? How does he do it?

He holds my chin and lifts my face gently. "Are you okay?"

"Yes," I answer automatically. But the truth is that I'm scared. No, I'm panicking.

I feel like I just woke from a long dream. My nerves are tingling, expectant. My body craves something that will never happen. I've been there before. I won't let a man touch me again. I step back, even though I'd rather stay in his safe embrace forever.

"Did I hurt you? I'm sorry. I was just trying to stop your fall." He looks worried.

"No, no, everything is fine. I was just scared."

The look on his face tells me he doesn't believe me when I say everything is fine. But he stops asking, and I continue to follow him with the utmost care. I don't want to stumble again. Now I keep my distance, concentrating on every step I take.

"So you come here a lot?" I ask in a joking tone, imitating the pick-up lines I hear in the pub every day, trying to lower the thick screen that has come up between us.

He turns to me with a surprised and grinning look. I managed to get his attention, and maybe he will forget the awkward moment from before. Well, he won't forget. I know him well enough to know that already. Just like he didn't forget a momentary encounter on the street that shouldn't have had any meaning. He's very perceptive, and he doesn't forget. But he also never pressures me to reveal what I'm not ready to share.

"Actually, yes," he answers and surprises me. "It's one of my favorite places for a day trip. I told you I like to travel."

Yes, he told me that. "I also like to travel," I say, realizing that I enjoyed today with him. "It's so beautiful here."

"I'm glad. There are many more places I'd be happy to show you."

His phone starts ringing, interrupting our conversation. A crease appears between his eyebrows as he looks at the screen.

"I'm sorry. I asked not to be disturbed, so if they're calling, it's probably urgent." He answers the call while still walking, and I keep quiet so as not to disturb him.

"Why do you think you're being spied on?"

I listen to the fragments of the conversation.

"Are you sure?" Ethan stops and listens intently to whoever is on the other end. "They have confidential information? From your email?"

I give him a wondering look, but he doesn't notice me.

"So you're telling me it's someone on the inside. Damn it. Well, I'll talk to Jess immediately. Everything should go through me until further notice."

He hangs up, and his hands close into fists.

"Fuck!" He kicks hard at one of the stones on the path. I freeze at the sight of his unexpected fury. I recognize this anger. Michael had many episodes that started exactly like that when bad news from work made him angry. He would slam the front door, and that was my cue to get ready. No matter what I did, the punches would come. At first, he apologized and promised it wouldn't happen again, and I believed him. After a while, I no longer believed, and he no longer apologized.

I look around, my heart pounding in my chest as I search for a stick or something similar for protection, trying to think of how to protect myself. Ethan is much more massive and stronger than Michael. He's wider in the shoulders and taller than him by at least four or five inches. And the spectacular display of muscles I witnessed in the lake doesn't bode well for me. I can only get away if I surprise him. I pick up a small rock that looks sharp and hold it firmly in the palm of my hand.

Ethan turns to me, and I keep my hand behind my back, so he won't see the rock. But he doesn't seem to pick up on my mood at all, which tells me he's distracted.

"We have to go home. I need to go to the office," he fires in my direction and starts walking back in the direction we came.

Wait a moment. What happened just now? It suddenly becomes apparent that his anger isn't directed at me. I throw the rock away and rush after him, trying to ask in my calmest voice, "What happened?"

"I'm looking into the possibility of purchasing several companies to expand my cyber business. One of the companies we're interested in purchasing received a similar offer from one of my competitors."

"Does this happen a lot?" I ask, trying to keep up with him. "That competitors make offers for the same companies?"

"Not often." He tilts his head. "But it happens. The thing is, according to the terms of the competing offer, it's clear they knew the exact details of our offer. The VP of my cyber company, the one who just called..." he pauses, then goes on to explain, "is the only one who knew what was written in our proposal. Well, him, Ryan, and me, of course. And he swears the contract is saved on his personal computer and only there. There are no copies."

"Maybe the computer was hacked."

"That would be our first guess. But his personal computer is not connected to the internet for exactly these reasons. Whoever stole the offer needed physical access to the computer."

"That means someone on the inside did it," I say, likely completing what he would have said next. "Are you sure it wasn't the VP or Ryan who leaked?"

"I'd bet my life on Ryan," he says. "And Stephan and I go back for many years. He's reliable."

"I thought Ryan was just a friend? How is he related to the deals?"

"Ryan and I are more than friends. He's like a brother to me. We've known each other since childhood. He's also my lawyer, and his office draws up all the transaction contracts for me."

"And how do you know the other company isn't the one who leaked to get a better offer?"

"I can't know for sure." He looks at me and seems pleased with my questions. "But they signed a non-disclosure agreement, so if it turns out they're the leakers, and it always gets out in the end, they'll have to pay millions, lose the deal, and probably future deals as well, because no one wants to work with such people. One company did something like that in the past, and it collapsed after the incident became public. I find it hard to believe they would take the risk."

"Okay..." I say. I have an idea, but I'm not sure how it will be received. Michael never wanted to hear my opinion.

Ethan stops and looks at me with interest, waiting for me to speak. Encouraged, I continue, "So you know someone is probably checking Stephan's computer, right? Why don't you take advantage of that to expose the thief?"

He pauses, and I get the impression he's processing the idea, then his eyes widen. "Of course! I didn't think of that. We'll plant false information in it, so we can track whoever it is." Ethan approaches me, and for a moment, I think he is going to hug me, but he stops a short distance away, turns around, and makes a phone call.

Is it terrible that I wanted him to hug me?

From that moment on, he disconnects from me completely. Forgetting my existence. He takes wireless headphones out of his bag, connects them, and walks at a fast pace while making phone calls. I get a glimpse of Ethan Wolf, the serious businessman, and he's far different from Ethan Wolf, the charming man who spent the day with me.

I try to keep up with him, but he's in great shape and much taller than me. For every step he takes, I need two, and soon enough, I'm panting and moving at almost a jogging pace.

Phew. I have to do more exercise. I scold myself for my bad shape. Cleaning may have strengthened my arm muscles, but it hasn't contributed to my cardiopulmonary endurance. After twenty minutes of me running after him, I can't do it anymore, and I switch to a walking pace. He'll just have to wait a few minutes for me when he gets to the car.

He rushes forward, opening a gap between us, and after a few minutes, I can't see him anymore. I lose sight of him completely. I continue walking in the same direction but stop when I reach a fork in the path. Which direction did we come from? Why didn't I notice where the hell I was going? Everything seems the same to me. Trees are everywhere, and there are lots of walking paths here. I just need to keep walking in the general direction, hoping I won't get lost.

Maybe he really is planning to murder me in the woods. He'll leave me here as food for the bears. Or, more simply, I'll starve to death because I have no sense of direction. Yes, I can imagine the headlines now. "Woman's body found on trail at Lake Mohonk after starving to death."

Well, at least I'm making jokes. I had fun today. I don't remember the last time I could say I had fun. I've had good days since I arrived in New York, but real fun? This is new to me. Ethan was interested in what I had to say. He sees me. I caught him watching me a few times, and it didn't even scare me like I thought it would.

"Hope!"

I shake off the trail of thoughts that swept me away when I hear my name being called. Ethan sounds stressed.

"I'm here!" I shout back, and he comes running, his face scrunched up in worry. He doesn't stop this time and hugs me. "Shit, I'm so sorry," he murmurs in my ear. "I didn't notice you weren't behind me. I'm so sorry."

I don't flinch this time, allowing myself to sink into his embrace.

CHAPTER 13

Ayala

Distracted, I scrub the stubborn food stains off one of the tables. I keep analyzing that hug between Ethan and me from every direction. I still remember my body's reaction, the wetness between my thighs.

I like him. I like him a lot. Something about him makes me feel safe, like he could protect me from anything.

But nothing good can come of it. He doesn't know who I am and never will. It won't take long for him to realize that I'm broken, that I'm worthless.

Maybe he already figured it out because I haven't seen him since our trip. He sent an apologetic message saying that the problems in the company are keeping him busy and he can't come see me, but perhaps this is just an excuse. I know he has a lot of work. He's an important person and obviously can't be away from his business. I'm not his first priority, either, and we're supposed to be only friends. So why am I so disappointed?

My phone beeps and I hurry to check the message. Ethan is the only one who has the number.

It's a picture. He sent me a picture of himself sitting in a meeting room and making a sad face. *I'd rather be with you*, is written under it.

I run my fingers over his face and save it. This is the first time he's sent me a picture of himself. I also prefer to be with you, I think and stop myself.

No one will ever love you. You're just a little whore.

"Earth calling to Hope!"

I was lost in thought again. I look up at Nicky, who's closing the bar.

"We're going out dancing tomorrow. Are you coming?" she asks, and not for the first time. To this day, I've refused every invite that would require me to come out of my hiding place, but I've been here for a month now, and it seems no one is chasing me. No one has come looking for me. My first priority was to survive, but now, I also want to live. I deserve more. I deserve a life worth living. I think it might be the right time for me to start. Maybe my thoughts about Ethan are telling me I'm ready for more.

"Why are you inviting her?" Robin intervenes and stops the collection of dirty cups. She glares at me with hatred.

What have I done to this girl? I just clean tables and bathrooms and anything else Dana asks me to. I haven't exchanged more than a few words with Robin since I arrived.

"Why shouldn't I invite her?" Nicky glares at Robin, her forehead wrinkled in a frown.

Robin twists her mouth. "If you don't notice what's going on around you, then you're blind." She waves her hand and goes into the kitchen.

"Do you have something I could wear?" I ask Nicky, deciding to ignore Robin's nuclear outburst.

"Yes! Does that mean you're coming with us? Come to my place this evening. We'll find something suitable for you."

When we leave Nicky's apartment, I'm wearing a short black dress and some heavy makeup that I would never have dared to wear if it weren't for her insistence.

I don't recognize myself. This isn't me. Or maybe it is. I don't know who I am anymore. I was never given a chance to find out, always being who they wanted me to be. First, the conservative and cute girl my parents wanted me to be, then the woman Michael wanted me to play for him. I don't know what I want. I don't know what I like to do. Maybe it's time to find out.

At the entrance of the club, I can already hear the loud music inside and the sweet smell of smoke. We meet up with Michelle and Shannon, Nicky's friends. They look nice and greet me with hugs and smiles.

"Hi." Robin joins us, greeting everyone but me.

I smile at her.

My phone vibrates in the small handbag I borrowed from Nicky.

Ethan
Can I see you on Saturday?

I have an evening shift. I can't cancel.

I got a promotion. Dana suggested that I work as a bartender. One of the bartenders announced his departure, and she asked him to train me in the coming week. I can't miss shifts.

Ethan
In the morning, then?

He won't give up. I suddenly remember what he told me.

Isn't that your birthday?

Ethan
Yes. But I told you, I'm not celebrating.

I don't understand it. Is none of his family members doing anything for him? How can that be? My fingers hover over the keyboard. I do want to meet with him again.

Okay, see you Saturday morning.

I have to do something for his birthday. Maybe a cake? Or a present?

What can I do for him? He has enough money that he certainly doesn't need anything from me.

I pick my brain, trying to come up with an idea, but it's hard. We don't know each other that well yet, and his list of hobbies is suitable for a millionaire and not a seamstress like me.

"Why are you so fascinated with your phone?" Nicky pulls me when it's our turn to go inside, and I put the device back in my bag. I'll think of an idea later.

The club is filled with people of all shapes and sizes. I love it. I've never been to such a place. Most everyone here is dressed so revealing that I find myself staring shamelessly. My short dress is nothing compared to what I see around me. They're all dancing, though I wouldn't call what they're doing a dance exactly. It's much more than that, and it's insanely sexy. The lights and the sweat infuse an atmosphere that opens all the senses. The music is loud, and smoke billowing from machines and cigarettes fills the place. Giant screens show clips on the walls. It's mesmerizing.

I'm a little shocked, I want to run, but I also want to stay.

The girls line up in the middle of the floor and start dancing, and I try to imitate their movements. I'm tense, and I know I don't look as good as they do. I'm not as relaxed as them, but I try.

After an hour of dancing, they take a break and drag me to the bathroom. I look at myself in the mirror and see I'm sweating, and my eyes are shiny. My short hair is wild. I look happy, radiant even. I'm absorbing my sweat in tissue paper and watching Shannon roll something that looks like a cigarette.

She's inhaling from the cigarette and breathing down my face. The sweet smell reaches my nose.

"Want a hit?" she asks.

"What is it?"

"You never smoked a joint?" She raises an eyebrow. "Here, have fun."

For a moment, I'm not sure. But I want to try new things. I want to live. This is why I came here. I take the offered cigarette, have a toke, and cough hard.

Robin smothers a laugh. "She can't even smoke."

Shannon's laughing out loud. "Take another one."

I like it. My heart pounds, threatening to break from my rib cage. I'm excited and feel adventurous. I feel like going out dancing again. I take a third toke and return the rolled-up cigarette to Shannon.

We go out on the floor again, and I dance, feeling a lot freer than before. I love the feeling. I raise my hands in the air and let the music lead me.

Two men come and start dancing close to us. I see how one of them gets closer to Nicky and touch her hips. She lets him dance with her, hold her, then she turns around and puts her arms on him. She's into him. I envy how open she is, relaxed, and not afraid of touching. I'd like to be more like her.

The other guy tries to get close to me, and I hold back my automatic reluctance and allow him to get closer. I see Robin staring at me with an angry glare in her eyes. Is this about this man? Does she want him? She's welcome to take him.

He reaches out and grabs me by my waist, similar to the guy dancing with Nicky. I freeze. He's touching me. A stranger is touching me. I'm trying to relax and be more like the other girls, but the memories won't let go. A wave of nausea washes over me.

I break away from him and run to the bathroom. Some girls are standing in the hallway, waiting in line, but I don't stop. My stomach twitches again, and I cover my mouth with my hand as I run around them while ignoring the angry shouts.

I can barely hold it when I reach the toilet. I push past the girl who's about to step inside and puke all the contents of my stomach. Disgusted moans sound from behind me, and I realize I left the stall door open. I extend one hand and slam it shut. After the cramps calm down, I stand on shaky feet and lean against the door. My chest rises and falls rapidly.

I can't stand even a small touch. Will I ever have a relationship again? I'm broken beyond repair.

I ignore the constant pounding on the door when the tears start to fall with silent sobs that rack my body for a long time.

Don't break now. I ran away from him and saved myself. I'm stronger than this. I don't need men in my life. I make myself come to my senses, go out and wash my face.

My makeup is smudged, dripping with ugly black stripes on my cheeks. I wet my hands and rub my face, cleaning it all up.

I look again in the mirror with my eyes wide open. I don't need anyone but myself. I'll be fine.

After I've got myself together, I find Michelle and Shannon easily, drawing my attention to the center of the floor, but Nicky and Robin are gone.

I get close to the girls and let them know I'm going home, just in case Nicky comes looking for me. Although I'm pretty sure she won't be coming back anytime soon.

The air outside is cool, and my ears pound like I'm still in the noisy club. I decide to walk back to Lunis. We're not far from there, and walking in the cold air soothes me.

I'm disappointed with myself. I was sure I'd made progress and was ready. It's been a month, and I thought I could be a normal girl going out. But once a stranger touched me, I completely lost it. Maybe it'll never stop? Perhaps I'll always be broken? Michael was right all along.

But when Ethan hugged me, it felt good. I can't stop thinking about our time together, swimming in the lake, and the picnic. The perfect day he gave me. He made me laugh. And I didn't feel worthless with him. I felt like me.

CHAPTER 14

Ayala

Saturday morning finally arrives, and I take the subway to Madison Square Garden. Ethan's supposed to meet me there.

I hold the little cardboard box on my knees with care, and my backpack is full of food that I prepared in Lunis's kitchen yesterday. Dana doesn't care that I cook as long as I keep the kitchen clean.

"Hey, Ira," I happily greet the guard who's already waiting for me at the gate of the hall. "I brought you the cookies you liked." I pull a paper bag full of big peanut butter cookies from the box and offer it to him.

"Hi, sweetie. So today's the big day?" he asks while he takes out one cookie and looks at it with greed.

I smile. "Yes. Today is the day. When Ethan comes looking for me, will you send him in, please?"

Ira nods and opens the door for me.

The place is empty and dark. I find the light switches on the wall, and the lights come on. The place comes alive. I can't believe I made it in.

Ira made my life a lot easier when I found out he was a

romantic guy and a cookie lover. I've been here every day trying my luck with the guards. I tried to talk to their hearts, tried to bribe them with pastries. The first two wouldn't hear a word from me once they realized what I was asking. But Ira didn't need too much convincing in order to help me. I let him believe that Ethan was my love, and that was enough. He's a big believer in love stories, and the romance in the idea was enough for him to let me sneak in this morning to prepare my surprise.

I take the blanket out of my backpack and place it on the floor in the middle of the hall, then put the cardboard box in the middle.

I arrange the breakfast I've made—eggs, vegetables, and some of my homemade brioche.

I'm good at baking. Cooking and baking have become a big part of my life in the last two years. It was the only thing I could do while I was locked up alone in the big house. The only thing Michael let me do.

I turn off the lights again, sit back and wait. Tapping with my leg on the floor.

"Hope?" I hear Ethan's low voice echoing in the empty hall.

He's standing there, trying to figure out where I am in this darkness. The illumination from the door behind him lights him up like some Greek god who came down from the sky. He's wearing jeans and a white Henley shirt with the top buttons open, revealing a piece of skin from his chest.

I try to remind myself that I just want a friend, but the heat wave in my loins thinks otherwise.

"I'm here." I go to him with a smile. "Congratulations."

"What are we doing here?" he asks. "And how did you get in?"

"It's your birthday, so I asked for some favors," I say it like it's not a big deal, and it's easy to get a huge famous place for ourselves. Like I haven't been begging on my knees all week from anyone I could think of to make this happen. "Come on."

I turn the lights back on and expose the meal I put in the middle of the field.

He stops, and his mouth drops. "What's going on?"

He appears to be in shock, and I like it. I was able to surprise him. I was able to surprise the man who has everything.

I sit on the blanket and invite him to sit next to me. But he remains standing.

"When did you arrange all this?"

"After you wrote to me that you wanted to see me on Saturday, and I remembered it was your birthday," I explain. "I still don't understand why you're not celebrating, but I love birthdays. I couldn't just ignore it."

"I haven't been here in a while," he mumbles and looks around. "I have a lot of memories of this place."

I watch him walk around. I think he's moved, and his eyes are a little wet. I hope I did something good and didn't screw this all up.

When he returns and sits next to me, he appears calm and is smiling. I explain about the food, and we start eating. The sounds he makes when he enjoys the food are irresistible.

"Your food is better than the deli. Where did you learn to cook like this?" He moans with pleasure, and I feel my cheeks warming. I lower my eyes.

I wait for him to finish eating and jump up as soon as he puts down the plate.

I open the cardboard box, trying not to rip it, and pull out the cake. It's a three-layered birthday cake covered in chocolate cream, with the number twenty-nine on it. I worked on the cake for a few hours yesterday. I'm glad it survived the trip, and Ethan seems impressed.

"Did you make a cake, too?" he mumbles. "For me?"

For a moment, he seems so embarrassed by the gesture that I

think no one has ever made a cake for him before. But of course, that can't be.

"Yes," I confirm as I dig through my bag, looking for the candle I brought.

"I found it," I call when my fingers clasp the lost candle. I stick it in the middle of the cake and light it up. "Make a wish!" I'm ordering him.

Ethan stares at me, then closes his eyes. He licks his lips and takes a moment. What's he thinking? I wonder when he finally blows out the candle and opens his eyes.

"Let's taste."

The cake is rich and creamy, and I enjoy it. I'm glad it turned out well after all my efforts. I close my eyes and sigh with pleasure. When I open them, the golden eyes are staring at me. I feel the tension building. The air between us is thick. My heart rate increases by a few beats, and a warm feeling fills my stomach.

No, this isn't appropriate. I don't want to feel that way with him. I just want a friend.

He reaches out and wipes a smear of chocolate from the corner of my mouth. I shudder at the touch but don't flinch. I want him to touch me. God, I really want him to! What's happening to me? He looks at his finger and then licks it, and my stomach cramps in anticipation. I look into his eyes, and they're full of lust.

I can't look away. For some reason, I have a feeling that sex with him would be different. Not like I've experienced. Maybe I'd finally understand why everyone is so excited about it. I'm ashamed of my dirty thoughts. What's going on with me? I don't want anything like that in my life. I don't need a man. I just got out of a terrible relationship.

I shake off the thoughts that overwhelm me and decide to ask about a topic that will not provoke any such reaction.

"What's happened with regard to the problem in your company? The hacked computer?"

"Oh. Your idea was excellent. We managed to mislead the thief and find him according to the trail of clues. It was my head of finance, no less." A disappointed look crosses over his face. "I can't believe I fell for it. And above that, he's also the son of friends of the family. I used to choose all of my employees personally, but now I have too many to do it all myself."

"Maybe you should hire someone to do background checks on the employees," I suggest.

"Yes. I have someone for that. I never thought I would have to run a check on a friend of the family, but I guess you can never tell."

"So, did you buy the company you wanted?"

"Not yet. They haven't decided whether to sell to us yet. But at least the other company that stole from us got off the table after we showed them evidence of the theft." His jaw tightens in anger. "I hate it when they play dirty."

At this moment, I feel so normal. We're talking like two regular people on everyday subjects, eating cake together. It feels good. *How come I'm so relaxed around him?*

Ethan stops talking, and his eyes focus on me, examining me. Do I have cake on my face again? I stick my tongue out and run it over the corner of my mouth, checking. It happens so fast, I don't have time to react when his lips land on mine. My pulse increases and my breaths quicken immediately.

My mouth opens as if it has a will of its own, and Ethan's tongue is already invading me. The taste of the chocolate in his mouth is simply divine. I moan, unaware of my actions. His hands hold my face and bring me closer to him while his mouth is busy tasting me.

The kiss is not soft and delicate. It's demanding and yet, not overwhelming.

My nipples rub against his chest and harden. The friction of his shirt, the touch of his tongue on mine… My thoughts are fuzzy, and my insides feel like butter. These are not feelings I recognize. I've never felt this way. Never. I didn't know something like this was even possible.

I can't help myself and run my fingers through his hair, pulling it gently. He moans in response, sending a heat wave between my legs. Oh, God.

His lips detach from mine, and he lowers his head and starts kissing my neck. I know I should stop him, but instead, I tilt my head back, allowing him access. It's like I'm not in control, allowing him to do what he wants with me, and I'm at his mercy.

He leaves a trail of hot kisses down my neck and quickly moves toward my shirt, his warm mouth on my cleavage. His hand goes under my shirt.

"No," I shout and jump back in panic, gasping. "Shit," I mutter in a weak voice. *Breathe. Breathe.* I try to calm my rapid breathing and stop the panic attack that is fast approaching. I raise my hand to my lips and notice that my hand is shaking.

"What happened?" he asks, obviously confused. He's also panting, trying to catch his breath. "What's wrong?"

I touch my face and find it hot. And I'm sure my lips are swollen from the kiss.

I'm so embarrassed. I thought I would be comfortable with him. But even with this attractive man, I can't continue. I'm broken.

I stand, and my legs are shaking hard. "I can't do this," I say, and before I know it, my legs are carrying me outside, and I'm running.

CHAPTER 15

Ethan

I leave all the food with the nice man at the entrance, who seems very happy to receive it and walk out.

What the hell just happened? It was a passionate kiss, just like I imagined it would be. And that doesn't happen to me often—that reality is as good as I imagine it. Ever since I met this woman, I knew she would be like fire. I knew she would be hot, and I know for sure she kissed me back. It was not one-sided. So why the hell did she run away from me?

My cock is hard as a rock now. I can barely walk straight. Fucking hell. She's going to be the death of me.

I've been holding back for a week. Yes, I haven't fucked in a week. Ethan Wolf, the sought-after bachelor, suffers from sexual frustration. I've become a joke. I haven't gone to any of my mistresses since our trip to the lake because I can't stop fantasizing about this one woman. Those blue eyes drive me crazy.

All week I masturbated like a child, sometimes even three times a day, just to relieve myself, to relieve my stress. But nothing helps. I'm so fucking horny.

I was sure today it was going to happen. After all, she invited me here. She prepared all that food and that cake! Who makes a chocolate cake and licks it like that in front of me if she doesn't want to get fucked? I don't understand. All I can think about is her tongue wrapped around my cock.

You don't do something like that without anticipating sex afterward, right?

Masturbating won't be enough for me this time. I call Adele.

"I need you now," I say as soon as she answers. This is not how I imagined my birthday, but I need to fuck now. I need it hard and painful, and Adele will take it.

"Ethan... I haven't heard from you in a long time," she purrs.

I have no patience for that.

"I'm on my way to you." I hang up.

My phone is flashing a new message.

Olive
What time is the dinner at your parents?

Fucking hell. I completely forgot about it. Olive and I are invited to dinner today in honor of my birthday.

I hate these meals. Hate the pretense. I hate to pretend that everything is fine, that everything is forgotten. To pretend we get along, that they love me, that Dad doesn't hate me. At least they like Olive and enjoy talking to her, which gives me the opportunity to keep quiet. Because if I say something, I know how it will end. I know the outburst will come.

I'll pick you up at six.

I check my watch and realize I'll have to cancel the visit with Adele.

Exactly at six, I wait near Olive's apartment. She walks to the car, wearing a long dark purple dress with thin straps and a delicate black shawl resting on her thin arms. Her long hair is gathered in a braid.

"Wow," I tell her as she gets into the car. "If you were into me, I would definitely do you."

In response, I receive a hit on my shoulder. "Ugh, disgusting!"

I love her. I don't understand how I thought we weren't compatible. Probably something in her body language that conveyed no. She's amazing, sharp and funny and sometimes I'm sorry she doesn't like men. My mother was right to match us, as much as I hate to admit it. If she wasn't a lesbian, we'd probably be together.

"So you told them?" I open the conversation with the eternal question that I ask her every time we meet. I haven't lost hope yet. Eventually, I'll convince her to tell her parents. It doesn't make sense to live life without being able to be with the one you love. And I'm sure she's exaggerating. From my acquaintance with her parents, they won't take it as hard as she imagines. Conservative or not, it's not such a big deal.

"You know I didn't," she says. "I brought you something." She hurries to change the subject, not allowing me to argue with her, then pulls out an envelope from the tiny bag and hands it to me with a "Happy Birthday." She bends down and kisses me on the cheek.

"Olive, you shouldn't have bought me anything..."

"But I wanted to." She shrugs. "Who would I buy gifts for if not for my best friend?"

I open the envelope to find two tickets to next week's NBA game at Madison Square Garden. The coincidence causes my heart to skip a beat. Is it just a fluke that they both thought of the same location?

We arrive at my parents' huge penthouse. I glance out at the landscape and inhale, trying to hold on to some peace of mind before I go into the lion's den. Olive holds my hand, lightly squeezing it. She always knows when I need that encouragement.

Their apartment is huge and isolated. They moved here after the tragedy, and I don't blame them. I couldn't live in our old home anymore either. But I also couldn't give up my childhood home.

When they sold the old house a few years after it happened, I bought it through an intermediary without them being able to know I was involved in the transaction. They would never have sold to me if they knew. I couldn't let the house go to someone else, not after what happened. The house is there as a monument, reminding me every time I pass it or think of what I did.

The new house is beautifully designed, down to the last detail, and there isn't a drop of warmth in it. There is no evidence of Anna or of the fact that they once raised a girl. They deleted her from their life. I hated living here.

My mother welcomes us with a big smile and a fake hug for me, while it seems Olive gets a real hug. I walk into the living room and greet my father. He just nods his head, acknowledging my existence and nothing more. I bite my cheek.

He gets up, and we all sit down at the long table. I can't help but chuckle because the table is huge, and the four of us are sitting far from each other like we're at a royal event.

I close my eyes and inhale. Huge blue eyes show up, giving me strength.

"So, Olivia, how's your business going?" my mother asks with interest while someone from the staff serves the first course. I don't recognize her, mother must have changed the staff again, for the thousandth time.

My attention returns to the women at the table, and I watch them as they converse. Mom seems to like Olive, not that it's surprising. There's nothing not to like about her. She's perfect. Not like me.

Olive sighs and puts down her fork. "I didn't know how complicated it would be, Laura. I'm working on my business plan. I'm so lucky to have Ethan here to help me. Without him, I wouldn't have succeeded." She turns her head and looks at me with a smile. "He's the one who convinced me to make evening dresses and not just wedding dresses."

It's true. I help her, but I know she's trying to flatter me to soften them up. She still doesn't understand that it means nothing to them.

"Yes, all the calculations show that it will be more profitable if you design both," I say.

"Do you already have dresses ready?" my mother asks.

"Oh, I have a lot of samples ready, but I don't have a production line yet. I need to find a place first. And a budget."

Despite my attempts to dissuade her from this, she wants her parents to be involved in the business and invest in it, so for now, the progress is quite slow. They still haven't agreed. I didn't take anything from my parents, and I don't understand why she would want to. I can't even imagine where I would be today if Dad had a hand or a foot in my business.

I say, "You'll have no problem finding a loan. You have hundreds of thousands of followers who will buy every piece of design you put out. It's an almost risk-free venture."

"I'll be your first customer," my mom says and claps her hands. My dad mumbles something without looking at me.

I can't understand what he's saying, and my stress level goes up a notch. "What?" I raise my voice to make my point clear. But he doesn't bother to respond. Why do I even come here?

I look down at the plate and take a deep breath. *Don't get excited. It's just Dad acting like he always does.* I should be used to it by now. The conversation halts for several minutes while we all start on our meal until the silence is broken.

"Ethan," Mom says, her tone cold and formal, and I lift my head to look at her, knowing this can't be good.

"I heard you fired Clifford. Nightingale's son."

Yes. This won't be good.

"Correct."

"His mother called and asked me to talk to you. We're friends, you know, and they're a lovely family. They've always adored you. Maybe you'll give him another chance? He can't be that bad. Maybe another role?"

"It won't happen, Mom. I fired him for a very good reason," I add, trying to deflect from the subject before the conversation deteriorates.

"I know, honey, but—"

My father waves a hand and stops her words at once. I hate when he does that. Keeps her from speaking like she's his maid or something. And worst of all, she obeys.

"Laura, he said no. You have nothing to gain. You know how stubborn he can be, especially since you're the one who asked." The contempt in his voice is so clear, and the blood rages and boils in my veins. Even Olive looks around, anticipating what's going to happen next.

He talks about me as if I'm not present in the room, and I'm not ready to tolerate it.

"I fired him because he sold information to my competitors and betrayed the company. It was only by luck that I discovered it before the damage was irreversible. I spent the entire week trying to fix what he did," I say, on the verge of screaming. "I don't need advice on how to run my company, and I certainly won't bring back an employee who went rogue as a favor to someone else, not even for Mom."

"Wouldn't hurt to listen to some advice, Son. Especially after we've spent years getting you out of trouble," my father says, adding fuel to the fire.

I get up from my seat so abruptly that the chair I'm sitting in falls with a bang, and I ignore it. Mom cringes.

"It's been years since you got me out of trouble, but you'll never admit that, will you? You won't allow me to forget what happened. No matter how many companies I've founded, no matter how much my business has surpassed yours, I'm still the wayward son." I'm practically yelling now, but I'm also on a roll.

"I came here at Mom's invitation, but it's pretty clear you can't stand me being here. So don't bother inviting me again. I don't need to hear how awful I am, and certainly not on my birthday!"

Especially when I already know it myself.

I grab Olive's hand and pull her up. "We're leaving."

CHAPTER 16

Ethan

The dashboard screen on the wall in Savee's offices is flashing yellow. There's a new call, one more person who needs help.

I check the numbers listed carefully. We helped two thousand four hundred and sixty people last week. Not bad, yet not enough. Not as much as I would like. We need more money.

On paper, I have lots of money. What people don't understand is that a company's value does not translate into dollars in the bank. I plan to pour a significant portion of the proceeds from the sale of Wolf Fortress into this company, but that has to wait. It'll take time for the lawyers to finalize the details and for me to turn the shares into dollars. Too much time.

The app has been unprofitable for some time now, ever since I expanded the business to cover the entire United States. The expenses for the phone centers, psychologists, and equipment have long passed the stage where everything can be financed by advertisements. I could have kept the company smaller and made it profitable, but I have one goal. No matter how much it costs. To save more people.

The company eats a lot of my private money. It drinks it like wine. I started organizing charity parties, even though I hate such events, just to raise more funds for Savee. The donations help me save more lives.

But even if the app eats up everything I have and bankrupts me, I'm determined to keep it alive. This company is my redemption.

Someone knocks on the glass wall of the conference room, calling me to come in. I'm about to get an update on everything that happened this week. Out of all the companies I own, this is the only one I manage so closely. I come to the offices every week to check on the situation, update plans for the future, and see what budget I need to raise to meet all these goals.

I examine all the numbers and flip through the reports that are presented to me. It's not bad. At least we met the budget. But I want to expand the service further.

My CEO, Paul Sheridan, is one of the most dedicated people I have ever met. His desire to pass it on is even greater than mine, and he's doing it for the right reasons. His heart is in the right place. Even though I pay everyone a decent wage, he's not here for the money.

I trust him without hesitation, so when he walks into the room looking agitated, my body stiffens, anticipating what's about to come.

"Ethan," he greets me with a shake of his head.

I get straight to the point. "What's happened?"

"We received a call, and it was canceled immediately," Paul answers.

"Okay and?" So far, nothing out of the ordinary. It happens sometimes.

"The operator called back, according to procedures, and a man answered. He said he pressed the button by mistake."

Well, that can happen too. Although we tried to prevent something like that from happening, we didn't want to hide the emergency button so that in case of an actual emergency, it could be found quickly. Disadvantages versus advantages. I'm waiting to hear what Paul has to say next.

"The phone is registered to a woman. The operator asked to speak with her, and the man refused." Paul's face contorts in anger.

We have signed cooperation with all the phone companies. The application usage agreement includes a right to locate the phone if necessary. This information has saved lives more times than I can count.

"I sent a team there, and the man opened the door. They reported the house looked as if a struggle had occurred. But he didn't allow them in."

"What about the police?" I ask, even though I know what the answer is going to be.

"They refused to get involved. Our call was canceled, and they didn't receive any complaints from neighbors. I insisted, and they sent a unit there, but the man said that everything was fine and they couldn't get inside either. We can't do anything beyond that."

I hit the table with my fist. Paul is probably right, and there is a case of a battered woman hiding there. But we have no authority to continue handling the case. We can locate the phone, but the law doesn't allow us to enter the house.

"Send a team to park in front of the house. Engage only if there are any suspicious noises or if he or she leaves the house," I say. It's not in our budget to place a team to watch one house for hours, maybe days. But I have no choice. What am I supposed to do? Let her get beaten again? Let her die?

Paul nods and leaves the room. I watch him through the glass wall, talking to staff members and giving them instructions. They hurry to their positions.

I need more investors to finance these cases.

Back in my main office, I sink into my chair and lean my head back. It will take some time before I can pour more money into Savee. The fundraising event I organized will keep us above water for the next two months. But then what? I need to fill the void and bring in more investors. Crisis follows crisis, and I'm busy putting out fires instead of paying attention to the important details. The dismissal of Wolf Iron Shield's treacherous CFO doesn't contribute to my peace of mind.

All week I've been picking my brain over what happened. When I fired Clifford Nightingale, he was surprised and flatly denied it. He probably didn't expect us to expose him so quickly.

Bambi's idea was helpful. It shortened the process. The incorrect data we hid in the VP's computer ended up in one of the company's financial reports. There was only one way for this to happen, and that's if Nightingale got into the computer.

I smile when I think of her. She is so sharp. The way she asked the right questions and came up with ideas for solutions amazed me. I don't understand why she works in a pub instead of for one of my companies. She would fit in great in a management position. I need loyal employees. But can I trust her? What do I even know about her?

I thought I knew enough about Clifford. I didn't even run background checks on him. He used to hang out at our house when we were little kids. And where did it get me?

I can't wrap my head around why he would do what he did. He's supposed to be a friend of the family, and as far as I know, our parents are still friends.

For money?

He earns well, and his parents are pretty damn rich. He doesn't need money.

Personal agenda?

The company I want to buy has nothing to do with him. Not from what I could see when I checked. I can't find any reason he would want to sabotage my deal. Nor do I recall exchanging more than a few words with him during the entire period of his employment here. What could I have done that would make him want to kill my deal? I can't put the issue behind me until I find out what his motive was.

CHAPTER 17

Ayala

"Daiquiri," Nicky says and waits for my response.

"Hmm... That's easy. Light rum, syrup, and lime juice."

She nods in satisfaction. "Good, you learn fast. Do you think you'll manage on your own on the day shift?"

I'm spending a lot of time this week trying to perfect my cocktail-mixing skills. As someone who has never even drunk alcohol before, I have a lot to learn and a lot of recipes to memorize.

I'm determined to succeed. The work behind the bar is much more pleasant than cleaning toilets, and the tips are also good, but I have much fewer shifts. I share the job with Nicky and Evans, the two other bartenders at Lunis, so I no longer have the possibility of working every day. I need to find a second job somehow, to earn more money so I can leave here.

Ethan hasn't contacted me since I ran away on his birthday. Five days and not even a message. I debate whether to call him but decide not to. I know I ran like a coward, but he promised we'd be just friends, and he broke that promise. And whatever it was between us has ended. Yet, despite everything, I can't help but glance at my phone and hope to see the flashing light.

"You're dreaming." Nicky brings me back to reality. "Who are you thinking about?" She winks at me.

"No one," I blurt. "Nobody."

"Good, because for the concert tomorrow, I want you to meet someone." She raises a mischievous eyebrow at me.

"Absolutely not." Nicky invited me to join them for a concert. A new rock band that mainly does covers and is supposed to be good. I love rock music, and I've never been to a live concert before, but I'm horrified by what she just suggested. I don't need anyone to fix me up. The memory of my head in the toilet is still too recent. The memory of the kiss with Ethan is still too close to the surface.

"He's cute, and he's a friend of Shannon's. I think you'll get along. I'll invite him, and we'll all go together, not as a date, so it won't be too awkward." She continues to try to persuade me, and I surrender to her as always.

I have no intentions of dating a man anytime soon. I've seen what happens to me when I try. It might always be too soon for me. I need to get to know myself, to be alone a little and on my own. I'm just now understanding what I like and want in life.

But once Nicky gets started, she doesn't give up, and I know she'll invite him no matter what my answer is. It will be okay, I tell myself. I don't have to go near him.

The first customers sitting at the bar do a good job of distracting me from all thoughts of Ethan and going out with the unwanted date tomorrow. I run from side to side in the crowded bar, trying to remember the recipes without help from Nicky. She smiles at me and gives me a thumbs-up to show me I'm doing a good job.

I smile at the man who sits down at the bar. "What can I get you?"

"Whiskey Sour," he answers. "Has anyone ever told you a man can drown in your eyes?" He winks.

I try hard to keep a smile on my face. I have been told this many times. They also said I'm beautiful. Where did it get me? I'm working in a bar without an identity and without a future. Beauty has contributed nothing positive to my life. I'm thankful for the physical barrier that the bar creates between the customers and me. At least I no longer have to deal with unwanted contact.

This time, I organize by myself. I examine my clothes with a smile. My belongings have multiplied since I got here. Nicky and I went shopping together, and we bought some makeup and clothes. I spent more money than I could afford, but it felt so normal, two girls hanging out. It was worth it. I apply my makeup in front of the small mirror in the shower, apply mascara and lip gloss, and choose the short red dress I bought with Nicky on our crazy shopping spree.

The dress is too short. I tug it down, trying to make it longer with no success.

The concert is only a few blocks away, and I intend to walk. The evening air is getting colder, and I pull my jacket tight around me.

I arrive at the entrance and find Nicky and Shannon in even shorter dresses. They stand tall, show off their assets, and don't seem to care about the male attention around them. I straighten my back, trying to feel like one of them. Shannon stands beside a handsome guy with long hair in a ponytail and brown eyes. His hand is wrapped around her waist.

He smiles at me and holds out his other hand for a squeeze. "Chris."

I shake his hand. "Hope."

The name still doesn't come easily to me, but the handshake goes through without a problem. I'm getting better at this.

The other guy now takes a step forward and extends his hand. "I'm Jonathan."

I examine his face. He has a pleasant smile. Blue eyes, light hair. He looks good, more than good. This is the guy Nicky wants to set me up with. I glance at her, and she nods slightly and raises an eyebrow in question. I give her a nod of approval. Okay, it could have been worse.

We enter the hall and find places close to the stage. The large stage is full of the band's equipment, and screens are set on both sides. The place fills up, and what seems to me at first like a lot of space becomes very crowded.

My heart is pounding because of the physical proximity to so many people rubbing against me from all sides. I try to get some distance, but the position we took at the front of the stage doesn't allow it. The crowd is excited, shouting and calling for the band to come on.

When the band starts singing, the crowd goes wild. I try to enjoy myself and forget what is happening around me, but I find it harder and harder by the minute.

I try to dance, but the feeling of pressure from the crowd only increases. Someone touches me, clinging to me, waving sweaty arms. I can't breathe. There's not enough air. My palms begin to sweat, and my breathing becomes shallow. I decide to step back and find a place to stand in a less crowded area.

"I'm going to the rear of the room!" I shout to Nicky, and she nods. I don't know if she even understood what I said, but right now, I'm concentrating on not passing out here in front of everyone.

I make my way to the rear, trying to avoid random contact with sweaty bodies. Far in the back, the crowd is thinner, and there's more air. I put a hand on my chest, inhale deeply, and try to calm my pounding heart.

Jonathan comes after me and stands beside me.

"Everything okay?" he asks, a look of concern in his eyes.

"Yes. It was too crowded there. I couldn't breathe."

Jonathan smiles at me and moves himself to the rhythm of the music. I try to concentrate on the music, on the low voice of the singer. I can't help but remember the way Ethan sang in the car. He could easily replace this singer... I imagine him, and my breathing calms. I dance and move to the beat of the music, raising my hands high.

Jonathan comes closer and stands behind me, and before I realize it, his hands are on my waist, and he's moving with me.

I gasp, trying to control the next panic attack I know is coming. Inhale... Exhale... I try to calm the trembling that takes over me. I can do it. His hands are on me.

Damn it. I can't do it.

I can. I have to conquer my fears.

I decide not to remove Jonathan's hands and concentrate on my breathing. It doesn't help. Where did all the air go? I start to choke, and a wave of nausea washes over me.

"I don't feel so good. I'm going home," I say, hurrying outside.

"Wait. I'll accompany you," he calls after me, but that's the last thing I want right now.

I wave my hand as I go. "No. No need, thanks."

"Can I have your number?" he yells after me, but I have no intention of stopping.

Outside in the cold air, I breathe slowly, trying to catch my breath. I'm so disappointed in myself. I can't spend an evening with friends without having a panic attack. And he only touched my waist. He didn't even try anything, really.

What if it's like this forever? What if I'll never be normal again?

I'm shivering. It's cold. The temperature dropped since we entered the building, and I didn't expect that. I zip up my jacket. I rush back to Lunis, warming my palms by blowing on them, but I'm still freezing.

I wake up late on Friday, and my chest hurts. Yesterday's stress, maybe? I check my phone, but still no message from Ethan. Why do I feel this pinch of disappointment? He's just a man who wants to sleep with me. No different from all the others. He doesn't want us to be friends, and I want nothing else. It's better this way.

I get out of bed, shaking a little. Is it cold here? I think I'm developing something. I must have caught a cold last night.

I have an evening shift today that I must work, but tomorrow I have a day off. I just need to survive this evening, and tomorrow I can rest.

By evening, I'm feeling worse. I swallow down two pills to help me get through the shift. The pills do their job. I'm feeling better, and I put on a smile and run around the bar, serving everyone.

But as the end of my shift approaches, the effect of the pills has worn off, and my body is weakening, my head is getting heavy, and my eyes closing.

"Are you okay?" Nicky grabs my arm after she senses my momentary hesitation before I lift the heavy tray.

"Yes, everything is fine." I nod. A little cold won't kill me.

"She's pretending again," Robin says with a sneer. "'Oh, I'm not feeling well. Can you replace me while I go to rest?'" Robin mimics my voice. "Do you think that after being promoted, you can escape cleaning?"

After all the time I've been scrubbing toilets, tables, and floors, how can she think I want to get away with washing a few glasses at the bar? "What do you want from me, Robin? I've done nothing to you," I snap at her.

"Ever since you got here, everyone's been lurking around you. Dana gives you priority in everything for no reason other than how you look."

"What do I look like? How is that related?"

"Haven't you noticed the groups of men at the bar since you started? Everyone comes to see the beautiful angel with the big blue eyes. You steal all of our tips. Why do you think you got a job as a bartender even though you don't even know how to pour beer?"

I open my mouth and close it again. I get good tips at the bar. But Dana gave me the job because she cares about me, not because my looks bring in clients. I'm sure of it. And if Robin hates me for that, good thing she doesn't know that Dana also gave me a room above the bar. It would blow her mind.

"Leave her alone, Robin," Nicky says, coming to my aid. "If you get fewer tips, think about what you're doing wrong. She's not to blame for your problems."

I want to tell her I don't need her to intervene for me, but I feel bad and welcome her help.

As soon as the shift is over, I go to my room, take another pill, and crawl into bed. I'll just sleep a little, and in the morning, I'll feel better. I have all day tomorrow to rest.

CHAPTER 18
Ethan

"Why didn't you make the presentation on time? If there's a deadline, I expect you to meet it." The anger is bubbling up in me. I try not to raise my voice in the middle of the hallway, but it's hard to control myself today.

"I... There were problems with the numbers because the new head of finance didn't have enough time to prepare the reports, and everything was delayed," the employee standing in front of me stammers in the face of my fury.

Fucking hell. Do I have another crisis to deal with? All the quarterly reports didn't come out on time because I fired Nightingale. I can't afford a drop in profits because of this. I run my hand through my hair. "I expect you to work all night if needed to fill in the gaps. And call the new manager. I want to see him right away." What's his name? Fuck, I can't remember.

"What?" I turn as someone touches my arm and find Ryan behind me, holding a stack of binders.

"Can we talk for a moment in your office?" He doesn't wait for an answer and starts walking. I follow him into my office and slam the door shut.

"You can't yell at the employees." He sits in the chair in front of my desk and scolds me.

"Sure I can if they don't do the job," I shout at him, not even taking a chair myself. I haven't felt like this in a long time. Everything drives me crazy. Good thing the weekend is coming and I can relax at home. *You're just fooling yourself, Wolf. You know why you're angry, and it's not because of your employees.*

"I don't know what's going on with you, but your employees aren't to blame," Ryan says in a calm voice.

I run a hand through my hair and pace the office. I was sure the trip would do the trick, but it does little to relieve my frustration.

She made me a birthday cake... Even Mom never made me a birthday cake. She just bought one. What should a man expect after something like that? I don't know how to vent. Nothing helps.

Despite the rumors about me that I encouraged, there were already quite a few women who refused me. I'm not disturbed by it. There are enough women who are interested. I don't have to chase anyone. Why exactly does this one affect me so much? Why am I chasing her when I can go to anyone else?

Those eyes haunt me. And that kiss...it was so hot. If kissing her felt like that, I can't even imagine what sex with her would be like.

"I kissed Hope, that waitress," I tell him.

"She gave you a serious blow on the head and you keep chasing her after everything that's happened? Did she reject you again? Is that why you're so moody?" He smirks.

I keep silent.

"Wow. She did. She rejected you again, didn't she?" Ryan turns serious. "What happened?"

"I wish I knew." Why was she so frightened by a kiss she clearly enjoyed? What's the deal? Red lights flash in front of my eyes, a huge stop sign. Could she be a virgin? She is only twenty-two years old. It's a bit late, but not that rare. Maybe she's just inexperienced? That could explain a lot. Maybe she's just not used to being touched.

Sex with a virgin is not my cup of tea. A virgin doesn't know how to please a man. It requires a lot of investment on my part, and they rarely enjoy it. But if that's her problem, I can get over it. I can teach her.

I even like the idea a little. Being her first turns me on. Well, everything about her turns me on. I have to know if that's the reason. I'm willing to take it slow and be gentle with her. Maybe there's still a chance here?

"Did you want something besides scolding me?" I ask him.

"I brought you some documents to sign." He takes the pages out of a binder and places them on the desk.

"Great. Now get out of here." I push him away and close the door, pick up the phone and call her for the first time in a week, but she doesn't answer. Fuck, I waited too long, and now she doesn't want to talk to me. Well, I deserve it. But I won't give up easily. Ethan Wolf doesn't give up on something he wants.

I look at her picture, the one I took on Mohonk lake, and caress her image with my finger. I wouldn't be where I am today if I had given up after every obstacle along the way.

Lunis is closed at these hours, and I knock hard on the side door, but no one opens it.

Does she know it's me? Is that why she won't open it? No, no way. There isn't even a window in her tiny room, so she could peek out. Maybe she won't open the door simply because she thinks it's someone who came to the bar. Yes, that must be the reason. She has no reason to open to a random drunk who wants to enter the bar when it's closed. I consider shouting out but prefer not to draw attention to myself. I send her a message. And then one more.

Shit, maybe she's not there at all. It's still morning on Saturday. She's not working at the moment, so she must have gone out. What a fool I am. I didn't think of the possibility that she might have a life.

The closed door tempts me. No, I can't make that mistake again. I sit down on the steps by the door. I can wait. I take another look at the door. Fucking hell. I'll just go inside and wait for her there.

I can hear Ryan yelling at me. I imagine the jail bars closing on me. I did it once and barely got out. How will I explain a second time?

It's better to wait for this evening when the bar opens. She'll be on duty, and I can talk to her without breaking in. But there will be customers, and she'll be busy.

I sigh, knowing I can't wait until this evening, and I'm pretty sure she won't report me. I get up, open the door carefully, pray that the alarm code is still the same as the last time I broke in here, and breathe a sigh of relief when I disarm it.

The door closes behind me, and I go up the stairs. Her room is dark. I stand in the doorway and knock on the doorframe to alert her of my presence. No answer. I was right. She's not here. But I'm willing to wait. I have patience, and I have nothing else to do. At home, I just go crazy thinking about her. I walk in, my eyes trying to adjust to the dark, and then I see her.

She's lying on the mattress, covered with a blanket, and her eyes are closed.

Asleep at this hour?

I get closer. "Bambi," I whisper, but she doesn't answer. "Hope," I say a little louder. Still no response.

I bend down to the floor to get closer to her and notice she's shivering. I reach out and touch her. Fucking hell, she's burning up.

"Hope," I call again, shaking her a little. Her eyes open, and her blue gaze stares at me. Her eyes shine in an unnatural glow.

"Ethan? What are you doing here?" She tries to sit up and coughs like her lungs are going to explode.

That doesn't sound good at all.

"You're sick," I point out.

"I've just got a little cold. What are you doing here?" Her gaze examines me.

I ignore her question. "It's not a cold. You're sick. You're feverish."

"It's nothing." She coughs again. "It will pass."

"I have to take you to the hospital." I'm worried about her. Her face is so pale, and her eyes look huge and dark against her white skin.

"No!" she shouts. "I don't need a doctor. And I don't have money," she adds. "It's just a cold."

"I'm not leaving you like this. I'll pay for the treatment." She needs to be checked out, and I'll be damned if I let a woman in that condition stay in this little room alone with no heating, no food, and no one to take care of her.

"I don't need a doctor. I'm fine," she insists.

"Then stand up." There's no way she can function in her current state, and I'll prove it to her.

"What?" She looks at me, and her forehead crunches.

"Stand up and show me you can manage here alone." I stand with my hands on my hips, challenging her.

She tries to get up, leans one hand on the wall, and rises, shaking like a blown leaf.

She wears a long hoodie that reaches her mid-thigh and long socks. No pants. Even in her current shabby state, she looks sexy. Nerdy and so sexy.

She has a fever. Stop thinking about her like that.

She sighs and leans against the wall. Well, there's no arguing anymore. She can't take care of herself. I approach her slowly, put my hands behind her, and lift her. She feels light and small in my arms.

She rests her head against my chest, and I exhale.

"I just need to get some rest. That's all."

"I'll take care of you."

Am I going to take her to the penthouse? A woman I barely know? I look at her. Her eyes are closed, and her body feels small and fragile against mine. I guess so. I go down the stairs carefully, cradling her in my arms. Put her in my car and drive home.

I put her in my bed and watch her sleep. The first woman to get into my bed, and she's a mystery. I don't even know her real name, yet I can't walk away.

Her temperature is too high. I cover her with a blanket and turn on the heating, and she's still shivering. She looks unwell, weak, and as pale as the sheet on which she lies. She needs a doctor. I agreed to no hospitals but said nothing about a doctor.

I pace back and forth between the living room and the bedroom until the doorbell startles me.

Finally.

"Dr. Shinar. Thank you for coming." I gesture with my hand toward the room, and he follows me.

We go in, and as if on cue, Hope gives him a display of her terrible cough. I bite my lip. At least I don't have to explain to him what's wrong.

"Ma'am. I want to check you out," he says and sits down on a chair next to the bed before turning to me. "Maybe you should go out and give her some privacy." I turn to leave.

"No! I want him to stay," she says.

I stop. That's about the last thing I expected to hear. "I'm right here by the door," I tell her, and she nods.

The doctor asks her to open her mouth and examines her throat and ears. He takes her temperature, then removes a stethoscope from his bag and asks her to take some deep breaths. A displeased look comes over his face.

"Okay," the doctor says, gathering his tools back into the bag. "I recommend going to the hospital and getting checked out. Without blood tests and x-rays, the diagnosis may not be accurate."

Hope moves her head from side to side. "No."

He frowns. "You might have pneumonia. I'll prescribe you broad-spectrum antibiotics and an inhaler to ease your breathing. But if your condition doesn't improve within twenty-four hours, go to the hospital. Please," he insists, and I see the anxiety on her face intensifies.

"To lower the fever, paracetamol, ibuprofen alternately, warm baths are also possible." He zips up his bag and stands. I accompany him to the door, and he stops just before leaving the apartment.

"Mr. Wolf, within twenty-four hours on antibiotics, she must show improvement," he emphasizes to me, and I nod.

Damn it. This woman only gets me into trouble.

CHAPTER 19

Ayala

I don't understand what happened. A whole week passed by with him ghosting me, not a sign of life, and now I'm in his bed. At his house. I don't know what he wants from me. I have nothing to give him.

I should be worried about my presence here. Lying in bed helpless, he can do whatever he wants with me, and I will have no way to resist. But I don't. I'm not afraid of him.

I feel terrible. The shaking doesn't stop. My muscles hurt, and my legs are numb. I couldn't even resist when he dragged me here and also brought a doctor to check on me.

If Ethan hadn't come, I don't know what would have happened to me. After everything I've been through, dying from a cold would be the irony of fate.

I look up at the sound of footsteps just outside the room. Ethan enters and approaches the bed. He studies me with narrowed eyes, maybe checking to see if I'm going to turn into a corpse soon. I'm not at my best. Right now, it's hard for me to breathe.

"I think we should lower your temperature. You're feverish."

The look on his face registers concern. Does he care about me? Why?

I nod. I don't have the strength to answer. The air has a hard time getting into my lungs. Can't waste energy on words.

"I brought you some pills to reduce fever." He hands me two pills and a glass of water, and I take them with a trembling hand and drink.

"The doctor also suggested a bath. Do you want to?"

Bath. It sounds very nice. I would love to immerse myself in hot water, but getting out of bed and walking to the bathroom seems impossible to me. Maybe I'll wait a bit for the medicine to take effect.

His eyes narrow into suspicious slits, and a small crease appears between his eyes. "No?"

A small sigh escapes me. "I want to," I say, afraid that if I refuse, he won't propose again.

My answer sets off a chain of actions. It seems he was just waiting for something to do. I watch as he goes and fetches a towel from one drawer, taking it into the next room, which I assume is the bathroom. The sound of running water confirms my assumption.

"Do you want a new shirt? Your clothes are soaked with sweat," he points out to me, his expression not changing.

He's so serious. Cold and unsmiling. I love to see his smile.

"Yes," I answer, shivering. "Why is it so cold here?"

The crease between his eyes deepens. "I'll get you another blanket." He turns to leave the room. "Fuck, what did I get myself into?" he curses in a low voice, but I can still hear it.

He doesn't want me here. He just feels obligated because I'm sick. The pinch of disappointment hurts. I would get up and leave right now if I could.

Ethan returns to the room, holding the blanket, and places it on the corner of the bed. Then he stops and waits.

I command my body to get out of bed, but it doesn't obey. I have a feeling that if I try to stand, I'll find myself on the ground. I glance at the floor as it suddenly seems so far away.

"Can you help me?" I ask in a whisper.

His eyes close for a moment, then he nods and approaches me. He doesn't want to be here right now. He doesn't want to be near me. The insult hits me. Maybe he's even disgusted with me, with my condition. I want to tell him there's no need, but he's already close, swinging me lightly into his arms and taking me into the bathroom. Carefully he places me on my feet, his hands still holding me by my waist, supporting me.

What am I doing? How do I continue from here? My chest rises and falls rapidly as I struggle to get air. The stress adds to how crappy I feel. I need to relax. *I got undressed next to him in the lake, and he respected my privacy. It will be fine.*

He bites his lower lip, studying my expression. I can imagine what I look like right now. Sweaty and miserable.

"Do you need help with the clothes as well?" he asks when I don't move.

I nod. I have no choice. I can't do it alone. My limbs are too weak and soft like noodles. I'm afraid of falling. I have to trust him.

"Raise your hands," he says, and I obey.

He pulls the hoodie over my head and throws it aside, leaving me standing in front of him in my panties.

To my relief, he keeps his eyes fixed on my face, not showing even a hint that anything in my body interests him.

I close my eyes and slide my panties down until they fall to my heels, and carefully lift one leg at a time to remove them. I wrap my arms around my body, trying to hide.

I'm naked. I've never been naked in front of anyone but Michael. And this is not exactly the situation in which I imagined it happening. I'm shaking, sweaty, and have a high fever. What does he think? I open my eyes but don't dare to look at him, afraid of what I will find in his gaze.

I lift one leg and put it in the tub. He holds my arm and helps me stabilize while I put my other leg in and sit down, hugging my knees to my chest.

Now under the cover of the water and foam, I dare to lift my head to look at him.

His gaze burns into me. God, the way he looks at me as if I'm desirable, as if he wants me.

I must be hallucinating. It's because of the fever. After all, he doesn't want me to be here at all.

"Will you manage here alone for a few minutes?" he asks, his voice more hoarse than usual. "I'm going to run out to pick up your prescriptions."

I nod, and he leaves quickly as if someone is after him.

I relax in the warm water, close my eyes and let the water relax my muscles. It's nice. After a few minutes pass, I feel better. I examine my surroundings. The bathroom is huge, certainly bigger than the room where I live. It's ridiculous.

White tiles cover the walls, and a light blue cabinet with double sinks sits opposite the tub. A large wooden surface under the sink creates a warm atmosphere. Wealth is no stranger to me. Micheal was rich, but there was no happiness in money.

What am I doing here? Alone with a man, I barely know? Naked in his bath? This is stupid. Irresponsible even. But what choice do I have? I didn't invite him into my room. He just appeared and took control of the situation. And he was right. Without medication and help, I wouldn't have managed alone.

The bath is helping, and I feel a little better. The shivers have stopped.

You like him, Ayala. Admit it.

God. My cheeks heat as I realize the truth. I do like him. Not that it matters. I can't let a man touch me. I'm ruined. Broken. It's only a matter of time before he realizes that.

I wonder what sleeping with him would feel like. If it will hurt like it did with Michael, or if he can teach me to like it. I shake my head. What the hell am I thinking?

"Hmm. Hmm." A deep voice comes from the door. Ethan is back, and he's looking at me like that again.

A wave of heat spreads in my stomach.

"Do you need help to get out?" he asks politely.

I shake my head. I think I can manage on my own. He leaves, and I get up and cover myself with the towel he placed next to the bathtub. I still feel my cheeks burning.

This time, he knocks on the door before opening it. "I brought you a clean shirt." He places the garment on the sink. "Are you feeling better?"

"Yes, the bath helped, thanks," I say, trying not to betray the fact that I was thinking inappropriate thoughts about him a moment ago.

"Can you get out so I can get dressed?"

He leaves the room, and I hurry to put on the shirt he gave me. It's big and long and reaches almost to my knees. Luckily, as he didn't bring me pants. I wear my old underwear inside out and regret that I don't have a clean pair. I go out, bracing myself with my hand on the wall.

He turns when he hears me step out.

"Wait. I don't want you to fall."

He rushes to me and wraps an arm around my waist, then leads me to the bed. The touch of his hand causes my breathing to pick up again.

I wait for the signs of the anxiety attack to come. But nothing. I'm not afraid. I'm excited.

"You're not breathing well," he says, noticing my panting. I sound like a snoring pig, but not for the reason he thinks.

He rummages through the bag and takes out the pills and the inhaler he bought, placing them in my palm.

"Take the pills three times a day. Take one now, and I'll set a reminder for you."

I hurry to do as he says, used to obeying.

I lie down again in the spacious bed and get under the blanket to warm up. No, that's not the truth. I get under the blanket to create a buffer between us. If I could, I would run away from here now before all these rising emotions weigh me down more. But in my current situation, I need his help.

I'm sure he'll want something from me later. Men don't do such things without expecting a favor in return. That's the way they're built. Always wanting something from you. I learned it the hard way, literally. And the way he looked at me before, I think I know what he expects from me.

True, he's attractive, and I like him, but I'm not there yet. I can't give myself to him.

I just hope I wasn't wrong in my assessment, and he will only take what I'm able to give.

CHAPTER 20
Ethan

The faint light coming through the curtains wakes me in the morning. I stretch slightly and then remember I'm not alone.

There's a woman in my bed, and one I want to fuck, but instead of hearing her scream my name, I had to make sure she wouldn't die. There's a first time for everything, I guess.

What could I do? Let her stay there by herself? There's no one else to help her. I know there isn't because Jess sends me weekly reports, and I'm still not even close to understanding who she is and where she came from.

I turn my head to look at her. Her face is turned away, and she's lying on the edge of the bed. Just a little more, and she might fall to the floor. Her irregular breathing betrays the fact that she's awake.

Is she that afraid of me?

I indeed kissed her on my birthday, even though I promised we'd stay friends, but I was sure she wanted it. She even kissed me back. Hell, I'm still sure of that much. I would never force myself on a woman.

I sit up. She still doesn't move, pretending to be asleep.

"Bambi," I say in a low voice without touching her. I don't want to run my scared doe away.

I notice a slight movement under the blanket. She heard me, but I think she moved a little further away, if that's even possible.

I dislike this. "Turn to me, please. I know you can hear me." I did nothing to deserve this. I was the perfect gentleman. I took care of her and didn't ask for anything.

For a moment, there is no movement, but then she turns, looking at me. She's still not at her best, but she looks better than yesterday. Those mesmerizing blue eyes stand out like two flashlights against the pale background of her face.

She looks like a painting, not like a real woman. And those full red lips, demanding that I kiss them. So fucking beautiful. I can't remember the last time I wanted to fuck someone so badly. That is, wanting a specific woman and not just to fuck.

"How do you feel?" I ask, keeping my thoughts to myself.

"Better. Thanks for taking care of me yesterday." She looks down, and her dark eyelashes look like fans against her cheeks. "I think the fever broke. How long did I sleep?"

"Almost twenty-four hours."

I stare at her, waiting for her to look at me again. It's now or never. I have to know. "Why are you afraid of me?"

"I'm not." But she flinches, proving my point. "I just don't enjoy being touched."

I can't believe that. When she kissed me, she enjoyed it. "Are you a virgin?"

"What?" Her eyes widen at the unexpected question, which came out of nowhere. She's silent for so long, I think she isn't going to answer, but then she shakes her head. "No."

She's lying.

"It scared you when I touched you. It seems logical to me you have no experience." I try to explain my theory and convince her to tell the truth.

"I'm not a virgin," she insists, with that scared look on her face again. "I just don't like being touched."

So what is she so afraid of?

"You liked our kiss." I raise an eyebrow and study her reaction. She remains still. "You don't have to be embarrassed." I'm getting closer to her, and her gaze is fixed on mine. "Not from me."

Now we're lying in bed facing each other, almost touching. I study the look in her eyes, giving her a chance to back off, but she stays still, close to me. I see the desire and fear reflected in her eyes, swirling at the same time. She wants me to touch her.

I close the distance between us, bringing my lips closer to hers. Giving her the extra moment to push me away, then I take her mouth.

I try to be gentle, not to scare her, not to exaggerate. And God, it's hard. I've been dreaming about this for weeks. My mouth on her sweet pussy. Her tongue responds, swirling with mine, which feels wonderful. It's good to taste her sweet mouth. My body wakes up, and the kiss is no longer gentle. It's full of passion and lust. I suck her tongue, and she moans. She's fire and flames. I just have to light the match.

My body clings to hers, to those amazing curves I've wanted to feel for a long time. Too much time. I press my hard cock to her body, and she recoils, pulling away as if I poured cold water on her.

Shit. I moved too fast.

"Show me what you like," I whisper to her, trying to calm her down. Don't close yourself to me again. "Show me how you like to touch yourself."

Her cheeks turn pink. I'll have to free her from this shyness. There's nothing to be embarrassed about. It's just the two of us here. Watching her masturbate and orgasm in front of me... Fuck. I think I can come just from looking.

"Touch yourself," I encourage her.

"I don't... I don't..." She hesitates, and her cheeks turn even redder. She can't complete the sentence, and then it falls on me.

"You don't masturbate?"

She shakes her head. Her eyes turn away.

"But why?" Hell, I don't think I've ever encountered something like that.

"I...don't..." Her voice is weak.

"So, how do you like to come then? Would you like me to touch you? Can you come from penetration? Clit rubbing?" I'm trying my best to understand. I want to know what will do her good. I want her, and she must enjoy it. She's so uptight.

But she's silent.

I keep looking at her. "You can tell me anything." I want her to open up to me.

"I can't come," she whispers in a small voice.

I'm not sure I heard right. "What?"

"I can't come," she says again, and this time I'm sure I heard it right. "I'm not good at sex."

Wait. Wait, wait. The world suddenly stops spinning. Did she say what I think she said? Has she never had an orgasm? How is that possible? She's twenty-two years old and has had sex, according to her claim. Maybe it's a medical issue? Maybe there are women who can't orgasm? I don't know.

It blows my mind. I was ready for someone inexperienced, ready to take it slow, but this is something completely different. And what does she mean, "not good at sex?"

"Not good at sex? Why do you think so? How many partners have you had?" It's rude to ask, but she isn't making any sense.

She raises one finger.

"One? Just one?" Ridiculous. Must be some jerk who doesn't understand women. "Why do you think you're not good?"

She looks at me, her cheeks flushed and not from the heat. I suddenly understand something. "Did he say that? That you're not good at sex?"

She nods.

Son of a bitch. "One partner says nothing about you and says more about him. If you don't touch yourself either, then you don't know what you like." She looks so embarrassed, but she's answering me and opening up to me. She wants me to know.

"I want to touch you." My voice comes out a little hoarse. The way she kisses, she must be amazing. I'll prove it to her. "Are you ready for me to touch you? I want to show you that you can enjoy it. I want to make you come for me." I hope I'm right, and it's not some medical problem or something, but nothing she said so far makes me think it was anything other than a bad partner.

I see she's thinking about it, hesitating, wondering whether to trust me. I'm already so turned on by the thought of her letting me touch her. Shit, I'm acting like a horny teenager. There's no way I'm coming in my underwear. *Control, Ethan, control.*

"I don't want to have sex," she replies.

"I didn't ask for sex. I'll stay fully clothed. I just want to touch you."

Her eyes widen as if she doesn't believe my words. "But... But..."

"But what?"

She moves her eyes to my crotch, where my erection is visible through the thin fabric. "You have a hard-on. You need to come."

I smile. "Who said I have to come?" I raise the corner of my mouth. "It's not mandatory. And besides, there are other ways to come besides penetration. Don't worry about me. I'll be fine." I refrain from telling her that at this rate, I'll soon come in my knickers without touching her at all.

When she nods, I take a deep breath. "I need you to tell me in words. Tell me you want me to touch you."

"I want you to touch me," she whispers. Her voice is full of hope. I must not disappoint her.

I move closer to her again. Her eyes close, and my lips land on hers. My tongue invades the paradise of her mouth. She kisses me back, her tongue swirls with mine, and my cock twists with the desire to be inside her. I keep my body away from hers so as not to stress her out again, as I promised.

I break the kiss and move to her neck, kissing and licking her soft skin. She tilts her head back, allowing me access. Her eyes are closed, and her mouth is open. I feel her pulse beating hard under my tongue.

I put my hand under her shirt, but she grabs my wrist and stops me. I wrap my fingers around her chin and coax her to look at me.

"Trust me," I say, my eyes fixed on hers. She lets go of my hand, releasing me, her eyes still showing concern.

I reach up to her shirt, not taking my eyes off her. Slowly, I gather the hem of the shirt and pull it up. She doesn't stop me this time and lets me remove it.

She's not wearing a bra. I look at her breasts, which I only got hints of before. Her heavy breasts are almost out of proportion with her delicate body. The pink nipples are protruding and hard, waiting to be tasted. I've been waiting so long for this moment.

I see she has a burn mark near her collarbone, but this is not the time to ask about it. Not now. Now I want to taste her.

"You're so beautiful," I whisper as I bow my head to her neck again, feeling her pulse with my lips, strong and fast. She's as excited as I am.

My hands are on her waist, caressing her warm skin. I take my time. My tongue makes a path from the neck down, passing over the scar, over the rough skin. She flinches but doesn't stop me. I continue, going further down until my mouth reaches her breasts. I kiss one and then the other, roll my tongue around the ping buds, wet them, and watch the marks I leave. Then I suck on her nipple, tasting it. Her back arches, and she moans. It's not too hard for me to tell how she feels. Her eyes are closed, and she doesn't speak, but her body speaks volumes, telling me she likes it.

I stay on her breasts, moving from one to the other, giving them extensive care. She has the most beautiful breasts I've ever seen. I want to bury my face in them and never let go. So beautiful. I'm enjoying myself, but I know she won't come like this, and I need to keep my promise.

I move one hand down to her panties. Her entire body stiffens. I stop and look at her. Her eyes are still closed. My fingers flutter over the fabric, and I feel it is wet. God, I'm not sure I can last much longer.

"You're so wet," I whisper. "You don't understand how arousing that is."

I continue to skim over the fabric, adding the weight of my palm as I rub my fingers between her legs, tracing the lips of her pussy. I think I hear a slight sigh coming out of her, and it encourages me to continue.

I run my finger back and forth on her slit, and she's so wet it's amazing. How did someone tell her she was no good?

I stop and use both of my hands to remove her panties. She shrinks and tries to hide.

"Do you want me to continue?" I ask again, hoping with all my heart that she won't stop me now. This is the moment I've been waiting for. Relief washes over me as she nods again.

My finger finds her wet slit, and I rub my thumb against her clit, starting at a slow, gentle pace.

Her pelvis moves. She presses against me, buries her face in my shoulder, her breathing increases, and her mouth is on my neck. I feel her clit swelling under my touch while her movements become faster.

I take one finger and insert it into the warm wetness. She stops moving and clasps my shoulders so tight it almost hurts. Okay, I need to go slower.

I leave my finger in place and continue with just my thumb on her clit, until I see her relax again. I concentrate, trying to read her rhythm. As she increases her movements, I add another finger. This time she doesn't stop, and I move my two fingers in and out of her.

Her eyes are closed the entire time. She's afraid to show me she's enjoying herself. Her hands are straight and rigid beside her body, careful not to touch me, not even accidentally. I want her to touch me so badly, but that's okay. There's a time for everything.

I'm dying to taste her. I crawl down the bed, place my head between her legs, reach out and find her clit with my tongue. Her pelvis lifts, and she grabs my hair.

I look up and see her looking at me, her eyes open wide and dark with desire. She's so sexy. It's crazy hot.

"What are you doing?"

"Tasting you," I answer.

She shakes her head, trying to pull me away.

"Trust me," I say again. "You'll like it."

I dive between her legs. She doesn't stop me, but I feel she is still tense. Frozen. Damn the man who took her virginity and left her so insecure about herself.

My tongue makes its way back to her clit. I lick around, suck and twirl, looking for what brings out the response I'm looking for. I send my tongue to her opening, tasting her sweet inside. The stiffness in her muscles slowly loosens, and her legs open further, allowing me easier access.

I feel her pushing her pelvis forward, and I pick up the pace, using my tongue and my fingers now, faster, stronger, adjusting to her body movements. She can't stop herself anymore, and she moans loudly. Fuck. It's so hot.

I feel her walls closing in on my fingers, and I arch one finger and stimulate the magic spot in her vagina. "Come for me, Bambi."

She squirms under me, her legs shaking wildly as she crosses the threshold, reaching her climax. She arches from the bed, trying to detach herself from me, but I insist, continuing to massage the sensitive spot, letting her ride the waves of her orgasm to completion. Until she falls back onto the mattress, gasping.

I remove my fingers from her, giving her a moment to sink back into reality. She blinks and opens her eyes with difficulty, watching me as if from a dream. I kiss her, allowing her to taste herself on my lips.

"Amazing," I tell her. "Just amazing."

Her eyelashes flutter again as she snaps out of her trance and looks at me like she's seeing me for the first time. Her eyes are wide and wild, and her cheeks are flushed. I love it. I've never felt like this before. My ego is about to burst through the ceiling.

She reaches for my crotch. "No." I block her. It's too soon. We'll have time for that. Her body tells me she's not ready for it yet. When we have sex, and we will, she'll want it just as much as I do.

Now that I've proved to both of us that she can come, I know it will happen. Giving a woman her first orgasm is one of the most erotic things I've ever done. I feel on top of the world. Without her even laying a hand on me, too. I didn't think I could feel like this without fucking.

I get up and walk to the bathroom, the tent in my boxers quite prominent. I rub myself until I come, imagining the amazing woman lying in my bed.

CHAPTER 21

Ayala

Oh, my fucking God. What happened just now? So this is what everyone is talking about? I didn't think I could... I didn't know. It's crazy! Everything Michael told me, that my body is broken, that I'm not good for sex, none of it is true.

I feel the tremors in my legs still. And his mouth. I can't believe I let him put his mouth there. And the things I let him do with that mouth... I didn't know that was even possible.

I get out of bed and put his shirt back on, wondering what I should do with my underwear. Just then, the bathroom door opens, and Ethan walks back into the room.

He's wearing the same tight boxer briefs, but his erection is no longer visible. His upper torso is bare, revealing a muscular and strong body. I saw him on our trip to the lake, of course, but not like this, not so close to me.

I can't help but admire the view. I've never seen abs like that before. He must work out for hours.

I want to touch him. I want to run my hand over those muscles, see if they feel hard or soft. I want to pass my hand over the thin strip of hair that descends from his stomach into—

"Like what you see?"

I realize I'm staring and shake off the stray thoughts that flood me. Since when do I fantasize about touching a man?

I tug on my shirt in an effort to cover myself.

He smiles. "Feeling shy? A moment ago, you let me go down on you."

I feel my cheeks burning even more.

He opens a drawer and hands me a pair of boxers. I take them from him and hold them in front of my body. Am I supposed to put them on in front of him?

"They'll probably be a little big on you, but I have nothing else right now. Would you like coffee and toast? Madeleine's not here today, and I'm not so good at cooking."

"Madeleine?"

"My housekeeper. She doesn't work on the weekends," he says, as if it's obvious that everyone has someone running their house.

He leaves the room, and I hurry to put on his boxers. They're long and look more like shorts on me. I'm sure I look ridiculous, but he's already seen me naked. He touched me there with his tongue. *A little late to be ashamed now.*

I leave the bedroom and pass several closed doors until I reach the kitchen. He's standing in the kitchen simmering milk for my coffee, steam coming out of the machine and swirling around him.

I sit down on one of the bar stools and look at him. He didn't bother to get dressed, and I find it hard to look at anything other than his body, this amazing male body. He seems so comfortable in his skin. I'm a little envious of that easiness.

He turns and brings me the cup with a smile. His hair is still damp and wild from his shower, and the stubble on his face is a few days old. He looks so good.

He sits down next to me, and I drink my coffee in silence. It embarrasses me to have him sitting next to me, almost naked, so close that I can smell him. And his nearness does things to me. Things I didn't know were possible. I want him to touch me again. I want to touch him.

"You don't need to be shy," he says, reading my thoughts. "Not after what we just did. Just tell me what you want."

I feel the blush rising in my cheeks again, and the knot in my belly tightens. How did I let him do all those things to me? How did I let him? I'm no better than a cheater.

"It's okay. I'm patient. I can wait, but talk to me."

I can't talk to you. You will never understand. No one will. If Ethan knew who I was, he would kick me out of here right now.

His phone rings, saving me.

"Shit. I forgot." He answers and says into the device, "Maybe we can postpone?" His eyebrows furrow as he listens to the other party.

"Okay, well, I'll be right there." He hangs up.

"Bambi, I'm sorry. I didn't plan for you to be here today, and I forgot I had a previous commitment."

I nod and get up, ready to collect my things. What do I have to take? He carried me here. I have nothing to collect.

"No, wait." He tugs on my arm, forcing me to sit back down. "I don't want you to go. Ryan and Maya are waiting for me. But I want you to stay."

"Ryan and Maya?"

"Yes. You've already met Ryan. Maya is his wife. We scheduled a luncheon, and I didn't realize it was already so late."

That wicked smile of his makes my stomach clench. Ugh, when will it stop?

Yes, I remember Ryan. He's the man who saved me when I thought I was going to prison for murder.

Ethan gets up and goes to the bedroom, and after a few

minutes, he returns wearing jeans, a t-shirt, and a black leather jacket.

"Promise me you'll stay here until I return. We need to talk."

His eyes don't leave mine until I nod.

I don't want to talk to him about what happened. I can't believe I agreed to him touching me. Where was my common sense?

"Make yourself at home. You can eat whatever you want. You've already seen the bathroom. If you want to take a shower, please do. I'll try to hurry. And don't forget your medicine." He retrieves his keys and stops in the doorway. "Wait for me."

When he leaves, I feel relieved. His presence here is strong and weighs on me, but now that he's not here, I can think more clearly.

Although Hope started a new life, I'm still Ayala. I can't believe I let him strip me and touch me like a whore. My parents' teachings are all thrown out the window the moment he's near me. But I'm not sorry.

I'm ashamed but not sorry. It was amazing, and now I believe everything I thought about myself was probably a mistake. I want to try again and see what else is possible. I want to get to know myself.

And my parents? Thinking of them is worth nothing. They weren't there for me when I asked for help. They sent me back to the monster. I remember the sting of betrayal when they believed Michael's version over mine. They took the side of a stranger over me.

I have no reason to think about them anymore. They don't exist for me.

I finish my coffee and wander around the house. Now that he's not here, I feel braver.

I find a lot of groceries in the fridge; it has everything. I take an apple and start nibbling on it.

His living room is decorated like it's straight out of a magazine, and I wonder if he uses it at all. Everything is exactly where it should be as if no one uses it.

I go back to his bedroom. The bed is still messy, testifying to what we did in it. I arrange the blankets and hide the evidence.

My pills are by the bed, and an empty teacup, too. Every time I woke up yesterday, there was a hot cup of tea next to me. How did he keep it warm all the time? I don't know.

I don't see my phone anywhere. It must still be in Lunis. Ugh.

I get in the shower and pass by the mirror. My short hair, which has grown a little longer, is wild, showing my bright roots. I need to dye it again.

My cheeks are still flushed. I'm wearing a long shirt that reaches mid-thigh and doesn't look sexy. I look more like a lost little girl.

When I'm done with the shower, I collect my shirt and underwear from yesterday and put them in the washing machine I find in the utility room next to the kitchen. There's also a dryer, so at least, in a few hours, I can wear my clothes instead of this enormous shirt.

What can I do until he returns?

The rooms interest me, so I walk down the long corridor and take a peek. He didn't say it was forbidden.

The first room is large. It's a gym with facilities of all kinds. One wall is covered in mirrors. Okay, he wasn't born with amazing abs. In the opposite room, I find an office. Desktop, document folders. I don't feel comfortable going in here, so I close the door. The next room is a guest room. I'm about to leave when I realize he could have easily put me here. Why did he put me in his room? Was it all planned to get me to sleep with him this morning? A man who was chosen as one of the sexiest men in New York can get any woman he wants. Why is he wasting his time on me? What does he get out of it?

I go back to the living room and sit on the bright sofa, swinging my legs. How long should I wait here?

There's a book on the end table next to the couch, and I pick it up. Maybe I'll read a book while I wait. On the first page, I see a hand-written dedication.

"To Ethan. Thank you for everything. I love you, Olive."

Not something long and gushing, but the signature... *"I love you, Olive."* It takes me a moment to make the connection, and a strong pain hits my chest. Olive is the woman in blue.

I'm so stupid. I didn't just break every rule I grew up on. I also did it with a taken man. A cheating man. He lied to me.

He just stands a little close to me, talks nicely, and I fall into the trap. Just like it happened to me with Michael.

I'm so weak. It's disappointing. Falling over and over again for the same lies. I have no character. I have no backbone. Where are all the promises I made to myself when I got here?

I'm a mouse in a trap. I pace the large living room. I can't stay here.

With a short rummage in his closet, I find a tracksuit, and I pull it on. The pants look ridiculous on me. I pull the laces and tie them tightly, so they don't fall, then roll the bottoms. That will have to do. I also take a jacket, it's freezing outside, and I'm still not completely well.

I don't have shoes either. I take a pair of flip-flops I found.

I step outside, closing the door behind me. I hope there are no thefts here because I can't lock it.

Shit. I forgot my medicine, and I don't have the money to buy more myself. I go back inside and take the bag, feeling a little guilty. He paid for a doctor and the drugs, and here I am, running away.

I have to go, though. If I stay because of money, I'm no better than a whore who sells her body.

The guard in the lobby looks up from his newspaper and

looks at me with narrowed eyes. He seems surprised by my ridiculous outfit, probably wondering how a homeless woman entered the building without him noticing. But I'm on my way out, not in, and by the time he decides what to do about me, I'm already out the door.

CHAPTER 22
Ethan

What bad timing.

Just when she's loosening up, just when I go through a crazy experience with her, and I want to talk to her about it, Ryan calls to remind me I promised to come to lunch with them and says it's very important to him it happens today.

I agreed to it at the beginning of the week, but I didn't know that Bambi would be at my house. Back then, I thought I should forget about her, that I must forget about her. But I failed.

So my theory was wrong. She's not a virgin, but she doesn't know what it's like to be touched by a man, a real man, I mean, because the maniac who fucked her—pun intended—is not a man at all.

I'm so lost in thought that I almost miss the entrance to their building. I brake and take a sharp turn into the parking lot.

Ryan welcomes me with a hug and a pat on the back like he always does when we see each other outside of the office and pulls me a beer from the fridge.

I see Maya already sitting on the sofa in the living room, and I approach her for a hug.

"Stunning, as always," I tell her. "If you ever tire of this asshole, come to me."

Maya smiles, and my head stings from the blow Ryan gives me.

I sit down in the chair across from them, and Ryan starts, "Do you remember the day I called you because I had a fight with Maya, and she left?"

How could I forget? That was the day that changed my life. The day I decided I wanted Bambi, who's now sitting in my house. "Yes."

"So it turns out I was an idiot because when she asked me my opinion on kids, it was after she found out she was pregnant."

He smiles, giving me time to understand what he just said. My gaze passes between them. They radiate happiness.

"I'm going to be a father, Ethan. A father!"

I get up from my seat and hug them. I suspected. When Ryan told me about their argument, I thought that might be the case, but neither of them had mentioned the matter since, and I remember the rule women taught me—you don't ask a woman if she's pregnant unless a baby is currently coming out from her vagina.

As if reading my mind, he says, "We waited until after the doctor's appointment to tell anyone."

I hug them again. "I'm so happy for you both! And you're an idiot," I say to Ryan. "I don't understand what she sees in you." I laugh. He's the best friend you could have.

"Maya, congratulations. You'll be an amazing mother." I smile at her.

Ryan and I raise our beers, Maya raises her glass of water, and we sit down to eat. I enjoy looking at them, at the small touches, the meaningful looks that say they understand each other without saying a word.

They look so happy.

Could I ever feel that way? Homey and happy? I imagine Bambi sitting next to me like Maya is now sitting next to Ryan, touching my arm and laughing.

It won't happen. I'm not a homey, corny type. I can't take care of her. I've failed before, and I would fail again. I should stick to what I'm good at—fucking and making money.

"Earth to Ethan." Ryan's voice pulls me out of my thoughts. "Are you even listening?"

I nod. "Yes. No. Sorry."

"What's bothering you so much? Did something new happen at the office? You can still consult me. I don't have a pregnancy brain." He laughs when Maya punches him, and I can't help but smile.

"Do you remember that waitress at Lunis?" I ask.

"The waitress, you couldn't take your eyes off of? The waitress-who-almost-sent-you-to-jail? That-waitress?" he says, and I see how Maya's eyes widen.

I glare at him, trying to kill him with my laser sight. He needs to shut up now.

"Yes. that one. I forgot about this lunch date, and I left her at my house. I'm a little eager to get back."

"You left her at your house?" Now his eyes widen. "You brought her to the penthouse? Didn't you rent a room?"

Maya's eyes pop out. *Reminder to self. Murder Ryan. He knows too much.*

"I know where my house is, Ryan," I answer. "She was sick and needed a doctor, and I..." I can't explain it to him because I can't explain it to myself.

"And your desire to play the saint and save her prevailed, as always. You're incapable of ignoring a woman in distress."

"No. That's not why." I deny it, but why did I take her to the penthouse? I could easily have sent a doctor to a hotel suite.

"Why don't you bring her over?" Maya asks.

"What?" Surprised, I turn my gaze to Maya.

"You could bring her to dinner with us. You seem to care about her. It would be nice to get to know her."

"No. No. It's nothing. There's nothing between us." I'm such a liar. Bambi occupies my thoughts all the time. Not only that, but I arranged for her permanent entry into my building, hoping we would continue to see each other.

"Ethan is in love," Ryan moans.

I stand and storm him, knocking him to the floor in a struggle.

"Okay, okay, I surrender!" he shouts.

Our relationship has always been physical, but we never fight. I love him like a brother. More even. I don't know how I would have survived the difficult period in my life without him and his parents.

Once back in my seat, I say, "Yes, she intrigues me," I admit. "But I'm not in love. You know relationships aren't for me." No, definitely not for me. She only interests me because she's a challenge.

"Relationships are for everyone," Maya argues. "Everyone needs someone to love."

I put a fake smile on my face. I'm not everyone. I lost my heart when I lost Anna.

"We gathered here for you, not for me." I divert the conversation back to them, which is easy to do because they're very excited. I happily listen to their chatter about the discovery of the pregnancy and the million tests that need to be done.

When I get home, get out of the car and walk to the elevator, I notice my stride is lighter. I feel almost...happy?

I want to see her blue eyes again, that bewildered look on her face after she comes. I feel like doing it over and over again just to see that look. I want her to come again while I'm inside her. Fucking hell, I'm getting a hard-on just thinking about it.

I open the door to my apartment. It's dark.

"Bambi? Hope?"

No answer. I hurry to check the bedroom. She's not here. She left even though I asked her to stay. *Damn it.*

Why doesn't she listen? What's the problem with waiting for a couple of hours? It's not like I left her on the street. She was in my apartment, which is much better than that shit hole she's living in.

I get back into the car and drive to Lunis.

When I get there, I take a deep breath and try to relax my tight muscles. The bar is locked, and she doesn't answer. I need to get a key to this place. Maybe it's better for me to just buy the fucking building.

I break in again. Her room is dark, and I don't find her inside. Not even in the shower. Where could she go?

I'm losing it. I call her phone, and a light flashes next to me. Her device is on the floor next to the mattress.

What an idiot I am. I left it here when I took her yesterday morning. That means she never returned. I go back outside and sit on the steps to wait for her.

Why don't I just go home and forget about her? It's the logical thing to do. Forget about her. She only brings me trouble. I run my hand through my hair, raise my head, and there she is.

She's standing in front of me, wide-eyed, hugging herself, wearing a huge sweatshirt, and barefoot. Are those my clothes? Fuck, I'm so mad I want to lay her on the ground in the middle of the street and fuck her until she screams my name.

I take a deep breath and rise to a standing position.

"Why didn't you wait?" The anger bubbles under the surface,

and I have a hard time keeping it there. I know she hears it in my voice, too, because she takes a step back.

"I had nothing to wait for. I feel better. There's no need for you to worry about me."

"Nothing to wait for? What about what happened between us? I asked you to wait so we could talk."

"It was good, and that's it. We have nothing to talk about."

"What? Good? It was fucking amazing, and you can't possibly think otherwise. And it can be better if you give me a chance to show you. This is just the beginning." I take a step forward, and she takes a step back. *Are we back at it again?*

"You have a girlfriend who loves you and who you take out to events. I don't want to be the mistress. I don't want to be the other woman." She sniffs as if she's holding back tears.

"Girlfriend? What girlfriend? Do you mean Olive?"

"Yes."

Shit. I should have clarified that first. "Olive and I..." I think of the right way to present this. "It's complicated. But she's not my girlfriend, and there's no problem with you being with me. I told you I'm single."

Those huge blue eyes fix on me. "She's not your girlfriend?"

"No. I mean, she's a good friend, but not a girlfriend. Not that way. We both have our reasons to be seen in public together." I try to be as clear as possible without revealing details from our contract. "Please don't keep running away from me all the time. Come, and we'll talk. I'm an open book." And I'm going crazy here. "Do you believe the gossip about me?"

"I believe she wrote to you she loves you."

"What?" What is she talking about?

"I thought I would read the book that was next to your sofa and saw that she signed it with love."

"Is that all?" I exhale. "I told you we're good friends. That's it." It seems Bambi got caught up in the words and took them out of context. "Why are you barefoot? How did you get here barefoot?"

"I had no shoes. I took your flip-flops, but I wasn't comfortable walking in them, so I ditched them on the way." She bites her lips. "And I didn't have money or a phone, so I couldn't take the subway. I walked."

I'm shocked. I don't know anyone who would walk from Central Park to here without shoes.

"Why did you put me in your bed?" Her hands are on her hips now. "I saw you had a guest room, so why was I in your bed? I know you didn't want to leave me here sick, but you didn't have to put me in your bed."

She's right. I'm not sure why I did that. "I wasn't thinking. I just walked into the house and went to my room."

"And it wasn't because you wanted to seduce me?"

I debate how to answer without scaring her. "Of course, I want to have sex with you. And I think it's safe to say that you want it too."

She shakes her head, but her body says something else.

"I don't seduce women. You make it sound dirty. Whoever has sex with me does it of her own free will. Anyway, I did nothing you didn't want me to do. I distinctly remember that I asked several times." I look into her eyes and hope she doesn't regret what happened now because if she says she didn't agree, it'll fucking blow my mind, and I won't be responsible for what happens next.

But she's silent.

"My car is here. Let's go. I want to talk, and I don't want to talk about it in the street." I hold my hand out to her, but she doesn't take it.

I see the hesitation on her face.

"What do we have to talk about? Why don't you give up? You can get any woman you want."

I don't want any woman. I want you. "Please. You owe me at least a conversation."

I wait in silence. No matter how she answers, I won't give up.

"Speak then."

Here? "Not on the street. Do you trust me?"

She's silent.

If she answers no, I'm not sure there's anywhere to go from here.

"Okay," she finally says. "But let me get some things from the room first. I have to get dressed. I don't want to be without clothes and underwear."

I grin. I prefer her with no underwear.

CHAPTER 23

Ayala

Here we are at his house again.

As soon as he's close to me, I can't stand my ground. I can't understand why he doesn't give up already. Is it because I didn't sleep with him? He won't stop until that happens? I'm not stupid. I know some men like the chase.

But do I want it to happen?

No.

Yes.

I don't know. I can't decide what to do. My body wants him, no doubt.

But my head screams no. I'm still on the run and without an identity. He can never know who I am. What kind of life can we lead like this? I need to build a life on my own. I need to forget about him.

But I owe him at least the conversation he wants after he took care of me and...gave me the first orgasm of my life.

My cheeks heat as the fresh memory comes to life in my mind.

When I'm alone, it's very clear to me what I have to do. I need to say no and build myself the life I want. But as soon as Ethan's near me, my thoughts blur, my stomach tightens, and I can't think logically. This has never happened to me before, and I don't understand what it says about me. About us.

I watch as he walks into the kitchen and pours himself a whiskey. As he brings the glass to his lips, I notice how similar the color of the liquid is to the golden glint in his eyes.

"Ever since I met you, I started drinking during the day."

His tone is scolding, and it annoys me. "I didn't invite you into my life. And I didn't ask for your help. I thought you could be my friend. I thought it would be nice to spend time with someone, but it doesn't seem possible anymore."

"No, I don't think it's possible," he throws at me. The glass stops halfway to his mouth, and he places it a little too hard on the counter.

I jump in panic at the angry sound. He strides from side to side. The kitchen looks small when his big body fills it.

"What do you want, Ethan?" I ask, keeping a safe distance from him.

"You. I want you. I've been trying not to think about you for weeks, but I can't." His eyes burn with a fire that scares me, not because I'm afraid of him but because of the intensity I see in his eyes. I'm surprised to realize that even now when I know he's angry, he doesn't scare me.

"And you're right, I don't want you to be my friend. But you need to know I'm not looking for a life partner either. It's not for me." He makes sure I understand him. "I do want to show you how good it will be between us. Much better than it was this morning."

I can't. Or maybe I can? I'm not looking for a partner, either. I didn't think I wanted sex with him but after this morning...

"It's just sex. Don't let one son of a bitch ruin the best experience of your life. Let me show you how it can be. I know you're attracted to me. I'm not wrong about these things." He smiles.

"I'm not looking for sex, and I don't want to sleep with you," I say, repeating my mantra, but I'm no longer convinced.

"You wanted to this morning. If I had continued, you would have had sex with me, and we wouldn't be having this conversation at all. But I stopped because I knew you would regret it later. And I wasn't wrong about that either." He tilts his head. "I want you to want it as much as I do, if not more. I'll ask again, do you trust me?"

I nod. I don't know how it happened, but I trust him. And he's right. I was ready to sleep with him this morning. But I was in the moment. I don't know what I was thinking. What if I have a panic attack in the middle of it? Or if it brings back the nightmares? Just when I'm getting better. I haven't woken up from a nightmare in a few days.

"I need to think." I need to sort out my thoughts.

"Okay." A disappointed look comes over his face, but he drops the subject. "Would you be willing to answer me one more thing?"

My curiosity is piqued. I nod.

"You told me you don't touch yourself. Why is that? No excuses. I can't believe you never tried."

Ah. This. "I've tried a few times," I admit. "But I've never been able to... *Ahem*... You know. I thought I couldn't, and I stopped trying. It seemed pointless to me." Michael only confirmed my fear when every time we slept together, it hurt, and I just waited for it to be over.

Ethan looks thoughtful. "I guess you were too stressed. Do you want to try again? Now that you know you can?" A spark lights up his eyes.

"Touch myself? Here? In front of you?" It's too embarrassing.

"Yes. You need to know what you enjoy. This will help."

"I can't." He's not serious.

"It's one of the sexiest things you can do with a partner. I'll start, and you'll see how sexy it is."

"Now?"

He nods.

I think of him touching himself, and I like it. I would like to see that. He unbuttons his pants and shoves them down to his ankles. His eyes are trained on me as he takes off the rest of his clothes. His body is a genuine work of art, and I can't take my eyes off him.

When he takes off his underwear as well, I choke and swallow. I see he's semi-erect, and he takes himself in his hand. The tip pokes out from his fingers. My breathing quickens. He's right. It is sexy as hell.

He slides his hand from the base to the tip. Then again, until it's fully erect, and he's bigger than I imagined, thicker. But his movements... That's what interests me the most. I've never seen a man masturbate. He's so sensual. His eyes are half closed in pleasure, and I know I'm the one he's thinking about. The throbbing between my legs increases, and wetness appears in my underwear. Shit. I didn't expect this. My heart beats at a tremendous speed, pounding in my chest, and I want to have such an effect on him. I want him to feel the way I feel now.

I take off my pants and shirt and put them on the sofa, but stay dressed in a bra and underwear. His pace increases, and he rubs himself faster, watching me.

"Fuck, you are so beautiful. Touch yourself for me. I want to see," he whispers.

I sit down on the couch and spread my legs. My arousal outweighs the embarrassment. He has already seen everything.

I move my panties aside and expose myself to him. His gaze clouds, and I inhale. It's an amazing feeling, knowing that I have this power over him.

I put my fingers on myself and imitate what he did to me before, hoping to stimulate the feeling he gave me.

It's not as good as when he did it, but when I watch him, it helps. I rub myself in front of him, increasing the pace. I moan out loud as a small lump builds inside me.

"Fuck, you are the most beautiful thing I have ever seen in my life. I'm going to come so hard because of you."

I glance over, watching him pick up the pace. His eyes close, and his muscles stiffen as he comes undone, shooting his hot white cum.

The sight of this man coming in front of me in this way turns me on completely, and waves of wetness flow between my legs. I think I'm soaking the couch. I increase the pace and feel the knot inside my body building up until I can't take it anymore. My whole body twitches as it unravels, taking me beyond my threshold, and I throw my head back in a wave of pleasure.

While he's still naked, and when I'm still recovering from the waves of my orgasm, he approaches me and kisses my head softly.

"I hope you enjoyed it as much as I did," he says, wrapping me in an embrace. "When you decide you want me, it will be even better. I'll wait until you're ready."

"I still need time to think." Yes, he taught me how to reach an orgasm and proved to me I'm not broken. But there is a big difference between that and sleeping with him.

"Shit." I jump up and pull on my shirt quickly. "I forgot I have a shift today. I have to go to the bar now and get ready."

"What? Now? No way. You're still sick."

"I feel fine. It didn't bother you this morning or now." I raise one eyebrow. "And I have to go. It's the weekend shift. It's crazy on the weekends. I can't leave Evans alone there."

"Evans?"

"The second bartender."

"Are you working at the bar now?"

I nod.

"Okay. But I'm coming with you."

"No way," I protest.

"I'll sit at the bar and order drinks. I'll be an outstanding customer. You won't notice I'm there, promise." He smiles from ear to ear.

Ugh. That irresistible smile.

I pour drinks, mix, and run along the bar while Ethan sits there and never takes his eyes off me.

Every time I glance at him, I see his eyes on me. And every time, that strange feeling in my stomach gets stronger. I'm feeling things for him I didn't want to feel.

He orders drinks but doesn't engage with me. He acts like one of the customers, just as he promised.

I serve a pink margarita to a customer and catch a handsome woman taking the chair next to Ethan. To my astonishment, her hand rises and rests on his arm, her body is turned toward him, and she smiles a seductive smile.

Bitch.

My hands clench into fists. Why doesn't he move her away from him?

I'm amazed by the strength of the emotions coming out of me. I'm angry. When I found out Michael was sleeping with other women, it didn't bother me as this does. Most of the time, I even preferred it. Why am I angry now? Ethan's not mine, and he owes me nothing.

Damn, I want him.

I glare at him, trying to tell him without words to push her away, but he either ignores me or doesn't understand.

Her mouth is getting close to his neck as she whispers something to him. I can't stop staring at the beautiful brunette whose lips are brushing his ear right now. How can I hate a woman I don't even know?

"What would you like?" I ask, making her leave him and turn to me. My eyes shoot burning sparks.

"Do you have a margarita?" She then turns back to Ethan and asks, "Will you invite me for a drink?" Her hand rests on Ethan's arm, and he turns his gaze to her and nods in agreement.

I bite my cheek hard and look into Ethan's eyes, hoping he can read my mind. *Look at me and explain why you're inviting this woman for a drink.* But he looks at his phone.

"Yes, we have a margarita," I say with a sweet smile and take her order.

I make her the drink and serve it to her, awkwardly placing it on the bar in front of her so the drink spills, soaking her dress. She jumps out of her chair and utters a variety of curses that would embarrass a sailor at sea. Where is that sweet smile from before?

"I'm so sorry," I apologize and hurry to hand her some napkins, but she rejects my outstretched hand, gets up, and rushes to the bathroom. I'm smiling.

Ethan raises an eyebrow in my direction but doesn't say a word.

CHAPTER 24

Ethan

Of course, I did it on purpose.

The brunette next to me whispered her intentions in my ear, and maybe on some other night, I would have liked it. But today, I'm only horny for one brunette, the one who works behind the bar.

I want to prove to Hope she wants me, so I let it continue. And going by her reaction, I proved that and more.

If that's not enough, I don't know what is.

Her reaction surprised me. I thought she would be angry, maybe yell at me. Her piercing looks burned a hole in me, that's for sure. But the drink she spilled? I didn't think she had it in her. A fire was lit in her that I hadn't seen before, and I liked it. It turned me on. As I thought before, you just need to light the match.

I follow her with my eyes, how her hair moves in waves around her face as she rushes from one side of the bar to the other, hurrying to serve customers. How the dark eyelashes shadow her cheeks as she looks down to do something at the bar. How her butt looks when she walks in those tight jeans.

My muscles twitch every time I see the other bartender, Evans, walk by her, his body rubbing against hers. I don't think it's by accident, and I notice she flinches when he does it. It's almost invisible, just the slightest contact, but it seems to bother her. She says nothing to him, and I feel like getting up and punching him.

Instead, I order more whiskey. I have to blur these illogical thoughts because I'm feeling things for her I don't want to feel.

But when he does it again, I can't stay silent anymore. "What do you think you're doing?" I call out to him.

All eyes turn to me. Fuck.

He approaches me. "Can I help you with something?"

"Yes, you can stop rubbing up against Hope all the time like it's not on purpose," I say in a low voice, not wanting the attention.

"I don't know who you think you are, but I don't rub anything with anyone. I'm working," he answers. Then he picks up an empty glass and turns to walk away from me.

My anger builds. I straighten and stand to my full height.

A waitress with a black ponytail brings a note with an order to Hope, and they both stop and look at me. Too late to back out now. If she doesn't say anything, I will.

"I'm warning you, if you touch her like that again, you'll be dealing with me."

Hope rushes out of the bar and over to me, grabs my arm, and pulls me aside.

"What are you doing?" she whispers, her eyes wide.

"Making him stop rubbing against you all the time. I see you don't like it. Why don't you say anything to him?"

"He works with me. It's a crowded place. I don't need you to intervene for me." She gets angry. "You have no right."

I raise my hands. Feelings that I don't recognize overwhelm me. "Fine, let him keep harassing you," I say, regretting the words before I even finish saying them.

She cringes when my comment hits.

"I'm sorry." I grasp her arm, but she shakes me off.

She turns and, without a word, goes back behind the bar, not looking at me again.

A crazy day at the office, back-to-back meetings, and I only get a little free time at lunch. I check the phone.

Olive
I have a problem with the numbers in the reports. Can you help?

Sure. Come to the penthouse at six, we'll talk.

I'm a little disappointed that there's no message from Bambi. It's taking too long. I need to conquer her and end this madness before these confusing feelings get stronger and become something I'm not interested in.

We need to continue the conversation from yesterday.

Hope
We have nothing more to talk about.

Ouch.

I'm sorry for what I said. Don't—

Ryan walks into my office, looking upset. He paces, rubbing his face. I don't remember seeing him so upset before. Maybe only after the fight with Maya.

"What's happened?" I dare to ask after a minute of silence.

"She..." he whispers, barely saying the words. "She had a miscarriage."

"What?" I get up from my desk and approach him. "Maya?"

He nods, his eyes sparkling with tears. "I know I'm supposed to be strong for her and support her. But she's crushed and crying. She said she wants to be alone. I don't know what to do."

"What do the doctors say?"

"That it happens. That one out of three pregnancies miscarries at the beginning, and we fell on the bad side of the statistics. I didn't even want kids. So why am I in so much pain?"

I hug him. I have no words to comfort him, so I close the computer and take him home. The work will wait.

Exactly at six in the evening, punctual as always, Olive arrives.

"I ordered us food from Bella Noche. Remember it? Our first date?" I lift the corner of my mouth into a half smile. It was a terrible date. She invited me to her bed, where she lay like a corpse. Luckily I stopped before something irreversible happened. Then she revealed to me she prefers women. The agreement between us helps her stay in the closet.

"No, I don't remember. In fact, I have erased that day from my memory, and I hope you have, too."

"Definitely not. The food was tasty. And besides, I'm sorry you didn't enjoy seeing the wonder of creation that is me." I laugh. "But I sure enjoyed looking at you. You know, a naked woman is a naked woman. I'll never erase it from my memory. I'm a man of breasts, and your—"

She waves an arm and hits my shoulder.

"Ouch."

"Ugh, Ethan. I can't believe you have a picture of me naked in your head. It's just in your head, right? You don't have a physical picture of me, do you?" She looks worried.

"I was only joking. And, of course, I don't have a picture of you."

"I would be happy if that terrible day had never happened."

I hold her hand, stroking her fingers.

"Olive, thanks to that day, I'm sitting here with you now. And thanks to that day, we're friends. Do you really want to delete that day?" I ask in complete seriousness. I was joking, but if she's serious...

"No." She shakes her head and interlaces her fingers with mine. "I know you don't like to hear this, but you have a big heart behind all that posing. I want you in my life, even if it means you imagine my tits every time we meet." She smiles.

"Hey, that's not what I said."

"But that's what you do." Her smile widens.

Well, I can't deny that. I like to imagine naked women. I pour wine, take out plates and the boxes filled with food, and spread all the reports she brought on the kitchen table to figure out what's wrong.

We sink deep into the numbers. It takes more than an hour to find and fix the mistake.

"How did I get confused in calculating the expenses of the fabrics?" Olive hits the table with her hand.

"Can happen to the best of us. You missed one. It happens." I pour us another glass of wine, and we move on to talking about strategies and potential places she found for rent.

"There are some good options here," I tell her. "You just need to decide whether to go for a store on the street or in the closed shopping center."

"Yes. And I also need a budget for the store's internet presence."

I move the reports aside to make room for the offers she

received and accidentally knock the glass of wine. Olive jumps back. I try to grab the glass without success. It flips over and the wine spills, staining all my clothes.

"Fuck," I curse, get up and remove my wet shirt. My pants are wet too. "I'm going to change." I turn to head for the bedroom, and my phone rings. I see it's Paul Sheridan calling.

"What's going on, Sheridan?"

"Ethan, sorry to bother you at such an hour. We have a legal problem."

I sigh. It's never good news. Certainly not if it's urgent enough to call after hours. "What's happened now?"

"About a month ago, someone reported a violent incident through our website and not through the app. The problem is that through the website, she didn't sign the user agreement, so we didn't have permission to locate her. Her husband is suing us."

I run my fingers through my hair. "Fucking hell. Did we save this woman?"

"Yes, and at the very last minute, too. She was hospitalized for a long time. But now he's suing us."

"This is just unbelievable!" I shout. "Saving lives and getting sued for it. What does the legal department say about that?"

"They're looking for a way to get us out of this, but right now, it's not looking good."

"Can she testify? Say she invited the unit into the house?"

I pace the living room, glancing at Olive. She's sitting on the chair in the kitchen, barefoot, her leg folded under her, a glass of wine in her hand. She raises an eyebrow in question, and I raise a finger, signaling just a moment.

I go to the big window and look out over Central Park. I take a deep breath and try to relax.

This is not the first time we've been sued. We usually win. Everyone understands that what we do is important and saves lives, but the costs of these lawsuits are high, whether we win or not.

We'll likely burn a few more million on nothing instead of using it to help more people.

"We're trying to convince her to testify. She's afraid of him."

The doorbell rings. I throw a pleading look at Olive, and she gets up to open the door for me. I have to finish this conversation first, before other interruptions. I turn to see who has arrived, just in time to see Bambi's eyes pass between Olive and me. Her mouth falls open. She stands there for a moment, then she turns and runs back to the elevator.

Shit. I glance down at myself and understand how the situation must look. "Just a minute, Paul," I say into the phone and shout after her. "Hope, wait!" I'm already halfway to the door, but Olive stops me.

"Finish the call, Ethan. I'll go explain. It will be better if it comes from me anyway."

I stop and watch as Olive puts her shoes back on and hurries after Hope. I return to Paul, much less focused than before, trying to end the conversation as quickly as possible.

CHAPTER 25

Ayala

"Hope, wait!" he yells after me, but I press the elevator button repeatedly, trying to speed it up. *Come on, open up.*

I can't believe I fell for his lies again, the emotional tailspin he put me into. I didn't think I would want to talk to him again, not after the bar scene. I couldn't believe he would say such an awful thing to me. That I allowed Evans to harass me. It hurt as if he had stabbed me. I tossed and turned in bed all night, trying to decide if there was any truth to what he was claiming. If I was repeating my patterns from the past.

And now, when I decide to come here to talk to him, I find him half naked, with this beautiful woman next to him. He said she isn't his girlfriend, but it's clear as daylight that they're sleeping together. It couldn't be any clearer than that.

The elevator doors open, and I enter, pressing the close door button. I blink, pushing the tears down. He's not worth my tears. I don't want to cry. My days of helplessness are over. I'll be my own master, and no man will make me cry again.

A hand comes between the doors and stops them from closing. I jump back, startled, and raise an eyebrow at the sight of that woman, Olive, entering the elevator after me.

Her.

Ethan didn't come after me. I can't decide if I'm disappointed or happy that he didn't. What does she want? To yell at me? I have no intention of stealing her boyfriend. It was all a big mistake.

The doors close, and the elevator descends while this woman is standing here, staring at me. I swallow.

"I know how it must have looked when you came in and saw us, but will you give me a chance to explain? It's not what you think," she says.

She doesn't blame me? I look at her with narrowed eyes. "Why should I believe anything you say? I don't know you."

"You don't have to believe me. But give me a chance to explain. After that, you're welcome to go."

What's the point of talking to her at all? But I'm curious. I want to know how she will try to explain it. "Okay."

"There's a small cafe on the corner. Let's sit there. My treat."

"I can pay for myself." Is she being condescending because I'm not wearing expensive clothes?

"I meant nothing by it," she says, raising her hands. "I invited you as a reconciliation offering."

I agree, and a few minutes later, we sit down at a small table in the cafe's corner, and I order some tea.

"My name is Olivia Danske. Nice to meet you."

I just shake my head and say nothing. We're not friends.

"I know little about your relationship because Ethan doesn't talk about ."

"There is no relationship," I burst out. "I thought we were friends, but it turns out we're not."

She shakes her head, and it's clear that she doesn't believe me. "It doesn't matter. I just wanted to tell you that there's nothing between Ethan and me. We're good friends. He's helping me with my business venture. He invests a lot of his private time to help me, but that's all."

I narrow my eyes. "He helps your business without a shirt?" I blurt. "And the gossips wrote you were engaged." I almost fainted when I read that, but Ethan insisted he didn't have a girlfriend.

"We're not engaged." She laughs and shows me her bare fingers. "That's a nasty rumor. And he took off his shirt because he spilled a glass of wine just before you arrived. That's all."

Spilled a glass of wine? Memories of the event where I was the one who spilled a few glasses of wine on him come to mind now. The manager there refused to let me work for him again after that incident. But even then, Ethan defended me.

I shake my head. "Why should I believe you?"

"Think of it like this. Why would I lie to you? If he was my lover, why would I convince you he wasn't? It doesn't make any sense."

She did have a point. If they were together, why would she convince another woman to be with him?

I don't understand.

The waitress comes and places two glasses, a pot of hot water, and a set of tea bags on our table. I fill my cup, then I take one bag and dip it in my glass.

"Are you really not a couple?" I ask again, taking a sip of the hot tea.

"No. We're only good friends."

"Then why do you let the newspapers think you are? Why isn't Ethan seen in public with anyone else?" It still bothers me.

"Let's just say that we both have reasons that serve us to let the newspapers think such things." She takes a sip, and we both fall silent.

Ethan said something similar. I think about everything she's told me. She seems to be telling the truth, and I can't think of a reason for her to tell me these things if she's with him.

"So what do you say?" she asks. "Tell me I didn't screw anything up between you two. I don't want it on my conscience. I've never seen him care so much about anyone before."

"What?" I don't hold back. "What do you mean?"

"It's obvious he likes you. I've never seen him this upset."

I snort.

"Believe me, I know him well enough to know when he cares."

"He just wants sex. He told me that himself."

Olive bites her lip. "If you want him, you need to have patience. You should look at what his eyes are saying, not what comes out of his mouth. Ethan... He's emotionally closed. He doesn't think he's worthy of love."

"Emotionally closed?" I repeat after her. What the hell does that mean? I rub my neck. He certainly knows what he's worth, and he has no problem saying it.

She nods. "Yes. I know it doesn't seem that way at first glance. He maintains that inflated almighty businessman pose quite well. But that's not who he is. After getting to know him, you'll realize he's so worth the time it takes for him to open up."

I scan her. What's she not telling me? "He's too domineering for me." I can't handle another Michael.

"No, Ethan is overprotective. It's totally different. He has a heart of gold." She waves to the waitress. "Let's go back. Hopefully, Ethan's finished his conversation by now, and you can make up."

We get up, and Olivia insists on paying for my tea. I allow her, understanding that this is her way of apologizing.

"What call?" I ask.

"Something to do with Savee. I don't know. I don't get involved in his business, but it sounds like there's some problem there."

I think about this app. Where would I be today if I'd used it? "I hope it's not a serious problem."

"I don't know, but he'll find a solution. He always does. This company is everything to him. He puts his all into it. He always says this company is his mission."

"His mission?" Savee handles cases of suicide, rape, and abuse. Is his mission to help me too? Maybe fate brought us together so that he could fix me?

We walk back to the building side by side. I'm dressed simply, in jeans and a t-shirt, and she's in an A-line dress that probably costs several hundred dollars and looks amazing on her. How can I compete with her? In this light sophistication, in her status and beauty? But she insists they're just friends. I don't understand it at all.

"Yes. He lost his sister, and since then, Ethan's determined to save as many people as he can."

"Oh, that's terrible. How did it happen?" I found nothing about it in the search I did. It wasn't written anywhere.

"I don't know. It was never public, and he won't talk about it. I know it happened when they were kids. I believe it's the reason he's so emotionally closed." She gives me a look that says, *I don't know any more than that, and I don't ask.*

Losing a sister in childhood sounds terrible. Car accident? Disease? And how come it wasn't published anywhere?

We arrive back at the penthouse, and Olivia rings the doorbell.

Ethan opens the door for us, wearing clean clothes, jeans, and a khaki t-shirt with the collar open. He gives me a long look before moving aside and allowing us to enter.

"I'm going, and I'll give you privacy," Olivia says from the kitchen while she collects all kinds of folders and documents from the table. It looks like they were working on something when I arrived.

"Did everything work out with Savee?" she asks when the bag is already packed and puts a hand on his arm.

I cringe a little.

"Not yet, but it will be." He shrugs, but I see the cloud in his eyes. He's not calm. I feel the need to hug him but hold back.

Olivia leaves, and the door closes behind her. I understand that the moment has come.

We stand facing each other, and my muscles are stiff, my whole body tense.

He smiles, and his eyes sparkle with affection. He's so beautiful, and his smile relieves some of my tension. Olivia was right. Everything is in his eyes.

"I'm glad you're back. Olive and I—"

"She explained everything," I quickly interrupt him.

"Everything? Really?" He looks surprised. Why is he so surprised?

He tilts his head to the side and examines me.

"Olivia told me it was your mission."

"What is?"

"Savee. Helping people."

"Something like that."

"She also said you lost your sister. I'm sorry."

It's as if a screen rises over him. His face loses expression. "Thanks. That was years ago."

Maybe it was years ago, but it's clear to me from his reaction that the pain hasn't dulled. I decide to change the subject and not dig into the wound. "You hurt me yesterday with the things you said."

"Wine?" He ignores my statement, walks into the kitchen, takes out a fresh glass from the cupboard, and offers me the wine that's on the table.

I nod, as I need a distraction from what's going to happen now.

He pours and turns to me. "What did I say?"

"That I allow Evans to harass me. That's not true. We're just working in a tight space."

Ethan shrugs. "Maybe. I don't know him. I barely know you. But I got angry and lost control. I'm sorry. I just wanted to help."

"Why does it bother you so much that he touches me if I don't care about it?"

"Because I'm jealous," he blurts out, surprising me with his honesty. "I want to be the only one touching you."

My cheeks burn. His low voice and his words send waves of desire through me. Maybe I should go? It's not too late. I haven't done anything irreversible yet.

But when he hands me the glass and our fingers touch, my whole body feels it. That touch plays on my nerves, crawling from my fingertips to my arms and into my body. I feel it everywhere, and I remember why I came here.

He can fix me. He can free me from fear, from this shadow that pursues me. If he can't, no one can.

I drink a little, and the glass shakes in my hands. I'm here, but I'm still scared.

He sits on the other side of the counter, just watching me, waiting for me to make the next move.

I sit there, my foot drumming on the leg of the chair, and I'm looking down at my glass. I don't know what to do. I've never done anything like this before. Michael was my only one.

Ethan moves so fast. One moment he's sitting on the other side, and the next, he's sitting next to me, his face close to mine, and I feel his breath on my cheek.

I bite my lower lip and glance at him. The gold in his eyes sparkles with passion. I know what he wants. My breathing increases, and already it's wet between my legs.

"Say yes," he whispers close to my ear, so close that my skin tingles.

I want to. I open my mouth, but no voice comes out. His lips are so close to my neck, and I want him to touch me. I want him to kiss me. I can smell him, the smell of wine and citrus and man, and I know it's going to happen. I want him.

"Yes," I say, feeling like I've lifted two-hundred-pound weights.

He moves away from me and extends his hand.

I take it.

"Come." He pulls me after him. "Your first time should be in bed."

"It's not my first time," I correct him.

"I don't know what you've been doing until now, but it wasn't sex. Today will be your first time." The look in his eyes is so intense. Can I stand it?

He pulls me into the room after him, leaving me with no time to hesitate. It's going to happen. I can't believe I agreed to it. We stop by the bed. His body is close to mine, and I'm so out of breath you'd think I'd just finished a marathon.

He lowers his head and puts his lips on mine. His kiss is soft and gentle. He takes nothing I don't give back, and I know he's just trying to calm me down. He wants more. He needs more. And so do I.

"I'm scared," I whisper through the kiss. "My heart is pounding."

"Mine too."

He takes my hand and places it on his chest, letting me feel his heart beating under my fingers. "I don't think I've been this excited before." His lips are on mine again, and I'm drawn in by his taste. I send my tongue into his mouth, and he accepts it, twirling mine with his. The kiss deepens, getting stronger, hotter. Dizzying me. I've never been kissed like this before, like I'm the only person in this world. And right now, he's the only one for me.

His tongue swirls around mine, and I dare and suck it lightly.

He moans into my mouth, and I feel another wave of pleasurable pain between my legs. What's happening to me? I'm not sure how I feel. My nipples are hard and demanding relief. My body demands relief. I try to pull him closer to me, touch him. I need more of him.

He stops, and a sigh of protest escapes me. Without taking his eyes off mine, he reaches for my shirt and pulls it over my head. His fingers are already undoing my bra clasp, and I wonder how many times he's done this before.

"Stay with me." He catches the look in my eyes again. "Don't go into your head."

How does he know?

"Do you want to undress me?"

I nod and take the hem of his shirt in my hand, and he bends down and lets me take it off him.

I can't help but stare at his smooth golden skin, those hard muscles, which look like they were drawn by the hand of an artist. A thin streak of hair descends from his abdomen into his pants, marking the way.

I take a deep breath, raise a hand, and drop it back. I can't do it.

"Touch me." He lifts my hand and places it on his chest.

He's hot and soft and hard. I run my fingers gently over his skin, trying to gather courage, caressing his chest muscles. I look up and see that his eyes are closed. Armed with new bravery, my hand slides down to feel his abs. They're harder than I expected them to be. His breathing increases as my hands are close to the button of his pants. I look up to meet his eyes. He swallows heavily and just gives me a small nod, requesting me to continue.

I unbutton and release the jeans, sliding them down to his heels. He kicks them aside and remains standing in his underwear.

I see the outline of his cock through the fabric and recoil. No. I can't do it. It's going to hurt again.

"Hey," he whispers. His hand caresses my chin and lifts my face to his. "Don't panic. You're with me. Look at me. We won't do anything you're not ready for." He coaxes me to look into his eyes. His eyes are filled with passion and softness, calming me down as he strips me of my jeans.

He reaches for my waist, holds me, and leans me back slowly until we're both lying on the bed.

He lies on top of me, but his body doesn't touch mine. He remains watchful on his elbows, keeping his distance from me.

I'm scared he'll find out the truth. I know he will. Why am I doing this? I need to get out of here. I need to run away. He brings his face closer to mine and holds my face for another kiss. I can't hide the trembling that grips me.

He puts one knee on the bed, and before I can understand what's happening, he turns us over so that now he's the one lying on his back, and I'm on top. I gasp.

"Now you're in control. You can do whatever you want with me. I am at your service." He burns me with his golden gaze and folds his hands behind his head.

There's no distance between us now. I can feel his hardness between my legs. I fight my initial impulse to get off of him.

"Calm down, my Bambi," he whispers. "You're safe with me."

I take a deep breath. I am safe with him. Everything we've done so far has proven to me I can trust him. If I can't overcome my fears with him, I never will.

I'm in control of this beautiful man.

I move my pelvis back and forth, rubbing against his cock, the throbbing between my legs begging for relief. I rub harder, trying to reach the excitement I felt when he touched me, but the fabric gets in the way.

I stop. He watches me, and I wonder what he will do, but he

just waits. I get up and remove my underwear. His gaze descends on my body, and I see his cock squirm in the tight fabric.

"Do you want me to undress, too?" he asks, and I nod. He removes his underwear, and I moan. I've seen him naked before, but now I know what we're going to do, and it's much bigger than Michael's, thicker too.

I'm waiting for him to push my head there, forcing me to suck him until he's done as Michael did, but he says the exact opposite.

"Don't look there."

I see the look in Ethan's eyes, the sadness. Shit, he's figuring it out.

I want to run away, but I don't want to stop, either. I want to overcome my inhibitions. I want to learn how to enjoy sex.

I look up, concentrating on Ethan's body, on his face, and I breathe slowly, in and out.

I kiss him again, then I put one leg over his hips and straddle him.

His cock is between my legs again, skin to skin. It's warm and hard and not as bad as I feared. I continue to rub myself against him, trying to get the right pressure on my clit.

He moans loudly, his breathing increases, and his eyes are closed in pleasure. Then he reaches for my hips, stopping me from moving.

He doesn't want me anymore?

"It's too good. I don't want to come like this. Do you want more?"

I dare to look down at our point of connection. I'm too excited to stop now. My body is screaming for release. "Yes," I say.

His cock is shiny, covered in my juices. God, this is amazing. I can't believe it's from me.

He reaches into the drawer next to the bed and pulls out a condom.

Shit. I didn't even think about it. Michael never used condoms. He took me to the doctor and made sure I was on the pill. But I haven't taken any since I ran away, and I have no way to renew my prescription. How stupid am I to lose my mind like that? Would I allow Ethan to sleep with me unprotected?

I move aside and watch as he puts the condom on himself.

"Do you want to stay on top?" he asks.

I shake my head. I don't know what to do. I can't. I want him to lead the way, to show me the way for myself.

He rolls me easily onto the mattress, and now he's on top of me again, the tip of his cock touching my opening. My muscles instinctively contract, bracing for the pain to come. It always hurts.

But he doesn't move. Instead, he lowers his head and kisses my neck, then licks my breast, takes the nipple in his mouth, and sucks hard. I groan and throw my head back on the bed. These feelings are stronger than me.

He continues to play with his tongue on one nipple while using his thumb on the other, causing waves of pleasure to flow down my body and waves of wetness to appear between my legs. I surrender to the feeling, concentrating on his tongue.

He pushes himself into me, slowly, inch by inch.

"Relax," he pleads, stopping halfway. I try, try to relax my contracted muscles. I exhale, closing my eyes. And then, in one gasp, he's inside me. I shout out loud.

I lie still for a moment, trying to get used to him, to his size. Waiting for that burning fire that always comes at this moment, but there's nothing. I feel fullness. I feel pressure. But it doesn't hurt. How come it doesn't hurt?

"You're so tight," he whispers, looking into my eyes. "Are you okay?"

I nod.

He moves, and his cock begins to thrust in and out of me.

Slow. Too slow. My thoughts surprise me. I need more. I raise my hips, trying to push myself closer to him. Deeper. Our blows become more frequent, more violent. I wrap my legs around his waist, trying to pull him deeper, enjoying the feeling of him inside me. I feel that small knot building, just like last time, this very pleasant feeling of pressure combined with pain.

He wraps his hands around my pelvis and lifts my butt in the air. He's deeper now, so deep it hurts. But it's such a delightful pain.

"Hell, it feels so good to fuck you," he moans, his body hitting mine again and again.

"Stronger!" I scream as I decompose, my inner walls contracting and closing in on him, hugging him. I feel the ecstasy washing over me, shattering me into pieces. I clench my fists on the sheet, trying to stay in the moment.

He stays deep inside me, letting the waves of my orgasm subside, then thrusts into me five more times. I feel his cock thicken inside me and the tremendous heat of his seed as he comes. He moans loudly and throws his head back. His eyes go foggy.

He's the most beautiful man I've ever seen. I can't take my eyes off him.

He was right. I was a virgin. What I did before was nothing like what we did just now, this act of passion and loss of consciousness. Sex of passion, sex like you see in movies. And I thought it was only possible in movies. I can't believe how much I've missed. I want to do it again. And again.

Ethan lies on top of me, his face buried in my neck, his shaft still inside me. The weight of his body over me and the scent of our mixed sweat is the most satisfying feeling I've felt in my life. Warmth and security.

He sighs and pulls out of me, takes off the condom, ties it and throws it to the side of the bed, then comes back to lay next to me, his arm resting under my chest.

I turn to the side so I can look at him.

Thanks, I tell him in my heart. Thank you for showing me how it should be, that everything Michael taught me was a lie.

I don't know if Ethan can see in my eyes what I'm telling him, but I see the pain in his.

"What did he do to you?" he asks quietly.

I knew he would figure it out. I shake my head and close my eyes in pain, then move away from him. I don't want anyone to know. I don't want him to know, to find out how weak I am. How broken I am. How I let a monster live by my side and hurt me for two years without stopping him.

Ethan closes his eyes for a moment and pulls me closer to him until I'm lying cuddled in his arms, my head resting under his chin. We stay like that, silent and together. I know at this moment I've crossed a line, the line I promised myself not to cross.

I have feelings for Ethan.

CHAPTER 26
Ethan

I wake up in the morning and immediately turn to check if my Bambi's still here, breathing a sigh of relief when I see her sleeping next to me, covered with a blanket. She's not even on the edge of the bed this time. I glance under the blanket at her naked body. She has a divine body. I'm just crazy about her breasts. Those pink nipples call to me, and I debate whether waking her up for quick morning sex will please or annoy her.

It's five in the morning, so I decide to leave her curled up in the warm blanket, kiss her forehead, and go out running.

What was between us was powerful and intense. I came so hard inside her tight and sweet pussy. I don't want to let her go.

I suspected, when she was reluctant to feel my erection, that she had a past. I suspected she'd been raped. I kept hoping I was wrong, but last night proved what I didn't want to be true.

It was clear in her every movement, every expression. She was afraid, and not because I gave her a reason to be, but because something from the past cast such an enormous shadow on her that she has trouble freeing herself from it. As soon as I asked, she shut down.

But she wanted me, despite her fears, and right now, it feels so right, so good, that I believe maybe, just maybe, she can heal me too.

When I return from my run, I find Madeleine working in the kitchen. "Good morning, Madeleine."

She washes some dishes in the sink and turns to me, smiling. "Good morning, *Kýrios* Wolf."

"When are you going to call me Ethan?"

She just shakes her head. "It's not respectable."

"How are the grandchildren?"

Her face lights up, and I can see how much she loves them. "They are amazing. Katrina is learning to walk now."

I smile at her. I know she spends a lot of time with them, and I'm sorry I'll never have that.

"Do you want the usual breakfast?" she asks, and I nod.

"Yes, please. And I have a guest today. Make her whatever she wants."

Madeleine's eyes widen, and her mouth drops open. "A guest? Of course, of course." She rushes and starts tidying the kitchen.

I smile at her excitement. I don't bring guests here. Certainly not ones that stay overnight. Nevertheless, her joy is not justified. Although I didn't exhaust my desire for sex with my Bambi, that's all it is. Sex.

"I know it's not my place to say..." Madeleine starts and stops.

I nod, asking her to continue.

"You're a good man. You deserve a woman who will love you. I don't know what happened to you in the past or who hurt you before, but not all women are like that. Open your heart. It's not good to live with a closed heart."

My lips raise into a tense smile. No one hurt me. It's me who hurt others.

I go to the bedroom and find Bambi still curled up in bed. I lean over her and kiss her red lips.

She moans slightly and stretches, her perfect breasts slipping out from beneath the blanket. I can no longer hold back and send an inquiring tongue to her nipple. Fuck. I have to fuck her again, but I'm just back from running, and I'm sweaty.

I see her eyelashes flutter open as she realizes this is not a dream. Those blue eyes are hazy from sleep as she looks at me.

"Ethan," she says with a voice hoarse from sleep.

Just hearing her say my name like that makes me horny. Fuck, I've been horny since I got up.

"Come, take a shower with me, Bambi," I ask her, hoping she will agree.

She stretches and gets up from the bed. My eyes widen as I take in her naked body.

Now that I've removed the initial barrier, she's no longer shy. I look in admiration at the triangle of paradise between her thighs below a flat stomach and large breasts that I have already come to admire.

She turns and walks to the shower, giving me a look at her butt, and I love it. I can imagine her under me as I pound that ass. God, this is so sexy.

I follow her, and when we get to the shower, she turns and looks at me, waiting for my next move.

I hurry to take off my clothes and throw them in the laundry basket, then turn on the water so it can warm up.

She's looking at me now, examining me as I examined her, her eyes curious.

I know I look good. I work hard for it. But strangely, I feel vulnerable under her gaze. I want her to like what she sees. I never cared before.

I go under the current and wait for her to join me.

I feel like a virgin myself. I don't know how to behave with her. I'm worried that if I touch her the wrong way, she'll run. I don't know what to do that won't possibly discourage her.

I stand under the flowing water in silence. She reaches out, her hand hovering over my body for a moment, then touches my chest. I inhale sharply, the touch of her hand like fire on my skin.

She looks at me, asking for permission, and I give it to her with a slight smile. Her hands roam over my skin. Caressing my chest, my body. My breathing turns heavy.

I try to control my reaction, but I can't anymore. I see the fearful look in her eyes as she looks down at my erection, touching her stomach. But she isn't flinching this time. Her hands continue to explore my body, crawling over my wet skin until she grasps my cock, wrapping the entire thickness in her fingers. I'm hard as a rock now, and I bite my bottom lip, trying to hold back.

She moves her hand up and down, and I moan. I have to stop her. It's too fast for her. I don't want her to panic.

"Bambi," I whisper and wrap my fingers around her wrist.

She looks up at me. "Let me."

I release her hand and bow my head to take her lips. She just stuns me.

I can't stand it anymore. I reach out to her, stroke her, and lightly pinch her nipples. She moans, and I know she likes it. I reach down, and my finger makes its way between her legs to find that sensitive spot.

I massage her, and her pelvis moves in circles, trying to meet my fingers. God, she is the most beautiful thing I have ever seen. I moan into her mouth as I kiss her again while her hand moves faster and faster on me.

"I'm coming," I moan, as a slight shiver runs down my spine. The powerful orgasm shakes me, and I mark her body with my sperm while she continues to squirm under my fingers.

She's not done yet. I kneel in the shower, and she gasps as I lift one of her legs over my shoulder, exposing her to me.

"I want to taste you," I say and press my mouth to her pussy, lightly licking her clit until I find the right position. Her pelvis thrusts into me, and I love it. I'm ready to be between her legs all day long.

I enjoy hearing her moans grow louder as she nears climax, and I slide a finger inside her hungry pussy, curving it inside her to stimulate her sweet spot. She's screaming now, writhing over me. I continue, eager to use up all the waves of her orgasm, to prolong it as long as possible. As the ripples in her body subside, she takes her leg off me and stands on unsteady legs.

I wrap her in a hug as the flowing water washes over us.

"I didn't know that was possible," she whispers into the hollow of my shoulder.

Her words make me sad. She has lost so much. I want to show her that everything is possible. I want to show her more. "I still have a lot to teach you. It will be even better."

I take the soap and start rubbing her soft skin, and when we are both covered in foam, I clasp her waist and hug her close to me, kissing her. My heart flutters with happiness. Feelings I don't know how to define, even to myself. But I feel good. I feel so good at this moment.

CHAPTER 27
Ayala

"I have to go to the office," Ethan says as I put my clothes back on.

I don't want him to go. I want to hold him tight and keep him close to me. I want more of him, to see how far he will take me, what more I can feel.

In the shared shower, when he stood there, so close and accessible, his beautiful body in front of me, I couldn't help myself. I didn't want to hold back. It was the first time I wanted to please a man. I wanted to touch him, feel him, make him feel like he did me.

I think he expected me to go down on him as he's done for me more than once, but I don't think I can ever do that again. Just thinking about it brings back all the terrible memories, and I shudder.

I finish getting dressed and sit on the bed, watching him button his shirt and take his suit jacket off the hanger.

"Madeleine is here," he tells me. "She will prepare whatever you want to eat."

She's here? Did we do it while she was here? What if she heard us? I feel my cheeks burning with shame.

He turns to me. "Everything okay?"

I look down and nod. All is well. I just want to bury myself in the ground. "She must have heard."

"She can't hear us from outside. And even if she did, I'm sure she knows what we do in the bedroom behind closed doors." He laughs. "Unlike my parents, she doesn't criticize me all the time."

His parents? My ears don't miss the piece of information he gave me just now.

"She's a superb cook, and she'll be happy to have someone she can feed." He puts on his jacket and turns to me, capturing my lips for a brief kiss. "I have to go." He takes the keys and phone from the dresser. "Goodbye, beautiful."

He leaves, and I already miss him. When did this happen? When did he become so important to me? I think it happened some time ago, but I didn't want to believe it was true. I can't deny it anymore. I'm falling in love with him.

It's clear to me we have no future, though. He made sure I understood that. What we have is just sex and nothing more. I know it can't be more, not when he doesn't know who I am. Should I tell him? Should I confess the secret that's eating me up?

No, it will end when he finds out. I'd rather take what he gives than nothing.

What I'm experiencing with him, the things I learn about myself, my abilities, my body, the orgasms he gives me... He cures me. It's worth everything. Even if I end up with a broken heart. I regret nothing.

I can't give up on these moments of normality, of the unexpected happiness that's come to me, the happiness that I never had before. I have to take it with both hands and keep it in the closed box of my heart.

I leave the room with hesitant steps, ready to meet Madeleine, not sure what to expect.

I discover a woman with white hair pulled up in a tight bun and a wide smile. She examines me from top to bottom.

"You're a beautiful little thing."

I lower my face. A lot of men have told me I'm beautiful, but they just wanted to sleep with me.

"I'm Madeleine Arditti, and what's your name?"

"Hope Brown," I answer and sit on a chair.

"What would you like to eat, Hope?"

"I'd love a coffee," I mumble.

"Coffee on its way. But what would you like to eat? Omelet and salad? That's what *Kýrios* Wolf likes to eat in the morning."

"Sounds good. What does *Kýrios* mean?"

"Oh, I'm sorry. I was born in Greece. Sometimes I blurt out words in Greek. I meant Mr. Wolf."

I wonder why she calls him Mr. Wolf and not by his name. He didn't give me the impression of a man who cares about official titles.

She continues to speak while preparing the food. "I'm not used to seeing Mr. Wolf's guests here. I see you will be good to him. He needs a woman in his life," she mumbles, and I wonder why she says she's not used to guests when he's obviously had a lot of women. Does he throw them out before she arrives? Probably.

I drink my coffee and eat, listening to Madeleine's chatter about her family. Despite these past several years, I miss my parents so much, the days when I lived at home, studied at the girls' school, and everything was calm and simple. Days that will never come back.

I tell her about my family, careful not to give any identifying details. The memories bring tears to my eyes. I'm angry at my parents, but I don't blame them. Not anymore. Time has given me proportion. They did what they thought was right. Michael was very convincing, and he had official documents. I'm sure they didn't mean to harm me. It's just a shame they believed him and not their only daughter.

"Have you been working for him for a long time?" I ask.

"It's been five years," she says, sticking her chest out. "Before that, I cleaned one of his buildings. And every morning when he arrived for work, he would greet me good morning and ask how I was. Every single morning. While the other tenants would pretend I didn't exist."

I know that feeling. Just like when I cleaned toilets in Lunis. People don't want to acknowledge the fact that there are people who need to clean up after them.

"When I told him my daughter was sick, he paid all the bills without asking for anything in return. This guy has a heart of gold."

Yes, he is perfect. I already know that. It's me who's broken, me who doesn't fit.

I see her eyes glisten with tears. "How's your daughter now?"

"Oh, she's perfectly fine. She healed, thanks to him. So when he asked me to come work for him, I agreed immediately, and I'm not sorry. I'm so glad he has you now. I worry about him. A man needs a woman to take care of him."

I put a fake smile on my face. Ethan clarified he has no need for me beyond sex. Besides, he's the one who takes care of me, not the other way around.

After I finish eating, I hug Madeleine and collect my things. I haven't talked to Ethan about the rest of the day, and anyway, I have an evening shift. He probably won't be back before it starts, so there's no point in me staying here.

During the midweek shift, only one bartender mans the bar, and today it's me. Although the place is not as busy as on the weekends, manning a shift by myself means I'm running non-stop to serve all the customers.

Dana told me how pleased she is with the way I've taken over all the work, that I could hold a shift by myself so quickly. I hope this means she will assign me more shifts from now on because I need the money. I want to earn enough to move into an actual apartment of my own, but I'm not sure I'll be able to achieve that with only the job here. Even in the suburbs, it is too expensive.

When I went to study business administration, I hoped to work in a large company, managing and planning marketing strategies. That was my dream. But to get such a position, I need a real identity. I need to think about how to get one. Enough time has passed for me to stop trying to just survive and think about my future.

The bar is packed, more than usual, and I have no time to linger in my thoughts. I serve drinks to customers and run back and forth around the bar. I place three glasses of beer under the tap and begin to pour, one after the other, as I feel the air in the room change and thicken.

I look up and see how all the eyes in the room turn to him, to his presence that can't be ignored. Ethan walks right up to me, wearing the same suit he wore this morning. My heart races faster, and I can't take my eyes off him. The way he walks, as if he rules the world, as if he rules me. He does rule me.

Cool liquid runs down my legs, and I jump back in a panic. The beer has long since filled the glass and is now sliding all over the floor, soaking me on the way. Shit.

He may be a Greek god, but I'm just a simple barmaid.

I take a rag, wipe up everything I spilled, and try to clean my jeans with a wet cloth.

I look at my sneakers, which are now soaked in beer.

"*Aaaah*," I growl through clenched teeth and throw the cloth into the trash. I can't believe I ruined my shoes.

Ethan claims a stool at the bar and watches me with increasing interest. Damn, why does he have to look so good in that suit? I want to be mad at him for distracting me in the middle of work, but I know the only person to blame here is me. He did nothing.

He waits patiently until I finish filling all my orders, then I approach him to take his. He grasps my palm, and his thumb strokes the inside of my hand, turning my body into a puddle of need.

I press my hips together and pull my hand back. How does he do it? I see the smile spread across his beautiful face, and he raises an eyebrow at me. Shit, he noticed.

"Whiskey, neat," he says, "and then we go."

"Whiskey on the way." I nod. "But I can't leave until the end of my shift. I'm here alone." I turn around and approach the waitress, who is waiting to pass me orders from the tables.

He gets up from his seat, and I follow him with my eyes as he walks toward Dana's office. Where exactly is he going? I want to stop him, but I can't leave my position at the bar. Shit.

"I knew you were a greedy bitch." Robin appears out of nowhere.

Jeez, she seems to follow everything I do. "I'm what?"

"That was Ethan Wolf. From Wolf Industries. He's a millionaire. Tell me you didn't know it."

"What do you want?"

"I saw you touch him. Are you after his money? He's engaged, you know. Do you steal engaged men too?" Her face twitches.

I take a deep breath. "It's none of your business, and he's not —" I almost blurt out to her that he's not engaged, but that's not information I should have. "Just leave me alone."

My eyes wander to the office every few seconds, waiting to see him leave. He has been with Dana for over fifteen minutes, and an unpleasant pressure forms in my stomach. What are they talking about for so long? It can't be good.

When they finally leave the room, they shake hands and hug like good friends. I stand there wide-eyed, staring as he walks back to the bar, puts some bills next to the glass of whiskey that's waiting for him, drinks it in one gulp, and walks out into the street.

Without a single word.

He left without talking to me. Why? I open the phone and send him a message.

What was that about?

By the end of the shift, I'm about to explode. Why doesn't he answer me?

As soon as I lock the front door after the last customer, I go to Dana's office. She lifts her head from the pages on her desk and smiles.

Well, at least she's still smiling. That's a good sign, isn't it?

"Sit," she says and points to the chair in front of her, and I sit down obediently.

"I had a visit today from Ethan Wolf. I understand you know each other."

I nod, and she continues. "He expressed a *dismay*." She cocks her head and emphasizes the word so that I understand it was a little more aggressive than the way she puts it. "He's concerned about you being here so late in the evenings. He doesn't seem to likc it."

"What?" I jump up from my seat. "He doesn't like it? I hope you set him straight," I seethe.

Dana laughs out loud. "He told me you'd react like that. He wants to offer you a position, and he wants me to release you from your job here for it."

Another job? What the hell is he talking about? I have nowhere else to go. "I don't want to leave. I enjoy working here. I live here." The feeling of anxiety overwhelms me. I feel sick.

"He offered to come in as an investor in the bar." She stops and pauses, letting me digest her words. "And I could really use the money. I'm sorry. I had to give you up to get the investment I need."

I sink back into the chair in defeat. "So I'm fired?"

"Not fired, no... Released from duties. You're welcome to continue living here as long as you need." She waves her hands.

"Oh, so he allows me to stay living here? How could you agree to that?" I'm losing it. He's just like Michael. Could it be that I was so badly wrong in assessing him?

"I'm sorry. He said he's going to offer you a new job. I thought you'd want it. It's a step up for you. And I need the money. Do you want me to talk to him again?"

I shake my head. I will deal with Ethan myself.

I know it's late. He's probably already asleep, but I don't care. I'll break down his door if I have to until he tells Dana to give me back my job. The only job I have, the only place that accepted me as I am.

I leave Lunis, armed with my rage, and notice a big man leaning against a black car in front of the entrance. When he sees me, he straightens and starts walking toward me.

Fuck. I'm immediately taken aback, unsure of this person's intentions. When he gets closer, I run. To my dismay, he runs after me. I have little chance of winning with him, certainly not in wet and sticky shoes, but maybe I can get to a busier street.

"Hope! Stop! Ethan sent me," he shouts.

Ethan? I stop and turn to the man with concern. He remains standing a safe distance from me and says again, "Ethan sent me to pick you up."

He knew I would be upset. My fists clench. "Are you going to take me to the penthouse?"

He nods, and I stomp back to the car and drive with him.

When we stop in front of the building, the driver turns to me and hands me an envelope. "Ethan asked me to give it to you."

I go out into the street, and the car drives off.

I peek into the envelope. It's a key. Could it be a key to his apartment? This man confuses me terribly. He got me fired, then leaves me a key?

I greet the guard at the entrance and give my name. He scolds me through narrowed eyes. My stained clothes don't make a good impression, but he's clearly been instructed to let me in.

I use the key in the elevator, go up, and work the key in the door. I enter the apartment, ready to charge Ethan with my anger, but it is dark, and he's nowhere in sight. I cautiously move into the bedroom, not sure what to expect, and there I find him asleep in bed.

He's lying on his stomach, a blanket covering him to his waist, his upper body bare. The wolf tattoo stands out on his smooth back, and his face is buried in the pillow. I watch him for a few moments, like watching a sleeping lion, when you know that at any moment, he can wake up and devour you.

I don't care if he sleeps. He left me without a job.

"Ethan," I call, but there is no response.

"Ethan!"

He moves and rolls onto his side, his eyes barely open. "Bambi?" He smiles at me with a sleepy face. My heart skips a beat, but it's not enough to weaken the anger that flows through my veins.

"Come to bed." He reaches out to me, but I remain standing, far from his reach.

He rubs his eyes, tries to wake up, and straightens into a sitting position. "What's wrong?"

"What's wrong? You have the boldness to ask? You got me

fired from the only job I could find. That's what's wrong. And you didn't even stay to tell me what you did."

My scolding speech doesn't seem to bother him in the least. He yawns. "I asked Dana to release you from the job because I want to offer you something else."

"What else can you offer me? Do you own a bar? Do you want me to clean your house instead of Madeleine?"

He narrows his eyes. "No. I want to find you a position in one of my companies. We have several open positions, and I'm sure you could fit into one of them."

"A role in your company? Do you think I'm a charity case? How will I fit in when I haven't even finished my degree?"

"You studied for a degree? Which one?" He tilts his head.

Shit. That slipped right out of me. "Business Administration. But I didn't graduate, so it's irrelevant." Don't ask why I didn't. Please don't ask.

"Excellent. It's even better than I expected. I'm looking for potential, not degrees. If you studied it, it means that it interested you. Now let's go to sleep. We'll talk about it in the morning. I'm so tired." He yawns again.

I'm not ready to sleep. "I want my job at Lunis back. You won't decide where I work." It's like Michael all over again. I will not fall into this trap a second time. I'm no longer as innocent as I used to be.

"Okay. I'll talk to Dana in the morning and get you back your job. I still think you should at least hear what I offer before you decide." He lays down and snuggles into the pillow. "Can we please talk about it in the morning? My head is killing me."

I can't wait for the morning. "Why did you do this? Why did you come and take my job?" I raise my voice.

The look of surprise on his face appears genuine. He doesn't understand why I'm angry.

"I was just trying to help get you something better. I work in the mornings, and you in the evenings. I wanted you to have a job during normal hours so that we could see each other."

The warning bells in my head are ringing loudly. Michael wanted me to quit my job so he could see me more. That's how it started. That was the excuse. I thought it was romantic, but it wasn't long before I found myself alone, with no friends, no support, and no job. I was dependent on him. I can't let Ethan tear apart the fragile life I'm trying to build for myself.

I go out into the living room and stand in front of the window that overlooks the twinkling lights of the night. Inhale... Exhale...

I don't know what to do.

I hear light footsteps behind me, and then his arms wrap around me, hugging me from behind, and I sink into his embrace. I feel safe in his arms, and I can't ignore how different it is from what I knew.

"I'm sorry," he whispers in my ear. "I didn't think Dana would tell you about it today. Otherwise, I would have stayed. I planned to tell you in the morning. I thought you would be happy to have a better job. I'll call her in the morning and make sure you get the job back. She'll also get the investment I promised, and everyone will be happy. Please don't be angry."

I turn to him and see regret in his eyes. How does he not understand what he did?

"You took away the only thing I have. My job," I say, a wayward tear running down my cheek.

He nods, and kisses my tears away, then kisses my mouth sweetly.

"That was not my intention. Let me fix it," he says between kisses. "I got home, and you weren't here. I needed you here. And when you told me you couldn't leave the bar, I got carried away. I'm sorry I acted like an idiot. Let me fix it."

I smile. His words penetrate and conquer my heart piece by piece.

Don't take all of my heart. Please leave me some pieces. I'm gonna need them when you don't want me anymore. When I need to rebuild myself.

I close my eyes and ignore the fact that I'm walking blindly to the edge of the cliff and give in to his embrace, pretending he wants me the way I want him.

"Come to bed," he whispers and takes my hand, pulling me after him.

I think I'm losing the battle.

CHAPTER 28
Ethan

I'm running my usual route, thinking about what happened last night. I fucked up big time. I didn't realize how much until I saw the tears. I thought she would like a better job that earns more. I even left my driver with a key to the apartment so she could come here after work and sleep in my arms. It was only after I saw her crying that I realized I was wrong. But it's not all lost. She stayed, and that filled me with joy.

I'll call Dana soon and arrange everything. If Bambi wants to work in a bar, she can work in a bar. We can work this out.

I can't believe I want to be with her. What does that mean? I don't know, but it's already clear to me I've lost the battle. I thought that a good fuck could get her out of my system, but it did the exact opposite. I'm drifting too fast into the deep, and I don't know how to stop.

I check my messages on my way up the elevator.

Invitation to a fundraising event on Friday. I hate events, but if my assistant sent me the invitation, it's probably an event I would be interested in. I go to fundraising events if the cause suits me. Indeed, the event is for teenagers who've run away from home.

I confirm my attendance, plus one.

Automatically, I write a message to Olive to inform her of the event. But my finger hesitates on the key just before I press Send.

Maybe I'll take Bambi?

I like the idea. I imagine her dressed in a gorgeous evening gown, holding my arm as we step inside. Yes. I want everyone to see her with me. I want to declare that she is mine.

I need to talk to Olive. ASAP. I need to get her approval to dissolve the agreement between us.

I open the door with one hand and press the dial button with the other. It's only half-past six, but Olive wakes up as early as I do. It's a good time to talk before I sink into the whirlwind of my business conversations.

Madeleine's working in the kitchen, so I go to my room to talk privately. I trust her, but these are not my secrets to reveal.

"Olive," I say when she answers, "we need to talk."

"You want to end our agreement," she replies, finishing my thought. How does she always know what I'm going to say?

"Yeah. You know I love you, but I want to date Hope, and I don't want to hide it," I say, trying to be completely honest as I enter the bedroom and start taking off my sweaty clothes. Bambi is still buried under the covers. At least she didn't run away.

"I understand, of course. You should go for it. I knew this day would come when I saw her with you." Olive's voice trembles.

I sit on the edge of the bed. "You know I only want the best for you, right? Maybe it's time to tell your parents? You're a grown woman. You're independent. You're strong. I know you're afraid of their reaction, afraid they'll cut you off. Do you believe that the relationship with them is worth living this lie? Sleeping with repulsive men like me against your will? Is that what you want for the rest of your life?"

Now that we're breaking up in public, if she doesn't come clean, she'll have to date men again. I give her my speech for the hundredth time. I've tried convincing her to come out of the closet and live her life for so long, but she never agrees.

I hear her muffle a crying sob. "Ethan, you're the most non-repulsive man ever. She'll be happy."

"I'll help you with whatever you need. I have a venture capital fund. I'll invest in your company. Help you stand on your own two feet. You don't need your parents. I'll take care of you. Besides, they might still surprise you," I tell her. "Actually, I'm pretty sure they won't expel you just because you're a lesbian."

I hear her sniffling. "Will you come with me?"

"What?" My mouth opens.

"Will you come with me to tell them?"

"Yes. Whatever you want." I'll support her with all I can.

We talk for another minute before I hang up and turn to find Hope sitting awake in bed behind me, her mouth open in astonishment.

"Olivia is a lesbian?"

I raise an eyebrow. "You said she told you everything."

"She told me you're not dating, and you both have reasons to appear in public together. I thought that was all."

"Shit. I thought she told you. That's not good. You're not supposed to know that." I close my eyes. "Please promise me you won't say anything to anyone."

"I won't say anything," Hope says in a hurry. "Don't worry. What did you mean when you told her you wanted to go out with me?" Her blue eyes stare at me.

"I want you to come with me to a charity event on Friday."

A look of disappointment washes over her face. "Um... I can't... I have to work. I don't..." Her gaze turns down, and she tries to avoid looking at me.

Why doesn't she want to come with me? Is it still because of what happened yesterday? I promised I would fix it. We need to talk, but first, I need a shower. "I'm going to take a shower, then we'll continue this conversation."

When I get out of the shower, she's still in bed. I look at her, trying to read her expression. She doesn't look mad. So why is she still in bed?

She lifts the edge of the blanket. "Will you join me?"

I can't refuse such an invitation. I lay down next to her, drowning in her blue eyes. She bites her bottom lip, trying to persuade me to touch her, but I don't move.

She holds my gaze, then reaches out and touches my bare chest. My skin tingles, and she brings her lips closer, kissing me gently.

I return her kiss with my own, run my tongue over her lips, then suck them gently.

She moans, which is enough to light me up completely. She wears my shirt, which is several sizes too big for her. And I'm surprised to find out how sexy it is. I reach under her baggy shirt, happy to find she's not wearing a bra. I stroke the nipple with my thumb in smaller and smaller circular movements, feeling it harden under my hand.

I need to see her. See this beauty. I pull the shirt over her, leaving her bare in front of me, her pink nipples calling my name.

"Show me where you want me to touch you," I whisper to her, coaxing her to be brave with me. She looks straight into my eyes, the bright blue in hers meeting mine with intensity. She's up for the challenge.

She takes my hand and places it on her lower abdomen, then leads it on a direct route into her paradise.

I'm panting heavily. I want to be inside her so much. But I need patience.

I willingly cooperate, reaching down, finding her slit, and caressing it through the fabric until she moves her pelvis in coordination with my movements.

I move the cloth aside, revealing her pussy wet and swollen for me. I find her little button and massage it while my mouth explores hers, all her tastes. When she is thoroughly wet and ready, I turn her onto her stomach, dying to penetrate her from behind, to see her amazing ass as I fuck her.

She flips back. "No."

"Why not? I promise you will enjoy it. Maybe even more than last time. If you don't like it, we won't do it again."

She stares at me as if taking my assessment. Her eyes open wide. Then she turns onto her stomach again.

I'm running my hands over her perfect, round butt. I want to slap it with my palm, but she's not ready for that yet. Instead, I caress her, separate her cheeks and slide my fingers down between her legs. I move my fingers inside her slit at a steady pace. She is so sexy, so beautiful.

Her hair covers her face, so I can't see how she feels. I lean forward, brush her hair back and kiss her again, making sure I can see her expression. I need to see how she feels so I can stop in time.

I place myself between her legs and slowly rub myself on her, smearing my cock with her juices. I want her to be close to her orgasm when I penetrate her.

I bend down and take a condom out of the drawer next to me, and put it on.

"You're so sexy," I whisper in her ear, "I've been dreaming of fucking you from behind since the first time I saw you."

She freezes for a split second, and her body stiffens. Too much? But then she continues to move her pelvis against me.

"Do you like dirty talk?" I ask, and she nods, a shy smile on her lips. "And I like to be inside you. I like to fuck you."

I lift her butt in the air and put her on her knees, her head resting on the pillow.

I run my fingers over her anus, and she contracts. I will fuck her there too, but that will wait for another time.

I reach out and caress her clit again, then slowly position myself at her opening. My hands caress her body, going all the way to her narrow waist and her round butt, then I push myself in and wait for her to relax. She is soaking wet, but I feel she is tense and so tight.

I bring my hand around her stomach and send it between her legs to continue rubbing. I'm not moving, waiting for the stimulus to cross the threshold of fear. As soon as she lets go, I push myself in, this time all the way, in one big thrust until I'm stuck in her up to my balls.

I moan out loud because the feeling is sublime. Fucking hell.

"Are you okay?" I ask, panting.

She moans, "I feel so full."

"Do you want me to stop?"

"No! Don't stop. I want you."

I move, pushing myself in and out. Our hips collide with a loud noise. She surprises me when she allows herself to shout out loud. Fuck, she's so good. I have to imagine something else. I must not come before her.

She pushes into me, deeper, harder, looking for her climax, and I increase the pace, pumping into her hard.

I wrap my hands around her breasts, and they sway in my palms, heavy and full. I pinch her nipples, knowing she likes that. She screams and collapses under me. Her contractions are strong, so strong it hurts.

I wait for her orgasm to fade, still gliding in and out of her in continuous thrusts. I'm close.

I pull out, tear off the condom, and rub myself over her back, covering her ass with my white fluid, and marking her mine.

Mine.

CHAPTER 29
Ethan

"Shit!" I spit out the hot coffee after it burns my mouth. I deserve it because I'm answering an email and drinking at the same time. But nothing will spoil my good mood after the amazing morning I had. I'm sure the office thinks I'm bipolar after last week. Just a few days ago, I shouted at everyone, and today, I smiled at everyone.

The feelings I have for Bambi stress me out but also excite me at the same time.

I didn't think I was even capable of it, that I could have feelings for someone like this. I didn't want it, that's for sure. All the psychologists they sent me to after Anna worked on me for hours and built their mansions on the money my parents paid them. They got me to reset and reintegrate into society and stop the unrestrained rampage I was on. But they couldn't open my heart again. I was doomed. At least, that's what I thought until now.

These feelings are elusive. They snuck up on me without me noticing, crawled under my nails, under my skin, and went deep until I couldn't ignore them any longer. I'm just so happy when I'm with her. And I didn't think I could ever be happy again.

I can't stop thinking about her, even now when she's not

beside me. I'm just waiting for her to get home, and I can take her to my bed again. We need to talk about the future and see how we proceed from here. Although I got her the job back, the matter of these shifts makes it difficult for me.

I take a cloth and wipe the laptop and the floor of the living room from the coffee, sink back into the armchair and continue writing the email.

My phone rings, interrupting my work again.

"Jess," I answer. "What's up?" My voice reflects my happiness, and I don't even try to hide it.

We have several open tasks, and I wonder which of them has had such important progress that he's calling to update me after normal working hours. We have a fixed time on the calendar for regular updates.

"Turn on the TV, Wolf."

"What?" I ask again, not sure I understood what he wanted.

"The TV!" His words are short, and the serious tone of his voice has me getting up from my chair and looking for the remote.

I'm flipping to the news channel. In the background, I see a young man with curly hair talking to the camera. Beside him, and slightly behind him, is an older man with graying hair. Looks like the older version of the first one. Father and son, I assume. I recognize the father, but I'm not sure from where.

I turn up the volume to hear what they're saying.

"It's on. What am I seeing here?" I ask Jess.

"Just listen," he says. "And you should sit down." He hangs up, leaving me to look at the phone.

I focus my attention back on the screen. The reporter projects an image of a woman, and the air instantly drains from my lungs. My vision blurs as if a large hammer landed on me. I have no air. I sit down, collapsing on the couch like my limbs are made of rubber.

She looks different in the picture, younger and more innocent. Her hair is long, bright, and arranged in a fashionable braid, and she's wearing a luxurious suit. But there's no doubt it's her.

Those blue eyes, you can't mistake them. The image changes, and now a picture of Bambi with this curly-haired man is shown on the screen, being photographed at what looks like some kind of social event.

My hand shakes a little when I press the remote to move back to the beginning of the news piece. What the hell is this?

Why is my Bambi in the news, and what does this man have to do with her?

I stop and press play, waiting for the reporter to speak. I'm not sure I want to hear what he's going to say.

"The police are asking for the public's help in locating Ayala Summers, who has been missing since last August. Ayala, twenty-two years old, disappeared from her home and has not been seen since.

"Ayala suffers from anxiety and severe psychotic hallucinations. She's mentally unstable and needs medication. Her life is in danger.

"I'll turn the broadcast over to Mr. Michael Summers, who will now issue a press statement."

I can't seem to draw air into my lungs.

Ayala Summers? Hallucinations? Who the hell is she? Why does the name Summers sound so familiar to me? I try to dig the name out from the depths of my mind.

Summers is one of the largest law firms in the US. They contacted me several times, trying to convince me to transfer my business to them, but I never agreed to talk with them. I have Ryan, and our friendship is precious. I have no intention of replacing him.

You always knew her name wasn't Hope.

The picture on the screen changes. The man is now standing

behind a microphone, ready to speak, and I try to concentrate on his words.

Below his image now appears the inscription Michael Summers, husband of the missing Ayala Summers.

Her husband? I feel like they stabbed knives in my chest, and I'm bleeding on the carpet. Is she fucking married?

Married?

I keep watching, unable to stop, like watching a car accident as it happens.

"My wife, Ayala, has been missing from home for two months. I've devoted all my resources to bring her home safely but haven't been able to find her. We're worried about her."

He wipes a tear from the corner of his eye and continues.

"Unfortunately, Ayala is not healthy, and she needs medical care. Without it, she's mentally unstable and may harm herself. I want her to come back to me so I can take care of her and make sure she's safe. We're asking anyone who thinks they've seen the woman in the picture to contact the number on the screen and help us save Ayala."

His father approaches him and hugs him. They stay for a moment in each other's arms, comforting each other.

The image plays repeatedly on the screen with the phone number.

I get up, run to the bathroom, and puke my guts out.

I sit there for long hard minutes on the floor. My legs won't move. I'm not even sure I'm conscious. Everything I believed, everything was a lie. One big lie.

I force myself to come to my senses and get up, drink a glass of water, and after I recover a bit, I pick up the phone again.

"Jess."

"Did you see?"

"Is this true? Is that her?" I still hold this glimmer of hope that there might be some mistake. Maybe it's a bad dream, and I'll wake up any minute now.

"I'm sorry, Wolf, but yes. She's his wife, and he has documents about her psychiatric hospitalization. It looks like he's telling the truth."

I sigh. "How can that be?"

"I'm sorry I wasn't able to come up with that information in the investigation you asked me to do. I don't know why, but he never reported her missing. Not with the police, not anyone. Not until now."

"He said he's been looking for her all this time."

"Maybe he hired private investigators instead of going to the police. I don't know. But I couldn't find anything when I looked."

I close my eyes and inhale. "Thanks, Jess." I hang up.

The cup of coffee I drank earlier is the first to pass under my hand. I slam it against the wall, watching as it shatters and the coffee splatters everywhere. But there is no sense of satisfaction in this. I don't know what to do with myself.

I want to pull my hair out. No, I want to rip the hair out of her head. I want to make her suffer. I want to take my heart back.

I pick up the phone again and try to call her, but she's working and doesn't answer, so I type with trembling fingers.

> Is it true? Is this correct? You're fucking married? Did you fool me all this time?

I send the message, although I don't know what response I expect.

How could it be that I spent all this time with someone mentally unstable? Someone who needs psychiatric pills, and I didn't notice? How fucked up am I not to notice?

Or maybe I noticed and ignored it?

I replay the strange situations in my mind.

This entire show she put on, that she's afraid of me? I

thought she'd been sexually assaulted, but actually, she was fucking married and afraid of getting caught. I thought she was scared, but she just suffers from anxiety and hallucinations.

I remember thinking how strange it was that she walked all the way home barefoot. Who does that? And that she lives in a storage room? I knew there was something off. I knew it wasn't her real name. And now I know there's nothing real about her. Cheating fucking liar.

I don't hold back and write her my opinion.

That's why she didn't tell me anything about herself. I thought she was shy, but she wanted to hide the truth. What a fool I am. She's completely psychotic.

I close my eyes, and her image appears before me. Ethan Wolf, the businessman, the entrepreneur, with all the money and private investigators, and one little woman with big blue eyes knocked me to the floor.

CHAPTER 30
Ayala

Nicky and I work at the bar today, and I'm pouring drinks next to her. My body is moving to the music. I love the shifts with her. She's my only friend at Lunis, and we dance together behind the bar, which increases the tipping rate, much to Robin's dismay.

I think about Ethan all the time. My relationship with him went up a notch. Although, neither of us talks about our feelings. I know he doesn't want a long-term relationship, but he makes me happy, and I think he's happy with me too.

I've been pondering for a few days now the possibility of telling him the truth. Revealing my true identity.

Will he be able to accept it? Deal with the fact that I won't be able to live under my real name? That I'm still married? I would like to hope so. I want to believe he won't abandon me.

He invited me to this event on Friday. He wants us to go as a couple in public. Something that can never happen, and I don't want to lie to him again. I want to stop all the lies. I want him to know the truth. Our relationship is genuine. I'm in love with him, and the lies contaminate our relationship, tainting it with the poison I bring with me.

I have no choice. I have to tell him soon. I'll gather the courage, save every drop, and hold tight so we can get through the storm together.

We're about halfway through the shift when I notice that the constant chatter at the bar has died down. I raise my head and look around, trying to understand what I missed.

All eyes are on me. This is the first thing I notice, and I automatically take a step back, bumping into the counter behind me. What's going on?

The television above me is flashing a newscast, and I realize everyone's gaze is alternating between the screen and me. I hear through the noise my biggest nightmare. My name. My real name.

I turn to look at the screen and discover that hell has found me.

There, inside the small square, stands my dear husband, reporting me missing.

Missing.

My picture is all over the screen, and the only thing I can think about is Ethan. Oh shit.

I look at Nicky, and she looks back at me. My eyes open when I hear the story he tells.

"It's not true, Nicky," I whisper to her and hope she believes me. That she knows I'm not this crazy woman they're talking about. "I'm not crazy. He's lying."

She comes closer to me and squeezes my hand. "I believe you."

I'm trapped behind the bar. People are already gathering around me. I step back, trying to think of how to escape. Dana comes out of the office and looks at me. From the look on her face, I gather she saw the news too.

Dana shouts, saying to turn the TV off. "You're all thinking that the woman on the news looks like our Hope, right? But our Hope isn't missing. She's been with us for years and will continue for years to come. Come on, let's all go back to drinking. Next round is on me." Sounds of joy ring throughout the bar. People shake their heads and return to their business. I'm ready to kiss her feet right now.

"Go," she whispers to me, her eyes fixed on mine.

"What?"

"Go. You need to run away from here. I don't know how many of them were convinced just now and how long it will last. Too many people will recognize you here. If you don't want to go back to him, run." She clasps my hand with both of hers, and we hug.

I nod.

"Thank you, Dana. For everything."

She removes some dollar bills from her pocket. "Take it. You need it more than I do right now."

I take it from her with a trembling hand and hurry out of the bar and to my room.

I need to pack. I now have a lot more clothes than I came with and I'm not sure they'll all fit in my backpack. I leave the dresses and less useful items behind and pack only a few shirts and pants. I put on my coat, then I take the phone from the bedside table. I need to call Ethan. I need to explain.

I turn on the screen and see the missed calls and the messages.

He knows.

I sit down in defeat on the bed. My heart aches. I squeeze my eyes closed, and tears wet my cheeks. He thinks I'm a liar, that I'm crazy like Michael said. Of all the people in the world, I thought Ethan would understand. That he would know I was always real with him. But he believes the story they sold him on TV. I lied about my name and didn't mention I was married, but everything else was me. I was more myself with him than I ever was in my relationship with Michael.

I have no reason to stay here anymore. I type him a message and send it.

I turn off the phone and leave it on the dresser. I pull the hood of the coat over my head, put on sunglasses, and a bag on my back, and I go out into the street, keeping my head down, just like on my first day here, trying to make myself smaller, to not take up space, and not grab anyone's attention.

I can't stay in New York. I have to disappear, evaporate for a few weeks until this story is forgotten, and no one remembers my face.

It was a mistake to spend money on clothes and unnecessary things instead of saving for emergencies. I thought I could build a life here. I fell into complacency, and now I have to pay the price.

I hurry toward the bus stop, trying to decide where I should go, but then I realize something. I'm all over the news channels. Traveling by public transport is like pointing a big, shiny arrow at myself. Someone will recognize me. I need to find a place to hide in the meantime and wait for the commotion to die down. I've done it before. I can do it again.

After the wave passes, I'll start over somewhere else. Michael will give up, and the news channels will tire of the story.

And eventually, I'll be forgotten.

CHAPTER 31

Ethan

After calling my assistant and canceling all my meetings for tomorrow, I'm trying to decide where to go. I need some air. I need to walk, conquer the mountain, and clear my head. Gotta get out of here before I go crazy.

Because I am going crazy.

Ryan has called me dozens of times already. Olive too. Even Maya called. Everyone saw, everyone knows.

But I don't feel like talking to anyone right now. Maybe after I get out some of this energy and wash my eyes in nature, it will be easier for me to pretend that everything is fine, that I never cared.

How did she do so much damage in such a short time?

The bottle of whiskey is already half empty, and by the end of the night, I'll probably finish it all. I'm trying to achieve the long-awaited blurring of my senses, but I can't seem to get there. Her expression when she comes, those blue eyes when she looks at me, I can't erase it all in one day. I'm not sure I'll ever be able to erase her from my mind.

My phone beeps with a new message.

> **Hope**
> I'm sorry. Have a good life.

That's it? Is that all the traitor has to say to me? I thought she would apologize with more than that. Tell me how sorry she was. She can't be fucking serious.

Everything was a game for her. I slept with a married woman. Who knows how many men she's done it with before.

Fuck.

My fist hits the wall and makes a hole in the plaster. Blood oozes from my knuckles. I see the blood, but I feel no pain. I feel nothing but a sharp ache in my chest from the heart she's taken and trampled and now beats within her clenched fist.

I hit the wall again and again, but nothing eases the pain. Nothing helps.

"Ethan! What the hell are you doing?" I hear Ryan's voice. How did he get here? When did he come in?

He pulls me back, away from the wall. No! I need to silence the voices. I need something else to hurt, something other than my heart. I resist and struggle with him.

"Leave me," I yell at him. "Go home."

But he doesn't give up and fights me until I give up, surrender, and sink to the floor, defeated.

He sits down on the floor with me. I look away. I don't want to see him right now.

"Talk to me," he says.

What do I have to say? What can I say that will help?

"Ethan, where is she? Where's Hope?"

"You mean Ayala Summers? Because everything was a lie. One big fat lie," I say, spitting every word out.

"Did you go to her? Ask her about it?" He tries to grab my arm, and I pull it away from him. I don't want anyone to comfort me right now.

"No." I toss him the phone, allowing him to see for himself the last messages we exchanged.

"You called her a traitor and a liar?" He raises an eyebrow.

"That's what she is."

He bites his lip. "So you're just gonna let her go? Without talking to her? Without letting her explain?"

"What is there to explain? She succeeded. Tricked me big time." The anger comes out of me in violent waves.

Ryan pulls himself back up to his feet, checking his surroundings. I can see the shocked expression on his face as he sees the destruction I've caused.

The wall behind me is stained with my blood, and a small hole appears in the middle. My laptop is broken and scattered on the floor. And the half-finished bottle of whiskey lies on the carpet. It all sums up the situation.

"You know what this reminds me of?" he says in a low voice.

I cringe. "It's not the same." I look at him. "Not at all." But it is.

"It's just like with Anna. You tried to destroy yourself and everything around you. Anna died. You couldn't talk to her about what happened. You couldn't get closure. But Hope is still here. You need to talk to her."

"There is a big difference. I was to blame for what happened to Anna. It's not my fault that Hope, sorry, Ayala, deceived me. I have to get used to it." I smile bitterly. "She's a liar and a whore who deceived everyone, including me. She's the one at fault!" I shout.

"You're not to blame, Ethan. Not for what happened to Anna, and not now. But you're trying to destroy yourself either way."

I get up and try to hit him, but the alcohol flowing in my blood slows me down. He takes a step back and avoids my swing.

"Well, at least you're on your feet now," he says and grins crookedly, dodging another punch from me.

I sway to my feet. The room spins. The blood from my fingers drips onto the floor, staining it in beautiful little circles.

Drip. Drip.

Ryan looks at the floor. "You need to take care of that."

I don't feel like it. I want the pain. I want to use it. It helps me focus.

"When I fight with Maya, which happens a lot," he adds with a grin, "you're always there for me, giving me perspective. I won't take you drinking because I see you've already taken care of that, but I'll put out the mirror for you," he says. "You can't let it end like this. It's obvious you're madly in love with her. You need to talk to her. Give her a chance to explain before you throw everything away."

I try to protest, to say I don't love her, but there's no point. Because I do.

"What does she have to explain? She's mentally unstable. She has hallucinations. I can't believe a word she says."

"Did she seem unstable to you? You went out with her and noticed nothing. Ask yourself why. Because the whole story sounds suspicious to me, to be quite honest."

He walks into my living room, stepping around the broken glass.

I look up. "What do you mean?"

"Her husband—" I cringe, and Ryan changes his words. "Michael Summers claims she needs medication, right? But she works in an orderly job, she's attentive and speaks logically. She has no sign of illness. He said she was delusional and anxious. It doesn't work out."

"She has anxieties," I say. I remember how she recoiled from me at first.

"Anxieties from what?" Ryan asks.

"Men. Me. There were signs. I just misinterpreted them."

We stand in silence for a long minute. Then Ryan says, "I don't think it's anxiety. Not the kind he claims, at least." He cocks his head. "Is she still afraid of you?"

"No." I try to understand where he's going. "But she already knows me. She knows I won't hurt her."

"Exactly. She knows you won't hurt her. A psychotic mental state isn't something that suddenly goes away just because she knows you. It's not a rational condition," he points out. "And her husband said she was in a very serious condition. He explained she needed medication, that she was in danger, right?"

I nod.

"So if she doesn't take the medication, her condition should get worse, not improve."

"What are you saying, Ryan? Get to the point." I'm losing patience.

"I think she's afraid of men because something happened to her. Not because she's hallucinating." He looks as if he's going through all the possibilities in his head. "It fits."

Those were my thoughts at first that she was sexually assaulted. But I can't tell what the truth is. I can't trust her. "How can I tell the difference between truth and lies if I can't trust her? She lied to me. She could be psychotic."

An image appears in my mind, flooding me. A memory of an event I never gave another thought to, and now the scene plays in my head as if it were happening again right now.

I'm walking down the street near my office, and a woman with long blond hair is sitting on a bench, looking at a map. She looks lost, looking for something on the map.

My urge to help takes over, and I ask her if she needs assistance. Her face shifts up, and I'm startled by the sight. Her face... It's so bruised and swollen. Fuck.

It was her. Those blue eyes.

"It's her!" I shout.

Ryan looks at me as if I've lost my mind.

"It was her on the bench that day. I finally remember where I've seen her before. Oh my God, I can't believe I didn't make this connection until now. I have a great memory for faces. How could I forget eyes like hers?"

Ryan continues to look at me, question marks in his eyes, waiting for me to explain.

"A few months ago, I saw a woman sitting near the offices. I asked if she needed help. She looked like the picture they showed on TV, with long blond hair and her face..." I frown. "It was disfigured by beatings. Her eye was completely closed, and her face was black and blue and swollen. That's why I didn't recognize her when I met her a few weeks later. Her face looked completely different. Her hair looked completely different. But her eyes... I could never forget them. It drove me crazy all this time. I knew I had seen her before. I can't believe that was her."

I pace the room, running my non-bloody hand through my hair. "She ran away, and I thought that was the last time I saw her. I can't believe it was Hope. I can't believe it!" She must have recognized me but said nothing, letting me believe that was the first time we met.

"Fuck, Ryan. Her face." I look at him in shock. Ryan was right. He did it to her. She's afraid of him, and now she's alone, and he's after her. Instead of helping her, I sent her to survive alone. What if he's already gotten to her? What if something happens to her because of me? Fucking hell.

"Let's go," I say, picking up my phone and keys and rushing to the door.

"Where do you think you're going?"

"I'm going to find her!"

"You're fucking drunk. And dripping blood everywhere," he tells me in a calm voice.

Oh my God, I can't understand how he tolerates me. I look at my hand and the trail of blood I'm leaving behind. Now I have a goal. Something to do instead of wallowing in my anger. She should still be on shift. I go to the bathroom, wash, and bandage my injured hand. The world still turns. I can't drive like this.

"Are you taking me or what?" I ask Ryan, not waiting for an answer and leaving the apartment. He rushes after me.

I storm into Lunis. The bar is still open, so at least I don't have to break in this time. I glance around, but she's not at the bar or at the tables. I don't wait and go upstairs to her room.

A quick glance is all I need to understand that she's gone.

There are a few things left here, but the dresser is almost empty. She's not here, and it doesn't look like she's planning to come back. Fuck. Lord of Fucks.

I go to her dresser, hoping she left a clue to where she's gone, but there's nothing. I take one last look, and by the bed, I see her phone.

She left it behind. Damn it. I have no way of locating her. Under the phone is a folded note, and I open it carefully.

Ethan,

I'm sorry. I never meant for you to get hurt. I didn't want a man in my life, but you persisted and made your way into my heart. In a short time, you have revealed to me worlds that I didn't know existed. Thank you for helping me discover myself. I'll Love you always,

Ayala.

I'm suffocating. She's in love with me.

I should have come here as soon as I found out. Why did I let her go?

Because you're a son of a bitch who believes everything they say on the news instead of the woman you love, that's why.

On second thought, I collect all that is left of her belongings, the phone and the note. I'll return everything to her when I find her. Because I'm fucking going to turn the world upside down until that happens.

CHAPTER 32
Ethan

I storm into Dana's office.

"Why did you hire Hope?" I ask, pacing back and forth in the small office.

"Maybe you should sit down?" she suggests.

"Answer the question, please." I say please, but my tone doesn't ask for anything. I have no patience for games right now.

"She looked like someone who needed help."

"And that's it? You didn't know her before that? Maybe her family?"

"No. The day I hired her was the first time we met. She had bruises on her face, which she tried to hide with makeup. I knew she was in trouble, that she was probably being beaten at home. And I knew that no one else would take her on. I couldn't throw her on the streets."

"She said she was beaten?"

"No, but I could tell. My ex-husband used to beat me. I recognize the signs. I know all the excuses. It was obvious. I saw myself in her, so I needed to save her."

I close my eyes and exhale. Too many cases, too many faces.

My app is just a drop in the ocean. "Do you have any idea where she would go?"

"I got the impression that before she started working here, she lived on the street. She had no other place to live. So I don't know where she went. Why isn't she with you? I thought that—"

"You thought wrong." I leave the office.

I employed three full-time private investigators to look for her, but it's been three days, and still no leads. I'm losing my mind, and anyone in my way gets a taste of my rage. The employees, the managers... Even Ryan isn't immune.

"What do you want?" I answer when he calls. The line should be free for updates from Jess.

"I was hoping maybe you wouldn't come to the office today. You can work from home."

"No way. I have to be in the office. The workers need to see me." And I need the distraction.

"Ethan, you can't come to the office in this condition. You won't have any employees left if you keep yelling at them."

Fuck. I want to tell him to go to hell, but I know he's right. I can't be in the office like this, not until I find her. "Okay, I'll stay home."

I work myself hard in the gym at home, trying to take my aggression out on the treadmill and dumbbells instead of on the surrounding people. But running on the treadmill doesn't give the same effect as running outside. Maybe I should go out for a while. I get off and wipe my face with a towel. The ringing of my phone startles me.

"Jess? Tell me you found something."

"I got hold of her parents. They refused to talk to me at first. I lied and said I worked for Summers. She hasn't made contact.

They haven't heard from her since she disappeared. They didn't even know she ran away until recently."

"They didn't know? What do you mean?"

"Michael told them she was hospitalized after having a nervous breakdown, and they believed it. They're the ones who started the search after they realized she wasn't there. That's why I hadn't found anything until now."

"Fuck." She's been missing for two months, and he wasn't even looking for her? What kind of husband is he?

"She has no siblings, but there is a distant relative who lives in Philadelphia."

"Where?" I'm already putting on shoes.

"I talked to him, and he claims he hasn't heard from her in years."

"I have to check for myself."

"I'm sending you the address," he says and hangs up.

I receive a message with the details, and in two minutes, I'm already outside, ready to go.

The trip to Philly brought no results. The uncle continues to claim he hasn't seen her since she was a child. And neither a financial reward nor threats convinced him to say anything else. I drive back home, my jaw clenched so hard it hurts. How can you find someone who doesn't want to be found?

My phone rings, and I answer quickly.

"Anything new?"

"I found one woman who claims she saw her three days ago on the train to Brooklyn," Jess says.

"Brooklyn? Why would she go to Brooklyn? Does she know anyone there?" This makes no sense at all.

"I don't know. But she described her pretty well, and it fit the hours. She said she had a big backpack and was walking around at night, wearing sunglasses. It seemed strange to her, and that's why she remembers."

"Okay. I want you to check it out. Take as many people as you need, no matter how much it costs." I hang up.

I'm afraid to get my hopes up. To hell with you, Bambi. Give me a sign of life. Where did you go?

I know she can't fly. Jess would have found out if she had any passports, real or fake. We also checked all the trains and found no one fitting her description.

And I know she didn't return to her husband because he's still looking for her, that son of a bitch.

I take the car and drive to Brooklyn. If she's there, I'll hang around there until I find her. I call Jess from the road again to pinpoint the area when suddenly, an idea comes to me.

"Jess," I say as he answers the call. "When you said earlier that she was spotted on the train to Brooklyn, did you mean the actual train or at the station?"

"I'll need to check it. What are you thinking?"

"I have an idea. I just want to know if it makes sense."

I hear him talking on the other line but can't make out the words.

"Ethan?"

"I'm here."

"She was at the station going to Brooklyn, not on the train."

"Which station?"

"Thirty-third Street."

"Of course," I mumble. "I'm on my way there."

"Why do you think she's there?"

"I have an idea." I press on the gas and honk at some vehicles going too slowly for my taste. "It's close to where I first saw her. She probably knows the area a bit. She may have slept there before. Can you find out if there are homeless shelters or women's shelters nearby? I want you to send your team there to help me with the searches." It's impossible to know where she's hiding.

"I'm on it." Jess hangs up, and I navigate my way to the station. I was sure she would leave New York, but if she stayed, she's probably gone back to what she knows.

CHAPTER 33

Ayala

I peek out through the station stairs. There were no free beds in the shelter yesterday, so I had to sleep on the train, and I'm hungry. I cover myself with my coat again, zipping it up, thankful for the cold outside that justifies this hiding. I look like a teddy bear, but it's harder for someone to recognize my face. I hope. Just to be on the safe side, I add a scarf and bury my face in it.

I half expect a SWAT team to jump on me, but nothing happens. The people on the street are walking around, as usual, and no one notices me.

The street is busy. What if one of these people saw my picture?

I bury my face deeper in the scarf. Lucky for me, there are food shops right above the station, and I don't have to go far.

I walk fast and enter the store. The seller raises his head and stares at me. He continues to follow me as I walk through the store, and I shiver. I don't know if he's examining me because he thinks I'm going to steal something, seeing my strange clothing, or because he recognizes me. I'm not ready to take the risk, and I go back outside to look for another store.

I stand there, looking around, trying to decide where to go, and a familiar black Jeep pulls up on the sidewalk next to me, almost running over some pedestrians. How the hell did he find me?

The window rolls down, and Ethan's face appears. My heart sinks at the sight of him. I lost him.

No, he was never mine to lose.

"Get in the car," he commands, his voice dangerously low.

"Why? What reason do I have to come with you?"

He bites his lower lip. "If I found you, so can this husband of yours. Get in already."

Maybe I should go with him. It's not good to stay exposed on the street. I close my eyes and exhale. What should I do? He called me a traitor and a liar. But this is Ethan. And despite everything, I trust him.

"Get in. We attract too much attention." His eyes scan the surroundings, running backward and forward.

He's right. Micheal's looking for me. And now, the big vehicle, the argument... We're getting unwanted attention. It's only a matter of time before someone makes the connection. I open the door and get into the passenger seat. Ethan drives off before I can even put on my seat belt.

We drive in oppressive silence. I notice that one of his hands is bandaged, but I'm afraid to ask. I'm afraid to look at him, afraid to know what he's thinking. My mind is flooded with questions. Where is he taking me? What will he do now that he knows?

He dials someone and puts the phone on speaker. "Jess, cancel the searches. I found her."

"What? really?"

"Yes. Cancel everything." He hangs up.

Who the hell is Jess? "How did you find me?" I dare to ask.

He turns his head, and the gold in his eyes swirls. I can't read his expression.

"I hired an entire team to find you. I thought you had left New York, but then someone saw you at the station. I looked for you in all the shelters nearby, and I've been wandering the streets for two hours. And suddenly, there you were, standing on the sidewalk."

The muscles in his face soften, and I realize how tense he is.

We stay silent until we get to the penthouse, and I take off my coat in his living room. The air is so thick I could cut it with a knife.

The apartment looks different. Messy. There's a hole in the wall and a red stain that someone tried to clean. I exchange glances between the hole and his hand, wondering if they're connected. I have a feeling they are. How well do I know him?

He throws his jacket on the couch and turns to me, and for a few moments, we just stand there and stare at each other in silence.

And then he's on me. Lips, hands, body. He swallows me, conquers me. He's everywhere. His hands caress me like I'm a precious object that has just been returned to him. Wherever he touches, he leaves a trail of fire.

My body wakes up immediately as if we were never apart. My brain disconnects, letting my body take control as if I were an animal controlled by my needs. I take off my clothes, dropping them on the floor beneath me. He tries to take off his shoes without allowing his lips to leave mine and almost falls. We crave each other, we're impatient, desire skin-to-skin contact, and can't wait another moment.

When the clothes are finally out of our way, he swings me lightly up into his arms and wraps my legs around his waist.

He takes me to the couch, trying not to break any point of contact between us. We both need each other. We're desperate for each other. Everything else is unimportant. We're the only two who exist at this moment.

His thrusts are hard and fast. Like he's trying to hurt me. I moan and grab his butt, pulling him closer to me. I need him so much I grind myself against his throbbing cock. "I can't... I can't..." I gasp as the feeling inside me grows bigger, flooding my senses and shaking my body to its core. His pace increases, and I hold on to him as he thrusts himself harder into me.

"Fuck, Bambi!" he screams as he comes hard inside me.

We continue panting on the couch for what seems like an eternity after a powerful orgasm. I don't want to come back to reality.

Why did I agree to come back here? I won't be able to stand it if he asks me to leave again. We didn't even talk about what happened. Just fucked like animals before we said a word.

"Condom!" I shout in horror as I feel his semen dripping between my legs. "You didn't put on a condom."

He jumps to his feet. "Fuck!" he runs his hands through his hair, a movement I've come to know he does when he's stressed or frustrated. "Are you not on the pill?"

I shake my head. The feeling of hysteria increases. "No, my prescription ran out, and I had no way to renew it. What am I going to do?" The perfect moment was lost. Reality bites us in the ass.

"I'll pick up the morning-after pill." He tries to calm me down, but it's clear he's panicking, too. "I'll go now. You stay here, and we'll talk. Don't you dare leave!"

I watch him pick up his clothes from the floor and quickly put them on.

What did we do? How was I so irresponsible?

"Wait here." He takes one last look at me before leaving, leaving me alone with my thoughts.

Why did I sleep with him again? After he called me names and thought I cheated on him? How low can I go?

But he was looking for me, the angel on my shoulder reminds me. He went looking for me. And not only him, but he also said there was an entire team trying to find me. That means something, doesn't it? That he cares? At least a little? Must be.

My heart is his. The fragments I gave him, piece by piece, comprise almost my whole heart. I have little left to give, and if he takes more from me, I can no longer heal from it.

I take a blanket and curl up on his couch, waiting.

He comes back, a worried look on his face. He gives me the pill and sits next to me, watching me swallow it.

"As soon as we finish our conversation, I'll make an appointment with a gynecologist. I don't want to think about condoms anymore."

What? Is he talking about the future? Is he making an appointment for me? What does it mean?

He bites his lips again and runs his hand through his hair, and I know he wants to say something. I lift his bandaged palm and gently run my fingers over it. "What happened to you?"

He points to the hole in the wall. "I lost it," he says in a broken voice. "I completely lost it."

I remain silent, allowing him to continue.

"When I saw the news and realized you were married and...unstable..." He raises his eyes to mine. "Because that's what he said, right? That you're crazy? I thought the world was crashing down on me. And I responded in the stupidest way possible. I blamed you. I'm so sorry. I'm sorry for the things I said, for the awful words. I don't know what I was thinking."

"I deserved it," I interject. "I was a coward. For days, I debated how to tell you the truth. But every time I had a chance, I chickened out. It was on the tip of my tongue every time, and every time I stopped myself. I didn't want to find out how you would react. I didn't want you to throw me out." I laugh, but there's no humor behind it. "And in the end, it happened, anyway."

"You wanted to tell me?" His eyes widen.

"Of course, I wanted to. I wanted to tell you more than anything. I wanted you to know who I am so I wouldn't have to hide the truth. I hated lying to you."

I take a breath. "But actually, you've always known who I was. Although you didn't know my name, you knew who I was. I've always been myself when I'm with you." I try to make it clear to him, and I'm not sure I succeed. Tears flood my eyes.

"So, what's your real name?" He asks the most basic question, the one no couple should ask at this stage.

"Ayala Beckett. That's the name my parents gave me. Summers is my name by marriage." I say the name Summers with disgust. I will never be Summers again.

"You were the woman on the bench. Right? With the map? That was our first meeting?"

I nod.

"I knew I'd seen you before. I couldn't understand where from, and then everything became clear. Did he do that to you? The bruises on your face?"

I nod again.

"Is that why you ran away from him? Was he beating you?"

"Yes."

"Why didn't you go to the police?"

I can't stop the snort that comes out of me. "Why do you think I didn't? You saw him. Even you bought his story. I'm mentally unstable. He has documents. He has guardianship over me. And he's from a respectable and well-known family. He's respectful and believable. The police laughed at me. They said he's my husband, and I should go to the doctor and not the police. No one would believe me. Even my parents didn't believe me," I say, my voice cracking.

"You tried to tell your parents?"

"I ran to them the first time he—" I can't say the words. But I must, I must get it out of me, tell him everything. No more secrets. "The first time, he raped me from behind."

Ethan sits quietly. I watch as his hands clench into fists and his jaw tightens.

"He used to rape me all the time," I say in a low voice. "At first, I didn't understand that it was rape. He would just come home and demand that I have sex with him. He said this is what a wife is supposed to do for her husband. I didn't always want to. I didn't enjoy sex with him. It hurt most of the time and other times was barely tolerable. But he demanded, he forced me, and I gave in."

I take another deep breath and straighten my shoulders, pulling all the courage I can muster to continue. "One day, he came home after a bad day at the office. I didn't have time to say a word. He just dragged me into the kitchen, bent me over the table, and tore my pants off. I told him I was on my period, so he penetrated my ass. He didn't use any lube and didn't prep me. I screamed. I screamed so loud. I thought he was tearing me in half. He didn't stop until he was done, and then he just left me there, bleeding and...

"For a week, I didn't get out of bed. I couldn't walk. He told everyone I was sick. But I was broken. I thought about killing myself, but I didn't want to die. I wanted *him* to die. I wanted to kill him. And then I just wanted to leave him."

"That son of a bitch." Ethan gets up and starts walking around the room. He curses and hits the wall again. Opening a bigger hole, I cringe a bit. "If I see him, I *will* kill him. I'll fucking kill him!"

I go to Ethan and put a hand on his arm, trying to get him to sit down again, but he shakes me off. "I ran away from him to my parents. I thought they would protect me. But he convinced them too. He showed them all these documents. He told them I had hallucinations and anxiety and that I was a danger to myself. That I tried to commit suicide, that I tried to hurt him. He fed them lies, and they ate every one of them. They let him take me back. I was angry with them at first, and I cut off contact. But I understand now that they just made the wrong decision. They bought his game. They didn't mean to harm me. He's just very convincing. Even you believed him. I don't know how he got all those documents..."

I didn't want to cry, but the tears are running down my cheeks.

"You can buy anything with money..." Ethan mumbles. "So you weren't under psychiatric care?"

"No. Never. I didn't see any doctor, and I don't need medication. I know you don't believe me—"

"I believe you. I should have never believed him over you." He pulls me in, and I surrender to his embrace. "I won't let him take you from me." Ethan puts several inches between us and lifts my chin so I see his eyes. The look on his face is powerful.

I believe him. I'm safe here.

"How long have you been married?"

"A little over two years."

"Why did you marry him?" he asks, and I cringe with guilt. The guilt that haunts me at night. How did I let him do this to me?

"I... You have to understand that I didn't know it would be like that. I didn't know he would be violent. He was nice at first, gentle even. He convinced me that he adored me. He was rich and from a well-known and respected family. I come from an average, ordinary family. When he showered me with money and attention, I was dizzy. I thought he loved me. Everyone looked at me as if I'd won the lottery. He was also my first. When I slept with him, and it hurt, he said it would get better with time. But it never did. After a while, he said I was just bad in bed, and I believed him."

I bury my face in my hands. How did I not understand who he was then?

It takes me a minute to compose myself before I go on. "The real troubles started a few months after we got married. Problems started at his work. He'd come home frustrated and..." I stop and take a breath. It's hard to explain how I stayed after something like that. How I believed him at that moment. No one can understand how much you want to believe the apologies, and excuses, simply because you love him. Or so I thought.

"He apologized and begged me to forgive him. That it was a one-time slip. And at first, I forgave him. Slowly, it got worse. He'd throw things around the house, then hit me for no real reason. Then he hit me simply because I served him food he didn't like and threw hot soup on me." I rub the scar on my shoulder. "I filed a complaint with the police, but he forced me to drop it."

"Forced you?"

"Yes." I look down. "He made me understand that nothing but humiliation would come of it for me. Then, when he realized there were no consequences, it got worse. After the...you know, I ran away to my parents, but even from there, he brought me back, and after my return, he made it clear that I had no option of refusing him. I realized my only option was to disappear and start over somewhere else. I planned the escape for months."

I look up, studying Ethan's reaction. Will he want me to stay here after all of this? But I have no choice. I have to tell him everything. I can't go on with the lies.

"Then came another day he came home angry. My escape plan wasn't ready. I wanted to save some more money." I remember that day and shudder. "He'd lost an important case, and his father, who's also a lawyer, blamed him for the loss. Michael liked nothing. Not the food, not the way I dressed, nothing. He just punched me repeatedly, and then when I was on the floor, he kicked me until I lost consciousness."

Ethan looks at me as if in shock. He's frozen in place, and I'm not sure what he's thinking. But I have to finish it, so I go on.

"I thought he was going to kill me. That I was already dead. But after a few hours, I woke up alone at home, on the floor. Micheal was gone."

"He left you on the floor?"

I nod. "In retrospect, I think he hoped I would die, and he went out to arrange an alibi for himself. He'd messed up the house, so it looked like there'd been a break-in. I guess he planned to sell the police a story about a burglar.

"But I survived. I woke up in terrible pain. I think he broke my rib. My face was swollen. That was the first time he'd hit me in the face. Mostly, he avoided hitting my face so that I could continue going to events with him, posing as his wonderful and supportive wife." I pause for a moment, letting Ethan digest everything.

"At that moment, I knew that when he came back, he'd end my life. So I packed some things and the money I had and got as far away as I could. You saw me on that bench a few days later."

Ethan gets up and paces the room again. I watch him and bite my lip. Now he knows everything there is to know about me.

"I don't know what to do. Tell me what to do!" he shouts. "I'm so angry I'm going crazy. I want to find him and kill him."

"Come to me." I extend my hand to Ethan. He takes it and sits down again on the couch next to me. He's shaking with anger. "If you believe me, that's enough. I don't need revenge."

I notice that the bandage on his hand is turning red. "Ethan, you're bleeding," I say, but he doesn't seem to care.

"I knew you'd been raped." He glances at me. "I guessed because of your reactions in bed. But I didn't imagine such a story. I didn't know he was your husband and that the abuse lasted for two fucking years. I don't know how to deal with it." He reaches for my cheek but stops just short of it, flinching.

"You don't have to be afraid to touch me," I whisper. "I'm still the same woman you knew. You saved me. You taught me to live. You showed me that my body is neither broken nor spoiled." I caress his face.

"You're so strong," he whispers as he brings his lips closer to mine.

"I'm not strong. I'm weak. So weak that I let him control me for two years. Two years in which he took everything I had from me. My degree, my job, my money, my body, and my soul until there was nothing left of me. He left only a shadow. For two years, I did nothing to stop him."

I cry, and Ethan kisses the tears away.

"You are so strong," he repeats. "You survived hell. You tried to escape, and you didn't give up until you found a way." He kisses me, tries to pull me inside him, and I let him, giving myself to him in every way I know how.

"I love you," he whispers, and I freeze, thinking I didn't hear correctly. But he repeats it, making sure I hear it. "I love you, Ayala."

Hearing my real name in his mouth is more than I can handle at this moment.

"Do you mean that? After everything you've just heard about me?"

"I know a woman who saved herself when she had no one to save her." His eyes are dark now. "She's the most amazing woman I've ever known and the woman I love."

"I love you, Ethan," I whisper in disbelief.

He sweeps me up into his arms and takes me to the bedroom.

CHAPTER 34
Ayala

"I'm ordering some food for us," Ethan says, getting up from the couch, where we've been sitting for the last hour, and walking to the kitchen to choose a menu from one of the drawers. "I'm starving. Let's get some sushi."

He picks up the phone and starts dialing.

"Wait," I say, and he stops and looks at me. "I want pasta."

He's standing there with his phone in hand. Staring at me.

"What?" I ask as he just keeps staring.

"Oh, nothing." He smiles, and my insides warm up. "What kind of pasta?"

"Hmmm... Pasta Alfredo would be nice."

He dials a number. "Two pasta alfredo, please."

We lay in bed after dinner, my head resting on his chest, and I tell him about my childhood at the girls' school. About studying at Stanford and how Michael convinced me I should leave school to live with him. How he prevented me from working and kept me away from everyone I knew until I was alone.

When I say it out loud, I realize how stupid I was. How stupid I was that I didn't know until it was too late. Michael had shown me his true face only after he stripped me of everything I had when I no longer had any choices and nowhere to go. I rub my neck.

"I have to do something. Confront him. He needs to let you go."

"Michael declared me unfit, got legal guardianship over me, and he's my husband. I lost my legal right to an independent life because of the documents he forged. If he knew I was here, he could just send the police to bring me back to him. You wouldn't have any way to stop him." I try to convince Ethan to give up. The other reason I try to convince him to leave it alone is that I'm afraid he won't be able to control himself. That he'll kill Michael and only end up in jail. "We must do it legally so I can be free."

"I know." He runs a hand through his hair. "And I'm doing everything I can. I hope it will be enough."

"It must be enough." I've been hiding in the house for a week, unable to go out. If Ethan can't free me, no one can.

The truth bought us closer, and the fire that I thought would consume me now burns with a bright light, protecting me.

I trust him.

I caress his arm and run my fingers over the tattooed bird on his arm. I gather the courage to ask him about it for the first time.

"Tell me about it?" I realize the tattoo, the name under it, has a lot of meaning, especially since I realized that the symbol of his first company is almost the same.

"Anna was my little sister. The tattoo is in memory of her." He closes his eyes as if returning to those days. "When we were little, my parents took us on a trip to the East Coast. One day we saw a tiny bird with pink cheeks, and my mother said the bird was called Anna's hummingbird. It became her favorite bird, the bird named after her." His gaze clouds over with the memories.

"What happened to her?" I ask with a low voice.

He takes his time saying the words. "She killed herself," he says in one heavy breath.

I freeze, horrified. "How old was she?"

"I was seventeen, and she was thirteen."

My heart skips a bit. "Thirteen? God. Why? What happened to her?" I can't grasp it. She was only a young girl.

"Me. I'm what happened to her." He gets up from the bed, puts on his pants, grabs a shirt, and leaves the room in a rush.

I get up, wrap my naked body in a blanket, and go into the living room after him, just to see him slam the door behind him.

What does he mean? He said she killed herself. Did he make her kill herself? I don't understand. How does that even make sense? All kinds of things he said to me in the past come to mind now.

Things he's not proud of. Is that what he meant?

I go back to the room to get dressed and see that he left his phone in the room. I want to ask him to come back to me, to tell him I'm here for him. He shouldn't run away from me. I love him. But he's prevented me from calling. I can't go out looking for him, either. All I can do is wait.

He just needs to blow off steam. I brought up unpleasant memories for him, and he needs a moment to think.

I poke through the kitchen cupboards. Madeleine keeps the kitchen in better shape than a restaurant.

Flour, eggs, milk. I take out the ingredients for my favorite chocolate chip cake. When I'm stressed, I bake. When Ethan is stressed, he runs or goes to the gym. That's why he has these amazing muscles I can drool over, and I have this big butt. I turn my head to glance at my butt in the mirror. At least Ethan loves it.

When the cake is in the oven and the aroma fills the house, I have nothing left to occupy myself. So I pace, praying for the door to open.

Hours pass. he's still not here, and my concern turns to panic. I walk around the house, unable to relax. I sit on the sofa, get up and sit again. I go to the door and open it just to look. But there's no one outside. What if something happened to him? What if Michael knows about our relationship?

My phone rings, and I run to it, hoping that maybe it's Ethan calling me. Unrecognized number.

"Hello?" I answer.

"Hey, this is Ryan. You're still at Ethan's, aren't you?"

"Yes. But he's not here."

"I know. I'm going to get him. I need you to open the parking garage for us."

"Get him from where?" I furrow my brow.

"The police called me. They arrested him for assault. I'm going to release him on bail."

"What?" I yell. "Bail? Assault? What are you talking about?" God, my worst fear comes to mind, "Is it Michael?" I ask hesitantly.

"No," Ryan says, and I let out a breath. "I'll explain everything to you when we get there. Right now, I have to get to the station. Long story short, he went to a bar, got completely drunk, and an argument escalated. They called the police and arrested them both. This is what I know right now. I just wanted to let you know I'll be back with him soon."

I thank him and hang up.

Ethan was so upset when he stormed out of here. I thought he was just going for a brief run to vent his emotions. But drinking and assault? I bite my lip. I hope he's okay and that nothing physically happened to him.

When Ryan texts me to open the gate, I stand by the door and wait on them. When they appear through the elevator doors, I gasp, covering my mouth with my hand.

Ethan is completely drunk, barely standing on his feet. A blue mark is already forming on his cheek. His hand, which almost healed, is bleeding again, and there are blood stains on his clothes. He reeks of alcohol.

I approach him and touch his arm, but he shakes me off like a stray fly. I recoil in pain. I have never seen him in such a state.

He walks into the bedroom with wobbly steps, rage still present in each of his steps, and slams the door hard behind him.

I look at Ryan, but he just raises his hands. "He hasn't done anything like this in years. I don't understand what happened. It will cost him dearly."

"I didn't think he was going to hit someone," I mutter.

"Did something happen between you two?" he asks.

"No. But I asked him about the tattoo, the one on his arm? The hummingbird?"

Ryan opens his mouth, and a look of understanding comes over his face. "Yes, that makes sense. He returned to his old behavior patterns. What did he tell you?"

"Only that it's in memory of his sister and that she killed herself."

Ryan nods but doesn't say anything more.

"He also said she killed herself because of him. Is that right, Ryan? Did he do something to her? Is he dangerous?" We don't know each other that well. Maybe I rushed into this relationship too fast. Maybe he is like Michael. Maybe Ethan has triggers, and he'll change? Hit me?

"No. He's not dangerous. Well, perhaps dangerous to himself."

"What does that mean, Ryan? Dangerous to himself? What happened there?"

He looks at me as if examining me. "I haven't seen him get to this state in years. I thought he had put everything behind him, but it turns out he still holds the guilt. He's still punishing himself for her death."

"Please tell me what happened, Ryan." I have to know. I need to understand.

"He needs to be the one telling you this. I won't be able to say anything beyond what he's willing to share. Let him relax a bit and sober up. Maybe he'll open up to you. You're the first one he's told about his sister. This is progress."

"Can you stay? I'm afraid." I'm afraid to find out he's not who I think he is. I won't stand for it again.

Ryan puts a hand on my arm. "I can. But you're safe here. I'm sure of it. Will you take good care of him? He's vulnerable now. Don't let him get in trouble, please."

I nod and promise while I close the door behind him.

When I enter the bedroom, I find Ethan in the shower, standing under the stream, his head against the wall. He looks defeated. Not like the Ethan I know, the one who would turn New York upside down to find me, protect me.

What the hell happened there with his sister that he can't get over it so many years later?

I undress and get in the shower, then wrap my arms around him from behind. He flinches, and for a moment, I think he's going to reject my gesture, but he turns to me, his eyes red, and wraps his arms around me. I hug him, transfer my strength to him, and comfort him. We stand, silent, and the hot water flows over both of us, washing away the blood, the dirt, and the emotions.

I take the shampoo and raise a hand to his head. He helps me and bends a little to help me reach. I run my hands over his scalp, massaging it and lathering the shampoo. He surrenders to my touch, sighing. I can see that it calms him. I take my time and don't rush. Then I go over the rest of him, removing the blood and alcohol smell and re-expose the scent of my man. His wonderful masculine scent that I love.

There's nothing sexual in this, just two people comforting each other and helping each other overcome the past. He strengthens me no less than I strengthen him.

In bed, he presses me to him, hugs me tightly as if I'm going to disappear, and falls asleep in seconds.

I stay in his embrace because I know he needs me now. It's my turn to support him. To be here for him.

I reach out and turn off both of our phones. No running at five a.m., no running to the office before seven. He will talk to me tomorrow.

We wake up late. Ethan reaches for the phone, sighs, and tries to check what time it is.

He gives me an angry look.

"Why is my phone off? I didn't wake up in time for my run."

"Running isn't important right now. Your state of mind is. You needed the sleep, and we need to talk." I run my fingers over the stubble on his face, and he surrenders to my touch.

"I told you my secrets. All the horrible things I've been through. The humiliation, the pain, and now we're closer than before. You didn't turn away from me. I won't turn away from you either," I say in a soft voice, trying to convince him to open up to me. "No more secrets."

He shakes his head. "It's not the same. You were the victim. I'm the guilty party. It's different. You'll hate me."

"I can't hate you. I'm in love with you." I smile softly.

"I'm not sure you'll still love me after this story. I'm not willing to take the risk."

"You'll have to trust me, Ethan. As I trusted you." I remain silent, waiting. He has to decide if I'm worth his trust. If not, this secret will poison our relationship.

He rolls onto his back and looks at the ceiling. Puts an arm on his forehead and speaks.

CHAPTER 35
Ethan

"Just before my birthday, my parents went on vacation in the Caribbean and left me to babysit my sister Anna. Of course, I didn't want to. Who wants to babysit a little sister? We were close, we used to go to Knicks games together, but she was also thirteen, a rebellious teenage girl who wasn't willing to do anything I asked her to." He inhales sharply.

"As a teenager myself, as soon as my parents vacated the house, I organized a birthday party. I arranged for alcohol and bought beer. I thought I was cool. That I would be more popular. All I was interested in was how many girls would come and if I could get laid. I asked Anna to get out of the house. She decided to piss me off and stayed."

I turn to Ayala with a smile, but there's nothing in it except pain. How angry I was at Anna, and how catastrophic that moment was.

"The party was a hit. The house was full. Someone must have disclosed the party, and crowds of people I didn't even know flooded the place. We were drinking, having fun... At some point, I went to one of the rooms with a girl I liked. The party went on, I knew some girls were wasted, but I didn't care as long as I was about to get laid."

I pause a moment, taking a breath. "After the party was over, Ryan and I cleaned up the house as best we could. My parents came back and were shocked. They grounded me for a month and gave me all kinds of jobs to do. So far, a normal high school story, right?"

Ayala nods without saying a word. I look away from her, unable to face her. Unable to face the moment, she realizes that I'm not as good a person as she thinks.

"After the party, my annoying little sister's behavior changed completely. She wasn't annoying anymore. In fact, she wasn't around at all. She stayed in her room most days, alone and quiet."

I feel my pulse rise as the memories flood through me. The smell of metal and blood rises in my nose, and a wave of nausea attacks me. I'm going to throw up. I take deep breaths, calming my churning stomach, and continue.

"About three months after that party, I came home from school and saw water dripping down the stairs. I didn't understand at first what it was. I thought there was a leak. I went upstairs and saw water running under the bathroom door. The door was locked, and it took me a minute to realize Anna was inside. I knocked on the door, started banging on it. I was hysterical. I screamed, but she didn't answer. I ended up kicking the door until it broke. There she was, in a bath full of red water, her head drooping back. She'd cut her veins." My voice breaks, and I can't go on.

Ayala lets out a muffled cry.

"I remember calling the police, asking them to come. I did everything as if in automatic mode. I was cold, emotionless. I knew right away that she was dead. There was nothing to try. I just sat down at the end of the hallway, on the floor, and waited. When my parents arrived, mom started screaming. She screamed and screamed. She couldn't stop. Even then, I continued to sit there. I couldn't move. I just sat there for hours."

Ayala covers her mouth with her hand and takes it down. "You were in shock. You were obviously in shock. No one approached you? They didn't take you away?"

"No. I was invisible. Mom was hysterical. She needed tranquilizers. She wouldn't stop screaming." I can still hear the screams echoing in my ears to this day. "Dad took care of her and everything else. No one was interested in me. I sat there until morning. A day later, I found out Anna had left a letter in her room. At the party I had, the one I thought was so cool and fun? Someone raped her. She went down to look for me, but I was busy having sex. Someone noticed her and took her to her room. He raped her over and over throughout the whole evening. No one heard, and no one saw. All that time and she kept it to herself. Didn't tell anyone. Only in a letter. Turns out that her period was late. She was only thirteen but realized she was pregnant by him. She saw no way out but to die. Cutting her veins. Why didn't she speak to me? to someone?" I blink rapidly, trying not to cry. I shoot a look at Ayala, challenging her to take her eyes off me. To see what I was always afraid of, that she would no longer be able to look at me. But she does exactly the opposite. She comes closer and kisses me.

"You're not to blame for her death. It's not you who raped her, and you did not make her commit suicide. You were a teenager yourself."

"I organized the party. I'm the one who brought strangers into the house with a thirteen-year-old girl. She was looking for me... Because of me, she was raped." I know I'm guilty. I've done everything I can since then to redeem myself for it, but there's no forgiveness for something like that.

Ayala takes my face in her hands, forcing me to look at her. "Yes, you organized the party. But you couldn't have known that would happen. And your parents shouldn't have left you alone. I'm sure they knew you'd throw a party. You're not the first—"

"My father's never forgiven me. He hates me to this day. He can't even look at me. I can't forgive myself, either. No matter what you say, it doesn't make it any less my fault." I turn my back on her, disengaging. I can no longer hear the empty words.

She reaches out and wraps me in a hug, preventing me from moving away. "When you told me you got into fights as a teen, was it because of that?"

"Yes. But that's an understatement for everything I did. That year is quite vague for me. I felt like I was losing my mind. I was drunk most of the time. I broke into bars to get alcohol because they wouldn't sell it to me in stores. I went into a rage with anyone who looked at me wrong. I wanted to feel something. But nothing helped. I didn't even graduate, you know? Nobody knows that about me. I missed my whole senior year of high school. I got arrested a few times. My mom bailed me out every time, and my parents paid a lot of money to hide the things I did so that I wouldn't have a criminal record. Dad paid so that their good name wouldn't be harmed. They would bribe whoever they needed to so that the family name stayed clean."

"Didn't they try to help you?"

"They did their best, I guess. They sent me to therapists and psychologists who tried to convince me I wasn't to blame for her death. But I know I'm guilty. At some point, I stopped going to them. It didn't help."

"And how did you get out of this phase?"

"Ryan said something to me I'll never forget. When I got drunk for the umpteenth time and broke into another store just for fun, just to create destruction, I couldn't see my parents' accusing faces again, so I hid at his house. He told me that's not how Anna would have wanted me to remember her. And that I wasn't respecting her memory. He was right. Those words stuck in my head. When I sobered up a bit, I thought about how she would have wanted me to remember her, then I found a girl who needed help. It felt so good to help her. So, I thought, this could be it. This is what I need to do. And that's when I started Savee." I take in a breath.

"It took some time, of course, but I put everything I had into this company. I was on my knees begging for loans from investors." I remember recruiting Ryan for help and how he and I went to meeting after meeting to present our business plan countless times.

"Originally, it was a helpline for those thinking about suicide. All the help centers that existed until then were on the phone or not good enough, so I adapted the help to the spirit of the times. It went great, and the app gained momentum and made a noise in the media. We received a lot of donations, and slowly I expanded. I opened more companies. I succeeded beyond my wildest dreams. I killed her, but she's the one who built my career."

A snorting sound escapes me, something between crying and laughing. I make money from my sister's death.

"I love you," Ayala says. "And you have done nothing in my eyes to make you unworthy of that love."

But that's exactly who I am. Unworthy. I let my sister down. I let my parents down. I'm broken inside.

I shake my head. "You're so brave. You're my hero. You suffered in hell for years and didn't break. You remained strong. I can't believe how strong you are. Not like my sister—" I say, and my voice breaks again.

"You're mad at her, aren't you? Angry that she killed herself? Without explaining? Without asking for help? She was just a young girl, too young. A girl who didn't know how to deal with what happened to her. She wasn't weak, Ethan. She was just a frightened little girl. It's okay to be angry with her because of the path she chose. It's okay."

"If she had told me what happened, maybe I could have saved her… I could have…" Tears drip down my cheeks. How could Ayala be so understanding? How can she not see the ugliness in me?

She hugs me and kisses away my tears, and I caress her, drawing strength from her.

CHAPTER 36
Ayala

I pass my time at Ethan's house doing nothing. Madeleine keeps my mind busy and tells me about her granddaughter, who has now said, "baba," and I see how Madeleine lights up when she tells me about her.

At noon she leaves, and I'm left alone. I'm going crazy. I'm so bored and lonely. I want to go to work, but I can't risk it. I want Ethan to be here with me, but he's at the office, working. I can't believe it's been almost two months, and I'm still stuck in this apartment with nothing to do other than go out of my mind.

I've already read several books I found in his library, put a cake in the oven that no one will eat, worked out at his home gym, and now I'm just lying on the couch and trying to concentrate on a movie that doesn't interest me at all.

Nicky's name lights up my phone screen.

I answer the call, happy to hear my friend's voice. "Hey, what's up?"

"Robin killed herself," she says with no preparation.

"What?" I jump off the couch. "What happened?"

"I don't know. At the start of the shift, Dana informed us. Her parents said she left a note, but I don't know what she wrote there. Do you think it's work-related? Do you think it's something I did? I wasn't very nice to her. What if I pushed her too far?"

"No way. She was the one who wasn't nice. And she hated me, not you. She claimed I was stealing her tips and her men." I didn't know she was in a low state of mind. Shit, it's like the story with Ethan's sister. You can't tell how people feel inside. Maybe she was mean to me simply because she was suffering? Maybe I should have tried to understand her instead of getting angry. My stomach clenches.

"Will you come to the funeral?"

"I can't. I can't be seen outside. He's still looking for me."

"Ugh. Will it ever end? Do you have a solution?"

"Not yet," I admit. "But I'm trying to stay optimistic."

"Fingers crossed for you."

A few minutes later, my phone rings again, and I answer automatically, assuming it's Ethan calling from an office line. Few people have my number.

"Hello?" I answer, hoping he's calling to let me know he'll be home soon. Or he has a plan to get me out of the mud I've sunk into.

"Ayala." It's the voice that appears in my nightmares. The voice I can never forget. I freeze.

"You know who this is, right?" he continues, and I hang up and throw the phone on the table.

I start to shake violently.

How did he get my number? The phone is registered in Ethan's name. Does he know where I am?

I run to the door and turn all the locks in place. I lean against the door, panting. In a panic, I look around as if he's going to break out of one of the rooms.

The phone rings again. "Please stop," I beg it, but it rings and rings non-stop.

I take the device and press the power button. I don't want to hear that voice ever again. The shutdown confirmation message appears. My finger hovers over the screen.

I am strong. I remember Ethan's words. I'm not in the same place I was. I'm no longer a young and gullible girl. Michael doesn't scare me anymore. I won't let him scare me anymore. I'll tell him to go to hell.

I take a deep breath and answer.

"Ayala, it's not nice to hang up on your husband," he says.

I cringe. Maybe I'm not as strong as I thought. I take another deep breath.

"I think you forgot your place. You went on an adventure. It was nice, and now it's time to come back home before you embarrass yourself. Before everyone in the world hears about the whore you are, a married woman who ran away to sleep with a man who's not her husband." He spits the last word with disgust.

"You're not my husband," I say after I find my voice again. "You'll never be my husband again."

His laughter makes me shudder.

"You belong to me, Ayala. You can't make decisions for yourself anymore. You're not competent. You belong to me, and you need to come back to me."

"Over my dead body." I know Ethan won't give up. He'll fight until we can undo this marriage.

"I can arrange that." I can hear the grin in his voice. "But it's better for you to come home on your own. Or else."

"Or else what? Will you take me by force? Will you rape me again? Beat me until I pass out? You already did all that to me. I'm not afraid of you anymore."

"You're wrong, Ayala. I'm your husband. You're mine. You belong to me. You're at my service always. I can do as I please with you."

"I'm a woman, not a toy, not a belonging. I'm not here to

serve you. And you're a rapist! I want a divorce. Let me divorce you."

He laughs as if I told a joke. "There are no divorces in my family. You know that. My dad wants to run for governor next year, and scandals and an adulterous wife…? Well, that doesn't work for me. Come back on your own, or your new boyfriend will pay the price for your actions."

Ethan? What does he know about Ethan? Ethan is stronger than him.

"I'm not afraid of you, and neither is Ethan."

"Are you sure?" I receive a new message on my phone.

I open it with shaking hands. Photo after photo of Ethan, on his way to the office, in the suit he wore this morning.

I keep scrolling. The photographer is standing close to him now, right behind him. A gun is pointed at Ethan's back without him being aware of it, without him knowing he's a step away from certain death.

I gasp out loud. Is Michael going to kill Ethan?

"Come willingly, or your friend…" Michael makes a gunshot sound and laughs. "You have two hours to decide. Then I tell my man that he has a green light. Oh, and don't try to warn him. I'll know if you do."

He hangs up.

I collapse to the floor. Why did I answer the phone? Why didn't I just stay bored in front of the movie?

I have to warn Ethan. I pick up the phone to call him but remember the warning. Is Michael tracking our phones too? I don't know what to do. Ethan won't be back from work for two more hours. How can I warn him? I have to decide what to do. I can't bear the thought of something happening to him because of me.

I scream, but the walls don't answer back.

I can handle everything Michael will do to me. I've been

through everything, and I've survived. He won't be able to break me again. But I can't let him hurt Ethan.

I'm defeated. I've lost the war.

Like a zombie, I walk through the house, trying to absorb the sights and the smells.

I put the cake I made on the counter and sit down to write my farewell letter.

How do you say goodbye to the person who holds your heart? I sit with my eyes closed and my fists clenched for long minutes before I write.

My Love,

When I arrived in New York, I hoped to build a new life on my own, but fate had other plans for me. He summoned you to me. The stubborn man who appeared in my life again and again until I couldn't deny you anymore. You taught me what true love is. You taught me I am not damaged, that I am a woman worthy of love. I love you so much.

Even in my wildest dreams, I couldn't imagine you. You have given me so much. Now it's my turn to save you.

Forgive yourself for me because I need you to forgive me too.

I promise to be strong for you.

Always yours,
Ayala.

The tears drip on the page and wet it. I move it away, but I allow myself to cry, allow the tears to diminish me. I need to do it now because I won't let Michael see me cry.

He will never break me again.

I pack my clothes, even though I know I'll never wear them again, and when the phone rings, I'm ready.

With a heavy step, I walk out.

To Be Continued...

Ethan and Ayala Story Continues

Shattered Secrets

Ayala returns to the monster in her dreams, ready to pay any price to protect Ethan. But the price is high, and she might not be as strong as she thought...

Ethan is prepared to do whatever it takes to save her, ready to give up his business empire and even his life.

Can their love survive?

Shattered Secrets

Dear Readers,

If you enjoyed *Shattered Hope,* please consider leaving a review on Amazon — it would be greatly appreciated — even a few words are a huge help.

Write a review on Amazon:

https://www.amazon.com/review/create-review/?&asin=9659304501

SAY HELLO!

Join Karin's newsletter and never miss a sale or new release
https://subscribepage.io/karinwinter

Join the ARC team
https://subscribepage.io/HtWpKH

You can connect with her at
https://linktr.ee/karinwinter

Also by Karin Winter

Read on how Ethan's story begins in the short story UNWORTHY

Grab your FREE Copy

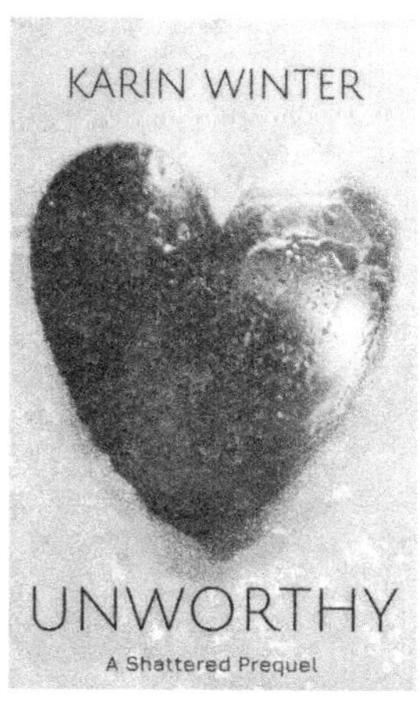

http://subscribepage.io/unworthy

Made in the USA
Monee, IL
10 September 2024

65375014R00163